COPPERHEAD ROAD

WINNIPEG

Brad SMITH

COPPERHEAD ROAD

A NOVEL

Copperhead Road

Copyright © 2022 Brad Smith

Published by At Bay Press April 2022.

Design and layout by Matthew Stevens and M. C. Joudrey.

Library and Archives Canada cataloguing in publication is available upon request.

ISBN 978-1-988168-62-3

Printed and bound in Canada.

This book is printed on acid free paper that is 100% recycled ancient forest friendly (100% post-consumer recycled).

First Edition

10 9 8 7 6 5 4 3 2 1

atbaypress.com

For John Smith and Lowry Siemens

Flathead Fords and moonshine whisky...
I think you guys would have liked this one.

To live outside the law, you must be honest.
—Bob Dylan

ONE

They park the Buick in a stand of spindly sycamore trees a half mile off the county road, along a shallow creek that emerges from the rock-strewn hills, flowing through the evergreens and into a meadow. They have boxed fried chicken and a few cans of beer. They spread out a blanket from the back seat of the sedan and eat by the side of the meandering stream, tossing the chicken bones into the current.

After drinking a couple of cans of Krueger's, Bobby decides on a nap. The back seat of the Buick is rich and plush, upholstered in mohair, and Bobby stretches out there, leaving the door open so he can extend his legs. The Buick is a nice car. As a rule, Bobby preferred a Ford because of the V8, but the big sedan was a good car for traveling, roomy, and easy to drive. It had a big six under the hood and was pretty fast. Not as fast as the Ford eight cylinder but not bad. They'd stolen the Buick just that morning, after the owner had left the keys in the ignition while he was getting a tooth pulled in a dentist's office in Forest City.

The shooting wakes Bobby a short time later. He sits up in the back seat and sees Luanne standing in the clearing fifty yards away, aiming the .38 at some empty beer cans she'd placed on a log beside the creek. She has fired off all six shots and is now reloading. The cans have yet to be threatened.

Bobby gets out of the car and stretches. He relieves himself in the tall grass behind the Buick, then wanders over to retrieve the remaining chicken leg from the box on the blanket. Stripping the meat from the bones, he watches as Luanne empties the revolver once more, again not coming close.

"Come show me how," she orders. Luanne has a voice that is at once whining and demanding, whether it is meant to be or not. It usually is.

"I haven't shot a gun in years," Bobby says.

"Thought you were a war hero."

"Nobody ever said that," Bobby tells her.

"You was in the war against the Kaiser," Luanne says. "Or so they claim."

"Being in a war don't make a man a hero." Bobby flips the chicken bone into the creek then wipes his fingers on his pant legs.

Bobby had been in the war against the Kaiser. He'd enlisted in '17 when he was just fifteen years old. He was nearly six feet tall at the time; the enlistment officer didn't blink when Bobby gave his dead cousin's name and birthdate. It seemed to Bobby that the marines weren't turning many away. But Bobby was no hero in France. Fact of the matter was, he was scared the entire time he was at the front. He suspected everybody he served with was every bit as scared. Maybe there were a few men—Alvin York and the like—who weren't scared. But even that big old Tennessean York must have known moments of fear. It was only human.

Luanne loads the revolver again before offering it over to him. Bobby reluctantly fires two shots, knocking over a can each time, then hands it back. "Point it like a finger," he says. "Why do you need to shoot a gun anyway?"

"Bonnie Parker could shoot," Luanne says. "Pistols, shotguns. Even a Tommy machine gun."

"And where'd it get her?" Bobby asks. "Six feet under."

"But she was famous."

"I'd rather be unfamous and above ground," Bobby says.

Luanne fires the remaining four shots and finally manages to wing one of the cans.

"That's enough," Bobby says, lighting a cigarette. "Somebody will come poking around. That Buick has been reported for sure by now."

"We're fifty miles from Forest City. Ain't nobody in this neck of the woods here looking for that car."

"You don't know that."

Luanne takes the gun and the box of cartridges to the car, and stows everything in the glove box. She gets a cigarette from her purse, lights it as she walks back to the creek, where Bobby is now sitting on the log where the beer cans were, smoking and skipping flat stones across the water.

"We'll head on over to Asheville after dark," Luanne says. "There's a trailer there, we can spend the night. Owner lives in Charlotte and don't hardly never come around. Leaves the key under the mat."

Bobby doesn't say anything for a time. He finishes his cigarette and flicks the butt into the water. "I ain't too sure about this," he finally says.

"About what?"

"You know about what."

Luanne sits down beside him. "I don't need you getting cold feet now. I tell you, this is a foolproof plan. I know these people. We tell 'em to dance, they'll dance."

"If you know these people, then the wife is going to recognize you. Or do you intend to wear a mask?"

"I got a wig," Luanne says. "Besides, old lady Hart don't know me from Mrs. O'Leary's cow. She's the type considers herself high society in Asheville and as such, she wouldn't never have nothing to do with me or my kin. I could pass her on the street and she wouldn't give me the time of day."

Bobby skips a stone and says nothing.

"You want to go over it again?" Luanne asks.

"I know the plan," Bobby says.

"We'll go over it anyway," Luanne says. "We don't need no

screw-ups. I stroll up to the house, knock on the door and ask for a glass of water. The old biddy lets me in and I produce the gun and tell her to sit down and shut her yap. That same time, you walk into the bank and ask to see the manager, old man Hart. You get him alone in his office and tell him to call the missus at home. She tells him some crazy woman is pointing a gun at her. At that point, he's going to give you anything you ask for. You take all the cash on hand and tell him he can't sound no alarm for an hour, otherwise we're gonna come back and shoot his wife in the head. You pick me up and we take it on the lam. We'll be over the state line before the cops even know what happened."

Bobby skips another stone. "What if they don't have a phone?"

"He's a banker," Luanne says. "Bankers have phones. They're like lawyers and politicians and all them. Jesus Christ Bobby, you ain't going to chicken on me now. Ain't I the one who picked you up when they let you out last week? Well, I didn't do it so we could rob no gas stations. That last one we didn't collect but seven dollars and change. I figured you to be somebody with some guts. Race-car driver and war hero and all that."

"I ain't no war hero, I keep telling you that. And I ain't so sure that I want to be a bank robber."

"What are you gonna do then, with this damn Depression on? Go to work at the Woolworths? I got news for you—the Woolworths ain't hiring. I hope you ain't gonna chicken on me, Bobby. I let you in on my plans, and I let you in my bed. You better come through for me. I got bigger fish to fry, bigger than you can even imagine."

"Such as?"

Luanne is quiet for a moment. She's been keeping this part of her plan to herself so far. "What's the one business in this country that ain't been depressed?" she asks.

Bobby shrugs. "I couldn't say."

"The moving picture business," Luanne says. "Which is situated out there in Hollywood, California. I was reading in *Life* magazine a while back, how they are always looking for stories to make their movies out of. So this is what I got figured. We do this Asheville job tomorrow and then head west. Whenever we need a little cash, we use the same plan, some small-town bank out in some hick town. Once we get to Hollywood, I sell my story to the movie people. But on one condition—I get to play me in the movies. I'll change my name of course; movie actresses do that. Did you know that Joan Crawford's real name is Lucy LeSueur? I figure to call myself Monique Marseille, which sounds real exotic. We can get Clark Gable to play you."

"You've been doing some figuring."

"I have," Luanne says. "I mean to become somebody. And you, goddamn it, are gonna help me, Bobby Barlow. You hear?"

Bobby hears. Luanne is an inch or two over five feet, skinny as a rake, and her two front teeth protrude past her upper lip, giving her the look of an aggressive cottontail rabbit. Her voice can cut cheese, as Bobby's grandmother used to say. Bobby isn't all that certain that the people making picture shows out in Hollywood, California, were going to be all that eager to make her a movie star, but then again Bobby doesn't know jack shit about the movie business.

He doesn't know jack shit about the bank robbing business either but he's about to find out.

The banker's house is on the outskirts of Asheville, on Boyd Avenue. They park across the street and watch the place for a time. Luanne has been chain smoking since they got up earlier. They had spent the night in the trailer she'd mentioned. They found a bottle of rye there—some bootleg hooch that tasted of kerosene—and finished it off before they went to bed. Bobby's head is now pounding from the cheap liquor and he hasn't taken any breakfast. Luanne didn't eat in the morning as a rule, but then she usually didn't get out of bed until it was time for lunch.

"How do you know she's even home?" Bobby asks.

Before he's done asking, the front door opens and a woman walks out, carrying a watering can. She is sixty or so, wearing a shapeless shift and a kerchief on her head. She waters the flowers alongside the front walkway, then stands there looking at them for a time, as if expecting to see some change in their appearance immediately. Then she scratches her armpit and goes back inside.

Luanne takes a blonde wig from her purse and tugs it into place. She puts on a pair of sunglasses, gives Bobby a smile, and gets out of the car.

Other than a single teller, standing at a wicket looking bored, the bank is empty when Bobby walks in. There is a large oaken door off to the side, with *HARVEY HART Manager* stenciled on it. The door is closed. When Bobby approaches the teller, he shunts aside the magazine he's been reading. Bobby has been thinking that the bank would be a busy place, with lots of people who might be able to identify him after the deed. He isn't wearing a wig or sunglasses, just his old fedora. He realizes he shouldn't have been surprised to find the place nearly empty. Nobody in the country has any money so what reason would they have to go to a bank? If they could find one still open, that is.

He tells the teller he is seeking a business loan and the man goes into the manager's office for a moment, then comes out and tells Bobby to go on in. Harvey Hart is sixty-five or so, and nearly as wide as he is tall, but then again, he isn't very tall. He is dressed in a blue serge suit with a red tie and is sitting behind a large desk built of wide-grained chestnut, wearing pince-nez on his nose. He smells of bay rum. Flicking his small gray eyes over Bobby's rough trousers and wrinkled shirt, it is evident that he has decided in a heartbeat that Bobby would not be receiving a loan from his bank.

"How can I help you?" Hart asks.

Bobby stands just inside the door. He is not asked to sit and would have declined if it was offered. Hart has a crystal dish containing jujubes on the desk. While he waits for Bobby to answer, he takes one and puts it in his mouth, sucking on it like a lozenge. Bobby notices the telephone on the desk. It is cool in the room but he is sweating profusely, rivulets running from his armpits down his sleeves. He feels as if he might faint.

"I asked what I can do for you, boy," Hart repeats. "I have a bank to run."

Contrary to that statement, it doesn't appear that there is much banking business in the works that morning, but it doesn't matter to Bobby. In that instant he realizes just what the little pince-nez-ed, jujube-sucking man can do for him.

"Not a goddamn thing," he tells the man and leaves.

Outside he gets into the Buick, thinks for a second or two about Luanne, waiting in the Hart house a few blocks south, the Smith & Wesson in her lap and God only knows in her heart.

Bobby fires the Buick up and heads north.

TWO

The bus for Knoxville left Union Station at seven that morning. With two large suitcases and a lunch she prepared the night before, Ava splurges on a taxicab to the station. Theodore does not see her off. They'd said their goodbyes the night before. Ava could see no reason for more tears.

The wind is out of the south and she can smell the pungent odor of the stockyards on the morning air as she gets out of the taxi. She goes inside and pays for her ticket before dragging her bags to the Greyhound that sits idling outside. The bus is less than half full. Ava takes a window seat and as they pull out of the station, she watches out the window to the city she's called home for four years and she wonders if she'll ever be back. Somewhere a few blocks north, Theodore is probably still sleeping. Musicians stay up late and sleep in. When he wakes though, she knows he'll be wondering the same thing.

The Greyhound stops frequently, and it takes a better part of two days to arrive at Knoxville, passing through countless small towns as well as Indianapolis and Louisville and Nashville. Ava reads her books and sleeps fitfully on the bus. Attempts to charm her along the way are made by a couple of soldiers, an encyclopedia salesman, and a man who claims to be a cowboy. He wears a black Stetson and cowboy boots, but his hands are as soft and pink as a baby's so Ava isn't buying his story, or anything else he's trying to sell.

In Knoxville the following morning, she is obliged to switch from Greyhound to the Tennessee Coach Company for the run south to Wilkesboro, arriving there around mid-afternoon. The salesman is also bound for Wilkesboro and suggests that Ava's family might be willing to put him up for a night or two while he conducts his business. Ava points him in the direction of the ancient Wilkesboro Hotel and leaves him sitting on his steamer trunk, pouting a little over the combined loss of what he hoped would be free accommodation and any potential for romance.

Ava gathers her bags and starts on foot along the red dirt road for Flagg's Hollow, two miles north of town. The day has grown warm and the road is dusty where it isn't littered with road apples from horses and mules, which still outnumber motorcars by two to one in Wilkes County. There are shotgun shacks along the roadside, with vegetable gardens in backyards and clothes hanging on lines. Chickens run in and out from under the buildings. Two old colored men sit in front of Lou's Blacksmith & Repair, lounging in the shade, a deck of cards laying idle on a table between them. Too hot even for a game of gin. Ava doubts there is much repair work to be had these days. Poverty hangs over the town like a cloak, just as it envelopes the entire republic. At the crossroads, she stops for a rest, sitting on her suitcase and removing her hat to wipe her brow. A boy of eight or nine comes out of a tarpaper shed and approaches nervously. Several other kids appear then too, hanging back, watching his lead.

"Can I have a nickel, please?" the boy asks.

Ava looks the kid over. His pants are too small and his shirt too big. She doubts he is the first owner of either garment or will be the last. His hair, beneath a stained tweed cap, is clipped close to the skull. A summer haircut, as is the fashion in these parts. His shoes have no laces and not a whole lot of sole leather.

"What would you do with a nickel?" Ava asks.

"Get me some licorice."

Ava glances to the other kids, now inching closer, possibly sensing that she is at least open to negotiation.

"If I give you a nickel, I'll have to give everybody a nickel."

The kid turns to look at the others, not happy that they have apparently ruined his chances. Ava stands up and goes through her purse for a quarter.

"You make sure everybody gets a licorice," she says. "I find out different, I'm going to come looking for you. You hear?"

The kid nods his head so vigorously his hat falls off. Ava gives him the coin, gathers her bags and continues for home. The dirt road curves as it descends down into the hollow. She sees the faded sign as she makes the turn, the white letters standing out against the weathered brick of the warehouse.

HOMER FLAGG & SONS MOLASSES COMPANY
EST. 1859

Homer Flagg was Ava's grandfather. He'd been a preacher and a farmer and the first man to produce molasses in North Carolina. He originally imported sugarcane from the West Indies. Later he grew sugar beets on the Flagg farm. The factory is built of red brick fired from the local clay pits, and is a hundred and fifty feet long, with a loading dock facing the road where Ava now walks. The building is not in good repair. The paint on the sashes and jambs is peeling and several of the windows have been shuttered closed. Two Model T Ford delivery trucks, one up on blocks, are parked alongside.

The Flagg home is on a rise behind the factory. The original house had been fired during the war between the states, by persons unknown, and rebuilt after the war ended, with the same red brick used in the warehouse. Farther along, and to the east is Darkytown, a scattershot cluster of houses and sheds and outbuildings. Most of the residents are sharecroppers or field hands for the larger farms in the area. Growing up, Ava had passed many a day there, playing with the colored kids her age.

Homer had died of the influenza in '19. Ava's father Jedediah at that time took over the farm and the molasses plant. He is also a preacher, following his father's and grandfather's lead. And at this moment, he is sitting in a slat-back chair on the loading dock, smoking a pipe and watching his only daughter make her approach along the dusty roadway. Now he stands, walks stiff-legged to the steps alongside the dock and climbs down to help her with her bags.

"Daughter," he says. "Welcome home."

"How is it, old man?" Ava embraces him, holds him close for a long moment before kissing him on his cheek.

That evening Ezra's wife Rachel cooks a big meal in honor of Ava's return. Ezra is Ava's older brother. He is tall and thin, with a full beard, and he is rigid as a barn beam, in every way she could name. Morgan is smaller and fairer than Ezra and is Ava's twin. She is closer to him than to anybody on the planet. Well, with the recent exception of Theodore, but that is an entirely different relationship than the one with Morgan. Ezra and Rachel have two kids, a boy and a girl, eight and ten. Rachel is quiet and somewhat insecure, although Ava catches her from time to time rolling her eyes at her husband's obtuseness.

After dinner in the big house, they sit outside on the porch. Morgan, on the top step, plays a few chords on his guitar while Jedediah is down by the pond with the kids, patiently baiting hooks with worms on bamboo poles and casting cork bobbers into the water.

"That's real nice, Morgan," Rachel says. "Does it have words?"

"Not as yet," Morgan says. "Something new."

Ava watches him as he bends over the guitar, trying out the sound. He has fine blonde hair and features. Ava doubts he could sprout a mustache. They both turned twenty-eight that winter but Morgan looks and acts younger. He'd always seemed younger than her, even when growing up. She'd been the tomboy and daredevil, always leaping before looking, often to her regret.

"Are you producing anything at all?" she asks Ezra then.

Meaning the plant.

"A few gallons a month," Ezra replies. "And having trouble selling that much. Laid everybody off. Most of the markets south, Georgia and Florida, have dried up."

Morgan strums the guitar once more and then sets it aside. "What happened in Chicago?"

"Same as everywhere, I guess," Ava says. "The people who aren't buying molasses aren't buying books either." She glances down to the pond. "How is father taking it?"

"You know the old man," Morgan says. "'The Lord will provide.' Well, he's taking his sweet damn time doing it."

"Don't blaspheme, brother," Ezra tells him.

Morgan looks over at Ava and smiles.

THREE

In times of plenty and in times of want, Sunday morning means church. It is the one constant for people of faith, no matter their daily travails. If anything, the Depression makes the church stronger. If there is no money for food, for clothes, for medicine, there is still the scripture. Not only does the scripture endure, it's free.

The church outside of Caledonia is a frame building on a rise above the town, with a cedar roof and high windows along each wall. It is in decent repair; it could use a coat of paint but in these times there is no money for that. The preacher hasn't been paid for nearly a year now. If the parishioners can't scrape together funds to pay the minister, then a gallon of paint is out of the question. He gets by on the meager donations to the collection plate each week, and his uncanny ability to show up on people's doorsteps at mealtime.

There is a cemetery with tombstones dating back to the 1600s behind the building and that's where Bobby is hunkered down, watching the congregation arrive, some on foot, some riding mules and driving horse and buggies, a few driving motorcars.

Bobby keeps out of sight, behind a crypt that houses an obscure general from the Revolutionary War. He is waiting patiently, watching the vehicles arrive. He is headed for Wilkes

County, a hundred and twenty miles away, and he is tired of walking. He has no interest in the rattletrap Model T coupes, the Dodge trucks or the Chevrolet sedans. He is waiting for a Ford V8. He'd left the stolen Buick an hour or so out of Asheville. He wouldn't risk the police catching up to him. Or Luanne neither. He can't say which of the two concerned him more.

After a time, he decides he is not to be rewarded this Sabbath and will have to settle on one of the lesser vehicles already parked in the churchyard. After mingling beneath the maple trees for a time, the congregation has now filed inside, and the organist is playing "Just A Closer Walk With Thee." Bobby scans the vehicles once more and decides on a 1929 Dodge truck. Dodge made a good flathead six.

But then he hears the familiar chug of an engine and the grinding gears from an inexperienced downshift. A moment later a 1936 Ford roadster pulls into the yard. A callow youth with slicked-down hair, wearing a white linen suit gets out of the car, looks at himself in the rearview mirror, runs a comb through his pomade, and goes inside.

The roadster is nearly new and Bobby can see the V8 emblem on the grille. He stands watching, wary that somebody might come outside, to go to the privy or retrieve something they may have forgotten. Inside the church, the preacher begins to sermonize. Bobby knows there will be another hymn coming shortly, and he waits for it.

When he hears the voices launch into "How Great Thou Art," he makes his way through the trees and tombstones to the churchyard. He glances into the roadster's interior, hoping to see the key in the ignition, but it isn't there. He retrieves a length of wire from his coat pocket and quietly lifts the hood on the passenger side, then runs the wire from a live connection on the firewall to the distributor. He gently closes the hood, gets into the car and hits the starter button on the floor. The engine fires up at once. He glances at the church. A small girl of five or six is standing by one of the tall windows, watching him. Behind her, the parishioners are facing the other way and giving the hymn their all. Bobby keeps his eyes on the little girl as he eases the gearshift into low. When he starts out, she waves to him and Bobby waves back.

Bye-bye.

The Ford is as smooth as silk. Bobby takes the county road down to the highway and heads north towards Wilkesboro. He figures the church service, depending on the preacher, would run anywhere from an hour to three, and that will give him plenty of time to get out of the county. By the time the car is reported stolen, Bobby might even be in Wilkesboro. He'll leave it in a lane outside of town somewhere and within a day or two the slick-haired swain will have his roadster back.

But then things rarely go as planned. Or at least, things in Bobby's world rarely go as planned. Coming to a stop sign thirty miles out of Wilkesboro, he spots a cardboard placard, nailed to a fence post at the intersection. The sign reads:

RACING TODAY 2 MILES

There is an arrow pointing to the right beneath the words. Bobby sits at the intersection for a moment. Wilkesboro is left. Wilkesboro, where he can be in less than an hour. Where he can ditch the stolen roadster and make his way to his Uncle Stan's place. His uncle is a smithy; maybe he can help Bobby find employment. A new start. No more gas station jobs. No more Luanne and her flighty dreams of bank robber fame and movie stardom. No more stolen cars. Well, aside from the one he's currently driving.

Wilkesboro it is. Bobby turns left.

But, as the pen is mightier than the sword, the pull is stronger than the will. He makes it less than a mile before he slows down, cranks the wheel, and puts the roadster into a skidding U-turn, dust flying. He heads back east.

The race is being held in a fallow field a few hundred yards off the main road. Two or three dozen men have gathered to watch as eight or nine vehicles, family sedans and farm pickup trucks for the most part, prepare to race. Bobby pulls up in the roadster and heads for the starting line—marked by two bales of hay. A heavy-set man with a bushy red beard appears to be in charge. He carries a pad of foolscap on a clipboard and is moving from car to car. He looks up as Bobby rolls to a stop, giving the roadster a critical once-over as Bobby climbs out from behind the wheel.

"Something I can do for you?

"If you're the man in charge, you can," Bobby says.

None of the other "race" cars were worth more than thirty or forty dollars. The big man looks at the roadster again.

"You intend to race this car?"

"Yes, sir," Bobby says. "More 'n that, I intend to win."

The big man shrugs his indifference. "Two-dollar entry, winner gets half. We won't get started here for a bit."

Bobby hands the man a dollar bill and the rest in change, then signs the sheet where the man indicates. The big man doesn't bother to look at the signature. Bobby gets back in the car and wheels the roadster to the rear of the pack. He reaches for a stick of Beechnut and chews while he waits. Men with sledgehammers and steel fence posts are still laying out the route. It is a half hour before the racing begins.

The race is just shy of complete chaos. Half the drivers are as raw as a north wind and have no idea what they are doing. Cars spin out in the dirt and crash through the fences. Green farm boys, driving pickup trucks "borrowed" from their fathers, hold the gas pedal to the floor. Two blow their engines to pieces. A Studebaker coupe overshoots the track and flips over three times. The engines are loud, the smoke and exhaust creating a thick cloud over the field. The fans—local youths primed with pints of busthead—are ecstatic.

Bobby maneuvers the roadster through the melee like an artist, sliding through the corners and flying down the straights. From time to time he scrapes fenders with the other cars, then pushes past them. He wins easily. Crossing the finish line, he slides the roadster to a stop and climbs out, cool as ice. Bobby is in his element, the only place he really feels at home. The man in the wild beard approaches, counts out ten dollars and hands it over. Bobby is congratulated by the crowd. Somebody hands him a jar of moonshine.

Soon there is talk of another race. Some of the farm boys want another shot at Bobby and his roadster, even though he'd trounced them all. Bobby is fine with the prospect. It would mean ten more dollars in his pocket for one thing but more than that, it is another chance to race. Truth be known, he'd do it for free.

He is standing along the fence, nipping at the pint, when the police car arrives. The decal on the sedan door reads: Alexander County Police. It doesn't take much to decipher why the sheriff has shown up. When the man climbs out of the car, he puts his hat on and heads straight for the stolen roadster. Watching from fifty yards away, Bobby hands the pint to the nearest farm boy and slips through the fence and into a cornfield. Within seconds he is out of sight.

The sheriff has a look at the Ford roadster. Noting the damaged fenders and grille, he beckons over the bearded man in charge.

"Who's driving this here vehicle?"

"Why, some stranger," the man says, looking around for Bobby. "Pulled in from nowhere, said he wanted to race."

"Where is he?"

"He was here not one minute ago. But I don't see him now."

"What's his name?" the sheriff asks.

"I couldn't say," the man admits. "Like I said, he was a stranger." He realizes something. "Wait now…he signed the sheet."

The man retrieves his clipboard from the running board of a truck and brings it over to the cop. He points out the signature, reading it himself for the first time. "Well, hell."

"Franklin D. Roosevelt," the sheriff says.

At that moment, the man who is clearly not the president of the United States emerges from the cornfield a quarter mile away, steps out onto the main road heading to Wilkesboro, and sticks out his thumb. An approaching Mack truck downshifts to a stop.

FOUR

Tilda doesn't show up to the house the next morning so it falls to Ava to make breakfast. There is plenty to eat in the house. Jedidiah keeps laying hens and he has always raised a couple of hogs for slaughter every year. There is a large vegetable garden behind the house, with corn, tomatoes, onions, okra and string beans in various stages of growth. Working in the kitchen makes Ava think of her mother, gone six years now. Even though Tilda has been with them seemingly forever, Ava's mother handled most of the cooking and she'd made an effort, not always successfully, to pass along what she knew to Ava. For her part, Ava has always been interested in things outside the house, things of a mechanical nature. She could drive a Model T when she was ten years old.

Her father and Morgan sit at the table while Ava fries sow belly and eggs, and steeps grits in a pot. Jedediah has the weekly Wilkesboro newspaper spread out before him. Morgan is searching the dial on the Philco, seeking the news out of Charlotte. A storm threatens and reception is poor; he gives up as Ezra comes through the back door, having walked over from his house along the ridge. He stops when he sees Ava at the stove.

"Why are you cooking the eggs?"

"Would you prefer them raw?" she asks.

He gives her a look and then sits at the table. He takes a

moment to regard the newspaper in his father's hands. "I don't know how long we can keep going like this," he says. "I don't know how long the country can."

Jedediah folds the paper and puts it aside. "The wolf is not at our door. There are many out there worse off than us. We have but a few dollars in the bank but this farm will provide for the family. I have faith that in due time Mr. Roosevelt will light our way."

"Another crooked millionaire," Ezra says. "He don't care about us."

"He's our president," Jedediah reminds him.

Ava comes over with a platter of food. "Now, boys, mother never allowed political talk at the breakfast table."

"Where is that colored woman anyway?" Ezra demands. "It's her job to cook the breakfast."

"She didn't show here this morning," Jedediah says. "First time in twenty odd years, I believe."

"I'll go over there after breakfast," Ava says. "Could be she's ailing."

"Or just plain lazy," Ezra says. "It's in their breeding. I read an article about it recently."

Morgan looks at his brother. "She's missed one day in twenty years and you're calling her lazy? I'd hate to see what you'd call industrious."

Ezra ignores Morgan and tucks into his breakfast. Over the years, he has gotten into the habit of dismissing both Morgan and Ava whenever they confront him, finding it easier to avoid an argument than to engage in one he will only end up losing.

"What about the men who worked for you, father?" Rose asks. "What are they doing now?"

"Some found work through the New Deal," Jedediah says.

"Not many," Ezra interjects. "And them that didn't are not doing well."

Jedediah turns a tolerant eye on Ezra. "The Lord will provide."

The statement is meant to end the discussion and it does precisely that. The talk turns to the weather and the new Cary Grant movie showing in town. They have finished eating and are drinking coffee when they hear Tilda's steps on the back porch. Ava stands up as she enters the kitchen. The housekeeper is trembling like a leaf in the wind and there are tears coursing down her cheeks.

There is no money for embalming, or even for ice to pack the body in, so the funeral is that same afternoon. After lunch, Ava bathes and changes into a black dress she'd last worn to her mother's funeral. Morgan had left earlier, headed to Charlotte with a few gallons of molasses, hoping to do some wholesale business with the mercantile interests there. He didn't appear particularly optimistic in this.

Ezra enters the living room as Ava is standing in front of the hall mirror, adjusting her hat.

"Where's Morgan?"

"Off to Charlotte. He told you that."

"He did not."

"Over breakfast." Ava removes the hat and walks across the room, to a vase filled with tulips. She snaps one at the stem and puts it in the hat band, then goes back to the mirror for another look. Ezra, never overly observant, finally notices how Ava is dressed.

"Where are you going?"

"To the funeral."

"What funeral?"

"Tilda's mother died last night," Ava says. "You might recall her telling us this a few hours ago. Is it possible that you're getting even more obtuse, brother?"

Ezra ignores the suggestion. "You are *not* going to a colored funeral in a colored church. Have you lost your mind?"

"I don't think so," Ava says. "But then I have long suspected that people who have lost their minds are always the last to know."

"This is not a joking matter," Ezra tells her. "Although these days it seems with you that everything is. I suspect that's the city talking. I forbid you to go to that funeral, sister."

Ava smiles at the word "city", and her brother's audacity in using it. She takes one last critical look in the mirror then turns to retrieve her handbag from the hall table. "When Mother was dying, Tilda sat with her every day for weeks. She slept on a cot in her room. She was there for our mother the times when I wasn't. The times when you weren't. Today I'm going to her mother's funeral."

Ezra's lips are tight. He has a habit of trying too hard to make sense of things he can't understand. "You should never have gone to Chicago."

"What does Chicago have to do with anything?"

"Come on," Ezra says. "Everybody knows; your kind of thinking is epidemic up north. The Jews and the intellectuals and the likes. Who are you to upset the order of things?"

"Who am I to upset the order of things? I had no idea I possessed such power. Tell me though—what order of things?"

"It's very simple. God did not intend whites and coloreds to intermingle. That's a natural fact. You did not see goats intermingling with horses, for instance. You do not see squirrels and rabbits living together."

"Those are different *species*, brother," Ava tells him. "You have a problem with color. But I recall seeing a white horse once having a very good time in a pasture field with a black horse. God didn't see fit to intervene that day."

"That is disgusting. I shudder to think what father would think if he was to hear you say that."

"You're the one that brought God into it," Ava says. "But it appears to me of late that God is more diplomatic than that. What I see is a God who has decided to bestow upon all people, regardless of color, the gifts of hunger and poverty and despair." She walks to the door then looks back. "*Why* he is doing that is another question altogether. Wouldn't you agree, brother?"

Outside she goes down the steps and heads out on the dusty red road leading into Darkytown. The Baptist church is just a few hundred yards away, a low-slung log building with a crude steeple fashioned from pine limbs. From all around, people are streaming from their houses, all heading to the funeral. Colored people.

There are a few white households along the way, inhabited mostly by families that had worked for the Flagg family over the years. Now a handful of people come out on their front steps, watching Ava as she walks. Apparently Ezra isn't the only one concerned with her upsetting the natural rhythm of things. Ava ignores their looks and walks on, her gaze fixed on the church house down the road.

She feels his presence beside her before she sees him. He is dressed in his best frock coat, wearing a wide-brimmed hat.

"You look beautiful today, daughter."

She slides her hand through her father's arm. "So do you, old man."

FIVE

Uncle Stan is Bobby's mother's kid brother, although he isn't a kid of any kind by now, having turned sixty the year before. He has a blacksmith shop at the southern edge of Wilkesboro, a crooked frame building that dates back to the pioneer days. There is a coal-powered forge in the shop and an Armitage anvil out front that weighs more than five hundred pounds.

"The one thing I ain't never worried about anybody ever stealing," Uncle Stan likes to say.

Bobby had showed up the night before, having hitched his way to town after his escape from the racetrack in the farmer's field. Uncle Stan lives alone now; his kids are grown and his second wife left him for one of the Baylor boys from Charlestown a couple years earlier. When she discovered that her new beau wasn't nearly as charming as she first thought and was in fact a drunken lay-about with a propensity for knocking her around, she returned to Uncle Stan. Or at least tried to return to him. He was having none of it and showed her the door. Uncle Stan isn't the forgiving type.

"I can't help you out much in the work department," he tells Bobby over breakfast the next day. "I'm shoeing a few mules. Fixing the odd plowshare or seed drill. Half the time I'm working on the cuff anyway, or barter. Hard to charge folks when you know they got no cash."

They are eating on the porch, biscuits and molasses. There is a pot of coffee from the night before, warming again on the forge a few yards away.

"You might make a dollar or two gathering bloodroot," Uncle Stan continues. "I hear that some still do. Finding a buyer might be tricky, in these times."

Bobby walks over to pour himself a cup. The coffee is stale tasting and weak. He suspects it had first been brewed a couple of days earlier.

"Man ain't likely to make his fortune gathering bloodroot," he says.

"Looking to get rich, are you?" Uncle Stan asks.

Bobby exhales heavily. "I guess not."

"How was it in the lock-up?" Uncle Stan asks.

"Boring."

"They don't put you to work there?"

"Not in county," Bobby says. "No work to be done there. Over at state they got a shop and all that. Road crews."

"You don't want to be there though."

"No, sir."

"Better quit stealing them automobiles then," Uncle Stan says.

Bobby nods and drinks the bad coffee. He wants to tell his uncle that he has every intention to quit stealing cars, but then he reminds himself that he's been out of jail less than a week and already stolen two. And held up a gas station near Stony Point. And almost robbed a bank in Asheville. He blames the last two incidents on Luanne but he can't deny his own involvement. Serving those two months, it had been his intention to walk a straight line when he was released. So far he'd been walking the crookedest straight line in history. He decides he best change the subject.

"They doing any racing around here?" he asks.

"Over at the Hollow still," Uncle Stan says. "Pick Johnson brought his Graham Paige coupe in, broke an axle over there the other night when he ran off the so-called track and hit a culvert. I welded her up and he gave me a dozen hen's eggs. But I don't

go near the place. Too damn loud for me; I'm near deaf already."
He regards Bobby a moment. "You got a one-track mind, nephew.
How do you figure to get into racing when you ain't got a job?"

Bobby has another sip. "That's a good question."

The roadster is a '28 Model A, sitting in the long grass behind the
Wilkesboro Mercantile. The car belongs to Lemuel Sims, the store
owner. He'd parked it there a couple years earlier, after the engine
started knocking. He decided he needed a truck for business
anyway so he'd just let the roadster sit. With money being the way
it was, nobody had even asked about the vehicle since.

Saturday around noon, Sims comes out the rear of the store,
intending to dump an ash can, and finds Bobby Barlow there,
walking around the Ford and kneeling to look at the tires and the
springs. Preoccupied, he doesn't notice the owner.

"Something I can do for you, son?" Sims asks.

Bobby straightens up. "You looking to sell this old Ford?"

"I'd part with her, I guess," Sims says. "The motor is kaput."

"Kaput how?" Bobby asks.

"I'm no mechanic," Sims says as he comes down from the dock.
"Started knocking to beat the band one day and I just parked her."

Bobby opens the hood side to have a look at the engine. He
reaches over and tries to work the carburetor linkage but it is
seized fast. He takes hold of the fan blade and turns the engine
over to make sure it isn't stuck as well.

"What kind of money?" he asks.

"I really never gave it any thought 'til now," Sims says and he
hesitates while he does. "Give me twenty dollars and you can haul
it away."

Bobby nods. It is a fair price, providing he could get it running
on the cheap. But he doesn't have twenty dollars. He pulls out the
dipstick. The oil is down a quart and black as tar.

"I haven't got but ten," he says. He slides the stick back into
the tube and when he does his shirtsleeve rides up to reveal the
tattoo on his forearm.

"Was you over there?" Sims asks, looking at the Marine corps emblem.

Bobby looks over. "At the Marne, 2nd Division. You?"

"83rd Infantry. Italy."

Bobby walks around to the front of the car and removes the radiator cap. The rad is full. He dips into the coolant and rubs it between his finger and thumb. Sims stands watching him.

"You see any action?"

"Some," Bobby says. "Me and a pal got assigned to working on the heavy trucks. Sometimes one would get stranded behind the lines and we'd have to go in and bring it back."

Sims watches as Bobby replaces the cap. "You say you got ten dollars?"

Bobby nods.

"That's close enough," Sims says.

Uncle Stan has a Reo truck that he uses for his farrier business. He and Bobby drive over that afternoon and tow the roadster home. Bobby frees the carburetor and cleans the plugs and points and has the car running within the hour. But just barely. Sims was right; the engine knocked as if it was about to fly apart. Bobby runs it for ten seconds and shuts it down. Thirty minutes later, he has removed the side plate and cylinder head and found the problem. A valve spring had broken and then the valve itself had snapped in two.

Uncle Stan has gone over to Yadkin County to shoe a couple of draft horses for a tobacco farmer. Bobby walks into town in the heat of the day, to Charley Walker's Texaco at the main inter-section. Charley has two gas pumps and a double bay garage. Out back, there are a number of wrecked cars; some have been sitting there for more than twenty years.

"That sedan in the corner with the crunched fender should have what you need," Charley says. He gives Bobby a long look. "I thought you were locked up."

Charley is seventy-six years old and has been fixing vehicles and farm implements in Wilkes County since the days of the buckboard. He doesn't pull punches when talking to Bobby, or anybody else for that matter. Charley was as capable a man as Bobby had ever known. He'd been in the Klondike during the gold rush back in '99. While panning a stream one morning he'd gotten too close to a grizzly cub and the sow had attacked him, mauling him and tearing his left ear off. An ex-army medic, a one-armed alcoholic who'd fought at Gettysburg, had sewed it back on in camp and the next morning Charley was back at the stream.

"I got out," Bobby tells him.

"I can see that."

"How much for a valve and spring?"

"You do the work, two dollars," Charley tells him.

After paying for the roadster, Bobby has two dollars and two nickels to his name. He hands Charley the two bucks and goes to remove the parts from the sedan.

Back at Uncle Stan's, he replaces the broken parts. He doesn't have money for a new head gasket so he coats the original with aluminum paint he finds in the shed. He torques the head bolts by feel and gives the engine a crank. After a half-dozen attempts, the car fires up, stutters a bit then evens out and purrs like a cat.

When Uncle Stan returns, Bobby has the roadster up on jacks and is adjusting the brakes. He starts the engine to show how well it runs.

"Well, you got yourself a car," Uncle Stan says. "What are you going to do with her?"

Bobby smiles. "What do you think?"

SIX

After the funeral Ava and Jedediah go to the graveside for the burial
and then head back for home. They have lunch and afterwards sit
on the front porch, drinking coffee. Down in the hollow, people
are gathered in clusters after the funeral, talking. Tilda had had
every intention of returning to work at the house that afternoon
but Ava had nixed the idea.

"You can come back on Monday," she'd told the housekeeper.
"Or whenever you're ready."

On the porch now, Jedediah stokes his pipe and lights it. Ava
has always loved the smell of his pipe tobacco. In Chicago, feeling
liberated, she'd even smoked a pipe herself until she realized that
she liked only the aroma, not the act of actually smoking, nor the
lightheaded feeling she got from it.

"So what now, daughter?" Jedediah asks. "Are you home for
good?"

"I'm not so sure about that," Ava says. "I wouldn't say that
Wilkes County abounds with career opportunities just now."

"Can you name a place that does?"

"I expect I can't," Ava admits.

"You could settle down and present me with some grandbabies."

"How would I manage that?" Ava asks. "To the best of my
recollection, I don't have a husband."

"Plenty of good Christian men in this valley."

Ava smiles and drinks her coffee. "You're looking to raffle me off, old man?"

"I am not."

"Good to know," Ava says. She looks up to see a black man approaching along the road, wearing a brown worsted suit and a straw fedora. "Who's this in the hat?"

"Luther Briscoe," Jedediah says. "He was at the church."

"Well, it is him," Ava recognizes. "He's somewhat wider than he used to be." She waits as Luther Briscoe leaves the roadway to cross the lawn, stopping at the bottom step to the porch. "Hello, Mr. Briscoe."

"Miz Ava's come home," Luther says, removing his hat. "Bless you."

"How are you?" Ava asks. She tries to estimate how old the man is. He has a daughter Ava's age but he also has a couple of boys who would be in their forties now, she guesses. Luther might be sixty-five or seventy, maybe older. He is known for his ability to play the banjo and harmonica.

"Getting by," Luther says. "Getting by."

"It was a fine service," Jedediah says.

"It was at that." Luther turns the hat brim in his hands. "Befitting the woman herself. Are you home to stay, Miz Ava, or just having you a little visit?"

"We were just discussing that," Ava says. "As of the moment, you could say I am carefully weighing my options." She smiles. "Truth is, I'm sitting on the porch and not weighing anything heavier than this coffee cup."

Luther returns the smile before turning to Jedediah, his eyes asking something.

"Go ahead," Jedediah says. "She's gassed and ready to go."

"Much obliged, Parson," the old man says. "Much obliged."

He returns to the road and heads for the molasses plant across the way. A moment later, they hear the sound of a truck starting and then the Model T with HOMER FLAGG & SONS stenciled on the

34

door comes around the building and rumbles out onto the road, heading south.

"What is that about?" Ava asks.

Jedediah puffs on the pipe. "Oh, he's been borrowing the truck every now and again. Goes up to Johnson City to visit his daughter. He was doing deliveries for us but we had to lay him off."

"His daughter is Angeline," Ava says. "Unless he has another I don't know of."

"Just the one," Jedediah says. "Two boys. One went north but the other is still here. The mother died two years ago."

"Angeline is in Richmond," Ava says. "We correspond on a regular basis through the post. She works for a dentist and she thinks she's going to marry him. I fear he might be leading her on."

Jedediah shrugs. "I expect she moved to Johnson City and didn't mention it."

"Didn't mention it?" Ava asks. "I got a letter from her a week ago, and she was on and on about the tooth doctor."

Jedediah's pipe goes out and he busies himself relighting it. He doesn't seem overly concerned about the discrepancies in old Briscoe's story, but then again it is his nature, as a preacher and a man, to allow his fellow man leeway in many things. Ava is less inclined in that direction.

"I'd say that's mighty odd," she tells her father.

Saturday night Morgan is playing some songs with his musical group at a roadhouse on the outskirts of Wilkesboro. Ava is going along. After supper Morgan puts his guitar in the rumble seat of his Nash coupe and pulls around to the front of the house to wait for her. After a moment, he sounds the horn a few times. Ava comes out a few moments later, tying a scarf around her neck. She wears a long skirt and an angora sweater she'd paid too much money for in Chicago.

"Where's the fire?" she asks.

"Trying to light one under you, sister."

They head out along the dirt county road. It has been another warm day but the heat is subsiding now. The wind is up out of the west and it is nice cruising along in the coupe, even though the vehicle has seen better days. It leaves a trail of blue smoke in its wake and the steering box is worn, causing the car to take up every inch of the road at certain speeds.

"So who's in the orchestra of yours anyway?" Ava asks.

"We call it a group, not an orchestra," Morgan tells her.

"What's the difference?"

"An orchestra is something you might see at a recital hall."

"And what's a group?"

Morgan hesitates. "Well, a group is just that. A group."

"You really don't know, do you?" Ava smiles. "So tell me—who's in this group?"

"Teddy Rickenboch you know," Morgan says. "He plays bass fiddle. And Dicky Murdock you don't. He's on accordion."

"Teddy Rickenboch from Spencer Creek?"

"Yes."

"I thought he went to Florida to work with his brother building houses for retired people."

"The company went under," Morgan says. "Teddy came home. He's back on the family farm." Morgan slows down. "Hey—they're racing at the Hollow."

Ava looks up to see a crude sign nailed to a post. There is a silhouette of a car and an arrow pointing north. Underneath it reads simply: TONIGHT. Morgan slows the coupe and turns to follow the arrow.

"What are we doing?"

"We're going to catch a race," Morgan says.

"I thought I was going to hear some music."

"You will," Morgan promises. "But we'll watch a race or two first. You ever seen this, Ava?"

Ava is bored in the extreme. "No."

"You're in for a treat."

"I somehow doubt that."

The Hollow is yet another farmer's field masquerading as a racetrack.

A thirty-acre pasture, it now has a worn track, roughly a hundred feet wide, around the perimeter. The farmer's gate is the entrance. A sign reading ADMISSION TEN CENTS is nailed to one gate post while ENTRIES TWO DOLLARS is displayed on the other.

Boss Harvey runs the show. He made a deal with the farmer who owns the field a year earlier. For ten dollars a night the field is Boss's to do with it as he pleases. They've been racing several times a month ever since.

Edgar Slack stands at the starting line, marked by two large rocks in the dirt, with a clipboard in one hand and a hat for the cash in the other, signing up the entries. Edgar is a hundred and thirty pounds, with curly hair and eyeglasses as thick as RC Cola bottles. His father owns the only funeral parlor in Wilkesboro and Edgar works for him. As a business, burying people is pretty much recession proof.

Bobby comes through the gate in the roadster, bounces through a drainage ditch and rolls to a stop beside Edgar.

"Hey, Bobby, you got her going, did you?"

Bobby shuts the engine down and climbs out. "Was there ever any doubt? Sign me up, Edgar."

"Two bucks to race," Edgar says.

"I spent my last dollar getting this thing running," Bobby says. "Sign me up on the cuff, will you?"

"Jesus, Boss Man will have my hide," Edgar says.

"Where is that tub of lard anyway?"

Edgar points. "Him and his two boys are filling that low spot with gravel. We got a sink hole there. But he'll be back and you know Boss Man would rather eat a bucket of worms than give out credit to anybody."

"Who made him dictator?" Bobby asks. "Cover me, Edgar. Shit, you got money coming out your ears. And you know damn well I'm going to win the race."

"I don't know nothing of the kind," Edgar says. "You don't got but four cylinders and half these boys are running V8s."

"But I'm the one who knows how to drive," Bobby says.

"Says you."

"Cover me, Edgar."

Edgar shakes his head but digs into his pocket for the two dollars and puts it in the hat. "I ain't going to make a habit of this, Bobby."

The race starts twenty minutes later. There are eleven entries, eight cars and three farm trucks, driven by sons whose fathers likely have no idea what is going on tonight. Most of the vehicles are either six or eight cylinders. Bobby's tired four banger is no match for them on the straights. Only in the corners can he make up ground, cutting tight on the inside, drifting into the turns and coming out fast. He manages to stay with the leaders until the last lap. Barreling out of the far turn, he sees a chance to take the lead and guns it. But he cuts it too hard and slides sideways in front of a Dodge sedan. The sedan hits him broadside, pushes Bobby and the roadster off the track and down a slope. The roadster tips onto two wheels and rolls over. Bobby is thrown free as the car crashes into an elm tree. The remaining cars—less two that have already blown their engines—rumble past and on to the finish line. The Dodge wins the race and the driver—Chick Humphries—immediately turns back up the track to where Bobby is slowly getting to his feet. He finds his fedora in the grass and puts it on.

"I'm sorry, Bobby," Chick says, rolling to a stop. "I couldn't get around you."

Bobby rubs his shoulder where he'd hit the ground. "Shit, I've been in worse wrecks on a bicycle." He walks over to look at the roadster, lying on its side. "Can you give me a hand, Chick?"

The two men manage to push the car over and back on its wheels. Bobby does a slow circle, limping around the vehicle, taking inventory.

"I got a rope," Chick says. "We can tow her in." He pauses, regarding the roadster. "There ain't that much left of her to tow."

Bobby kneels down. "Front axle's busted and the motor mount too. Shit—there's oil running out of somewhere." He straightens and calculates for a moment what it would cost to fix a wreck that isn't worth fixing. "To hell with it. I'm done running these four bangers anyway."

Leaning against the Nash a hundred yards away, on a rise inside the gate, Morgan and Ava watch the proceedings.

"Looks like the driver's all right," Morgan says. He squints through the dust and smoke. "Hey—you see who it is?"

Ava shakes her head.

"That's Bobby Barlow from Cub Creek. I never knew he was back in the area. You remember him. The man is a wizard with a wrench and he can drive. Last I heard, he was in the hoosegow for stealing cars."

Ava yawns and makes no effort to stifle it. "Can we go now?"

SEVEN

The roadhouse is called Mac's and is situated at the town limits, just off the pike. There is a baseball field behind the place and on Saturday nights the owner—who's name isn't Mac—sets up a makeshift riser at home plate and invites local musicians to come down and play. Spectators either sit in the bleachers or stand in the infield. Some remain in the parking lot, sitting on the hoods and fenders of cars. Given the economic circumstances in Wilkes County, there is no admission charge; the roadhouse does a fair business selling sodas and hot dogs to the crowd.

Walking to the bleachers as Morgan and his band are getting ready to play, Ava hears her name called and looks up to see June Patterson, squealing like a piglet and waving as if she's hailing a taxicab on State Street. June is gussied up like a china doll, as is her custom, in a frilly pink skirt and a sweater with a kitten embroidered on the breast. She has pink ribbons in her hair. Ava climbs up to join her along the top row of the bleachers.

Morgan's group begins with "The Wabash Cannonball" and then moves on to "The Ballad of Casey Jones." Morgan plays guitar and handles the vocals. He has a clear alto voice and has been singing to Ava for as long as she can recall, going back to lullabies and nursery rhymes when they were barely old enough to walk. She's always been envious of his voice and his musical talent. He's been telling her since they were children that she couldn't carry a tune in a washtub and in this he is right.

Around the time that Casey Jones buys the farm, Teddy Rickenboch snaps a string on his bass and they have to take a break while he replaces it.

"In publishing?" June repeats. "How'd you ever land a job like that? You never even finished college."

June likes to remind Ava that she is the better educated of the two. Ava had gone to college in Charlotte for one year, gotten bored and dropped out. June, on the other hand, had attended Asheville Collegiate for two years and graduated with a degree in the secretarial arts. To date, her diploma has landed her a position as cashier and stock girl at Handy Andy's Hardware in Hamptonville. The proprietor Andy is June's uncle on her mother's side.

"I just applied," Ava replies. "There was an ad in the paper. Had an interview with a man who smelled like gin and salami and got hired."

"What did you do there?"

"Well, I would purchase the rough manuscripts, edit them, choose the artwork for the covers and then send them off for printing and binding."

"You're kidding!"

"You bet your pearl buttons I'm kidding," Ava says. "Truth of the matter is, I answered the old boys' phones, fetched coffee, emptied their garbage cans and lied to their wives when they didn't go straight home after work. There were times when I thought I might jump out the window. Luckily, I got laid off before I did. Sometimes I think this Depression is the best thing ever happened to me."

The band begins to play again amid a roar of exhaust. Ava looks over to see several cars from the race earlier pulling into the parking lot beside the field. The drivers shut their engines down and climb out, all acting cock of the walk. Chick Humphries in his Dodge sedan is among them and Bobby Barlow is riding shotgun with Chick. All of them lean against the cars' front fenders to watch the show. Soon there are pint jars being passed around.

"Oh geez, grease monkeys," June says. "They always show up. Bet they don't have *them* in Chicago."

"Oh, I'm sure there's an urban version," Ava says. She watches the men as Morgan and the band swing into a raucous version of Jimmie Rodgers's "In The Jailhouse Now." "Looks like they enjoy their liquor. Or do you figure that's lemonade they're passing around?"

June shakes her head in disapproval. "It's downright scandalous. They drink and smoke and use bad language. You wouldn't want to get near one of them. They stink of gasoline and grease. A man wants to get close to me, he'd better smell of lilac or bay rum."

Ava smiles. "When you find a man in this valley who smells of lilac, I suggest you grab him and hold on with both hands."

Across the way Bobby is still moping over the loss of his roadster, a car he owned for exactly three days. He finds the music to his liking though—especially the rollicking Rodgers song—and it isn't his nature in any case to stay down. Not only that but upon arriving he'd become immediately aware of three young women, standing in front of the riser where the band played. The girl in the middle has shoulder-length auburn hair and wears a snug summer dress with tiny roses on it. Bobby looks over at Chick, who is tilting a jar to his lips.

"Who's that in the dress?"

Chick wipes his mouth. "Can't see from here. Want me to go find out?"

"I do not," Bobby says. He walks over and stops directly in front of the woman in question, turning his back to her as he claps along with the band.

"Excuse me?" she asks.

Bobby turns and feigns surprise to see her. "Yeah?"

"You're in the way." She has to shout above the music.

"Well, I apologize," Bobby says. "I didn't see you there."

"The dickens you didn't."

"What's that?" Bobby points to his ear to indicate he can't hear.

"I said the dickens you didn't!"

At that instant the band finishes the song. The woman's voice is loud above the crowd and she is embarrassed.

Bobby smiles. "You're right. How's a man supposed to miss the prettiest girl on the premises? What's your name anyway?"

"Myrna Lee."

"I'm Bobby Barlow."

"Oh, I know who you are," Myrna Lee says. "My brother is Jake Saunders. You used to come by the house."

"You're a Saunders?" Bobby says. "Hey, I know you now. Hell, you were still in pigtails last I saw you."

"For your information, I was never in pigtails, Bobby Barlow."

Bobby laughs. "Where's old Jake at these days?"

"Doing a stretch over to Camp Polk for counterfeiting," Myrna Lee says. "Gets out in the fall."

"Jake was always one to hang paper."

"Yeah and look where it gets him."

"Well, I have to say Myrna Lee Saunders, that you have done a spectacular job growing up."

Myrna Lee blushes. "Why, thank you, kind sir."

Bobby grins as he looks out over the spectators in the bleachers. "I wonder if I might stop by—" He stops, hesitates. "Say—is that Ava Flagg over there?"

Myrna Lee turns, slightly miffed that Bobby is looking at other women while wooing her. "The kewpie doll?"

"Beside her, in the dark hair."

"I couldn't say," Myrna Lee replies. "Since I don't know any Ava Flagg."

Bobby turns back to her. "As I was saying. I was wondering if I might stop by sometime, take you for a malted."

"I work part-time at the Rexall in town," Myrna Lee says. "At the lunch counter. Why don't you come there and pay me a visit?"

"I'm going to do just that."

A car horn sounds loudly. Bobby turns to see Edgar pulling

up in his father's Studebaker. He jumps out, looks around until he spots Bobby, then heads over.

"Looks like old Edgar's about to split a gut," Bobby says. He waits until the skinny boy comes through the fence. "Don't tell me you're here chasing your two dollars. Tell you what—I'll give you that roadster of mine and we'll call it even."

Edgar frowns and shakes off the debt. "I just stopped for gas at Charley Walker's Texaco. He towed in a wreck while I was at the pumps. I figured it might be of interest to you." In his excitement Edgar doesn't notice Myrna Lee standing there until now. "Oh, hi Myrna Lee."

Bobby sees that she has no idea who Edgar is, but she nods anyway. It figures; Edgar is the sort to worship girls like Myrna Lee from a distance. Edgar is the sort to worship all girls from afar.

"What's the car?" he asks.

"A '32 Ford coupe," Edgar says.

"Four cylinder or V8?"

"She's an eight."

Now Bobby is interested. "For sale?"

"Charley says yeah."

Bobby turns to point a finger at Myrna Lee. "I'll be catching up to you later, Miss Saunders. Count on it. Let's go, Edgar."

When they get to Walker's Texaco, the wrecked coupe has already been towed around back, but is still hanging off the hook of the tow truck. The entire passenger side is ruined—front fender crushed, running board torn half off, rear fender crumpled against the wheel. Bobby walks around the car while Edgar stands off to the side, pleased as punch to be pleasing Bobby.

Charley Walker comes out the back door of the garage when he hears them pull up. Bobby glances over at him.

"Who owns it?"

"As of tonight, I do," Charley says. "Belonged to some rich guy's kid. Kid was drunk, drove into a concrete bridge. The old man showed up, gave the kid five across the snotbox, then sold me the car."

Bobby tries to open the passenger door but it is jammed from the collision. "How much you give for her?"

"None of your business."

"None of my business," Bobby repeats. "Is the car for sale or not, Charley?"

"After a fashion, young Barlow," the old man says. "Here's the situation. My mechanic is in the hospital. They took out some shrapnel he's been carrying around in his back for near twenty years. I need a mechanic for a month or so. You want to work it off, we can make a deal on the car."

Bobby considers the offer as he makes another circle around the wreck.

"The thought of steady work scare you that much, boy?" Charley says. "Come here and look at this then." He lifts the hood side and props it open to reveal the engine. "The kid blew the original engine to pieces and the old man had this put in. Brand new V8, eighty-five horsepower, right from Ford Motor Company in Detroit. Hasn't got but a few hundred miles on it, according to the old man."

A glance at the engine is all Bobby needs. "I can start on Monday."

Charley closes the hood. "Be here at eight o'clock. You're five minutes late, I go looking for another mechanic."

EIGHT

After Sunday's service, the Flagg family has lunch at the big house on the hill. Afterward they sit outside on the porch and talk, while Ezra and Rachel's children play in the yard. Morgan's guitar leans against the railing. Ava stands with her hip against the newel post.

"That was a fine sermon, father," Rachel says.

Jedediah is lighting his pipe. "I have always found Corinthians to be a source of comfort, in good times and bad."

"I believe it's important to give people hope in times such as these," Rachel says. "I think the worshippers today felt that."

"All twelve of them," Ava points out.

"Now daughter," Jedediah admonishes. "It's not the size of the congregation, it's the heart of the congregation that matters. We need to keep in mind that our troubles are temporary." He puffs away at the pipe a moment, stoking it before continuing. "Many years ago, I had a distant cousin, a reprobate and unabashed heathen he was, but he had a saying I admired nonetheless. He would say—tough times don't last, tough people do."

Morgan reaches for his guitar and plays a couple of chords. "*Tough times, tough times, come again no more,*" he sings.

"Must everything be a joke?" Ezra asks.

"What do you know about jokes?" Morgan replies. "You've never told a joke in your life."

Ava smiles, listening. She is watching down the road, toward the colored church, which is just now getting out, people scattering to the four winds, some on foot, others in buggies behind horses and mules. A few drive cars. The congregation is large, forty or fifty people. Maybe folks who have less in life are more inclined to seek spiritual comfort.

Ava is waiting for Luther Briscoe to emerge and then she sees him, wearing the same suit and hat as a few days earlier. He passes the time of day with some fellow parishioners before making his way along the dusty road, heading north into the hollow. Ava comes down the steps and intercepts him at the intersection below the Flagg house.

"Good Sabbath, Mr. Briscoe."

Luther regards her warily. "Good Sabbath to you, child."

"How was your trip to Johnson City?"

"Oh," Luther replies just as slowly. "It was fine. Just fine."

"And Angeline? How is she doing?"

"She's doing real good," Luther says. "Real good."

Ava is of the opinion that people who have a habit of repeating themselves are quite often not being entirely honest, as if they are convinced they can make a falsehood true by mere repetition.

"Did I hear that she's working for a dentist up there?"

"She is," Luther says. "She is working for a dentist."

Ava slips a forefinger into the corner of her mouth and pulls it back. "I have a troublesome tooth here in the back. I wonder if I should consider going up to Johnson City to see this fellow Angeline works for."

She has succeeded in making the old man uncomfortable. He removes his hat as he glances over to the Flagg house, where the family is relaxing on the porch yet.

"Well now, he is a colored man—" he begins.

"I have no problem with that," Ava assures him. "As long as he's a skilled practitioner of the dental arts."

Luther takes a few moments. "The thing is—she is no longer working for him. She has taken a position elsewhere."

"And where is that?"

A family in an ancient chaise pulled by a brindle mule comes down the road. Ava and Luther step out of the way to allow them to pass, the reins slapping along the mule's withers, the leathers creaking on the shafts.

"She's working for a harness company," Luther says then.

Ava attempts to hide her smile. "A harness company? That's a step down from a dentist, isn't it?"

Now Luther, seeing his escape, feigns indignation. "There is dignity in all work, young lady. I should think that your father would have taught you that. Good day."

Ava, having heard all she needs to, lets him go.

The following Saturday she and Morgan sit parked in his Nash a half mile from the Flagg house, hidden in a stand of cedar trees that had been planted by Jedediah years earlier for a wind break. Shortly past ten o'clock they see Luther approaching the Flagg house on foot. He talks briefly with Jedediah, who is hoeing his vegetable garden, and then disappears behind the molasses plant. Moments later, the Model T truck comes rumbling out from behind the factory, heading down into Darkytown.

"Where the hell is he going?" Ava asks.

"His house?" Morgan guesses. "Maybe he forgot something."

Whatever Luther is doing, he does it fairly quick. After a few minutes, the truck reappears and heads their way. They stay in the trees until he passes and then give him a quarter mile lead before pulling out to follow. Luther would know Morgan's coupe by sight but there is no reason for him to think he is being followed. Morgan himself doesn't believe there is much of a reason to be doing it.

"I was thinking," he says as they drove, "seeing as this is going to be an exercise in futility, why don't we keep on after Johnson City and head over to Nashville? The Grand Ole Opry is on tonight."

Ava wears a tweed cap and one of Morgan's jackets, a leather aviator's coat from the Great War that had once belonged to their uncle. She fancies herself to be traveling incognito, like a spy in the

French countryside during the war. Following an elderly colored man across North Carolina isn't quite the same but she has always had a fertile imagination.

"We won't be going to Nashville today," she says. "And why do you think this is a futile effort?"

"I still say he's got himself a woman somewhere and there's nothing to this," Morgan replies.

"Then why wouldn't he say that, instead of making up tales of his daughter and harness companies?" Ava asks. "He's a widower; he's allowed a woman friend."

Morgan thinks about it. "Maybe he's getting horizontal with the woman and he doesn't want Father to know. Our father is a preacher, you'll recall."

Ava laughs. "Getting horizontal with the woman? Is that what you just said?"

"I was trying to be delicate," Morgan says. "What would you call it, sister? What do they call it in Chicago?"

Ava props her feet up on the dash. "Oh, in Chicago we would never speak of such carnal matters in polite company."

"You are full of beans right up to your ears," Morgan tells her.

Ava laughs again. They drive in silence for a time. Up ahead, the Model T is chugging along, barely making twenty-five miles an hour. It will be a long drive to Johnson City.

"You feel like something's changing, brother?" Ava asks.

"Changing where?" Morgan replies.

"Well, in the world."

"Not really, other than everybody's broke. And hungry."

"I don't mean that," Ava says. "That's just economics. But it seems like something new is happening out there. The music's different. Books are different. Take Henry Miller. Have you read his books?"

"His books are banned."

Ava gives him a look, her eyebrows raised.

"What?" Morgan demands. "You've read them? What's in there that folks are so excited about?"

"People getting horizontal, for one thing," Ava says.

"How did you ever get your hands on them?"

"Come on," Ava admonishes. "You want people to get their hands on a thing, just tell them they're not allowed to have it."

Morgan drives along, his mind now completely focused on Henry Miller. "You didn't bring those books home with you?"

"Of course I did."

"Better not let Father find them."

Ava smiles, shaking her head. "All those things we're not supposed to be talking about and reading about, Father and Mother did. If they didn't, you and I wouldn't be here having this conversation." She gives her brother a look. "And before you even ask— yes, you can read the books. Might be a good education for you."

"I'm educated," Morgan protests.

"You'll be better educated after reading *Tropic of Cancer.*"

"There are those who claim that book is immoral." Morgan smiles and gives her a look. "Aren't you concerned it might corrupt me? You know—destroy my faith in human nature?"

Ava takes a cigarette from her purse and lights it. "Sometimes I think you have too much faith in human nature."

"I hope that's not even possible," Morgan says. "Then again, maybe it's required that I have too much, seeing as you have too little."

Ava exhales, blowing smoke into the air. "Just drive, brother."

Johnson City is a large town, built hard on the banks of Boone Creek. Just west of the Blue Ridge Mountains, it had started out as a railway depot, one that impractically featured two rail lines of different gauges. During the Civil War the town had been renamed Haynesville, after the Confederate general Landon Haynes, whose claims to fame included selling diseased hogs to the local citizenry, stealing corn and shooting in the leg a local preacher who dared to criticize him. When the North prevailed, Haynes was swept into the dustbin of history and the name went back to Johnson City.

It is shortly past noon when Morgan points the Nash down

into the valley where the town is situated, trailing Luther Briscoe by a quarter mile. It is overcast and a stubborn mist hangs over the creek.

"You know Charlie Bowman is from here?" Morgan says.

"I did not," Ava admits. "Nor do I know who that is."

"Only the best fiddle player between here and anywhere," Morgan says. "He was one of the main players in the Johnson City Sessions, put on right here by Columbia Records, out of New York City."

"Now I have heard of New York City," Ava says.

"You got listening to that jazz music in Chicago and forgot about your own. Jimmie Rodgers was better than all those jazz singers put together."

"That is a matter of opinion, brother," Ava says, thinking about Theodore. "Watch him now, he's turning off."

Up ahead, Luther pokes along in the Model T. He hasn't noticed the Nash coupe following him from a distance, but then again he has no reason to think he'd be followed. When he gets to Johnson City, he turns onto Watauga Avenue, leading to the town's commercial district. There is a succession of retail concerns along the street, including a hardware store and millinery and a movie theater showing *The Trail of the Lonesome Pine*. When Luther reaches a derelict hotel called The Tennessee Arms, he turns into a laneway beside the building.

There is an alley behind the hotel, running parallel to the street, and all along the rear of the stores there. There are loading docks behind each place of business, built mainly of stout piers and wide planking. Luther backs the truck up to the dock attached to the hotel, a rickety platform with narrow steps along one side. He gets out and climbs up to knock on a heavy wooden door. A moment later Bones Pettifog emerges. Bones is over six feet tall and skinny as a snake, with a thick mop of hair and copper bracelets on each wrist designed to drive out the rheumatism, or so he believed.

"Brother Luther," he says.

"Hello Bones." Luther says. "How the accommodation business treating you?"

"Could be better." Bones fishes Zig-Zag papers from his vest pocket and begins to fashion a cigarette. "Truth of the matter is, I ain't hardly making squat renting out these rooms at four dollars a night. Now, if I was to have access to more of a particular beverage, might just be a different story."

"I brung five gallons," Luther says.

"I'll take your five gallons," Bones tells him. "You know that. What I'm saying is, I could sell twice that every week. Maybe three, four times that. You surely got a special way with that old corn, Luther."

Luther climbs into the back of the truck and pulls back a heavy tarpaulin to reveal the jugs of moonshine packed in burlap to avoid breakage. He hands the bottles one by one to Bones, who deposits them inside the door of the hotel. As Luther folds up the tarp to place it in the box of the truck, Bones pulls money from his pocket and begins to count it out.

"Like I said, brother Luther, if you could see your way to increase production, it would make me happier than a puppy with two peckers."

"I done told you," Luther said, "I ain't got but a little still in a lean-to in the hills out back of my house. Ain't nobody suspicioned me because I keep it little. I get to buying more corn and more sugar and pretty soon I'm sitting in the crowbar hotel, and you, Bones, are as dry as them Israelites out in the desert."

Bones hands over the cash. "Well, there's a market here if you ever need it. You got to learn to think big, Luther. Where would Henry Ford be if he didn't think big?"

Luther smiles. "When I see the commonalities between a rich white man making automobiles and a poor colored man cooking busthead, then you and I will sit in the shade and talk turkey."

Luther tucks the money in his pants and gets into the truck. Driving out of the alley, he doesn't notice the Nash coupe, with Ava and Morgan slumped down low inside, parked behind a coal wagon fifty yards away.

The diner is called Mabel's Good Eats and is located a few miles outside Johnson City, beside the two-lane blacktop on the way back to Wilkesboro. It's a colored roadhouse, with a long plank counter and tables inside and a barbecue pit out back.

Luther sits at a corner table. He'd enjoyed a meal of pork chops and collard greens and is now eating blueberry pie à la mode with coffee. The place is busy and Luther is focused on his dessert; he doesn't notice that two white people have entered. Everybody else in the place takes note and are staring. It's a rare occurrence for white people to come inside.

"How's the pie, Luther?" Ava asks, approaching the table.

Luther looks up at her and at Morgan, his eyes widening like a little boy who has just been caught with his hand in the cookie jar. He could insist all day long he wasn't stealing cookies, but he was going to have trouble explaining his hand in the jar.

"Pie's good," Luther replies. "Yes, ma'am." He glances around, clearly wondering how the two of them happen to be there. It is as if they had dropped from the sky.

Now Ava sits down across from him and Morgan follows suit. Luther reaches for his coffee cup and takes a nervous sip.

"And Angeline?" Ava asks. "How is she?"

"She's fine," Luther says. "Just fine. I, um, I told her you were asking after her."

"That's nice of you," Ava says. "You know, I should get her address from you. I might stop and see her one day. Who knows that I might find myself in need of some good quality harness? I assume they make a good harness where she works?"

"I expect they do. Surely."

"What was the name of the company again?"

Luther shakes his head. The ice cream is melting on his pie, dripping off the wedge and pooling on the plate alongside. "I don't recall at the moment," he says. "Um, might it be the Johnson City Harness Company?"

The waitress has been hanging back, watching Ava and Morgan arrive. Seeing them sit down, she approaches now.

"Would y'all like to order something?"

"Pie seems to be the thing," Morgan says.

"Blueberry?"

"Blueberry will do," Morgan says. "We've heard good things about it."

As the waitress walks away, Luther shovels the last of his own pie into his maw, gulps down his coffee and gets to his feet, putting his hat on. "I'd best be getting back. Parson be waiting on that truck, I expect."

"I doubt he's too concerned about the truck, Luther," Ava says.

"I best be getting back anyway."

"How's the moonshine business these days, Luther?" Ava asks.

"What's that?"

Ava repeats the question slowly, enunciating each syllable. "I said—how is the moonshine business these days?"

"I have no idea in the world," Luther replies. "Now I surely got to be going."

"*Sit* down," Ava tells him.

Luther sits, although he is not happy about it in the least. He removes his hat and holds it in his hands. "I should be getting that truck back."

"In due time," Ava says. "First, we're going to clarify a few things. Angeline lives in Richmond, which is, I would hazard a guess, about four hundred miles from where we're sitting right now. That's quite a commute for a woman who is allegedly working for the Johnson City Harness Company these days. Wouldn't you say?"

Luther drops his gaze to the oil cloth tabletop and says nothing.

Ava goes on. "Not only that, but a short time ago you sold five gallons of something to that beanpole behind that old hotel on Watauga Avenue. I can't say for certain what was in those jugs, but I suspect it wasn't mountain spring water."

Luther keeps his eyes on the table. His nostrils are flared and he is stewing now, growing resentful.

"These is hard times, young lady," he says after a bit. "Hard times."

"We are well aware of that," Ava says. "This thing called the Depression affects everyone."

"Some more than others," Luther tells her. "Ain't everybody living in a fine brick house on a hill."

"I lost my job, same as you," Ava says. "The only difference between you and me is that I'm not bootlegging and lying about it."

Now Luther looks up at her. "All due respect, Miss Ava—that ain't the only difference between you and me."

He reaches her with that remark. She knows it is accurate, of course, and in truth she admires him for having the gumption to point it out. Most people spend their lives thinking thoughts but never speaking them. Of course, there are those who go overboard in the other direction in that regard; whatever enters their head comes out of their mouth. But Luther Briscoe is not one of them.

The waitress arrives with the pie and coffee. Ava waits until she's gone before turning back to Luther.

"Point taken," she says. "But here's the sticky part of it all. We don't give a hoot in hell if you want to brew a little white lightning and sell it off. But you're driving a Flagg company truck. If the law catches up to you, I suspect they might just seize the truck and keep it."

Luther nods his head slowly. "I suppose I ain't never thought of that. But ain't nobody watching me and my five gallons."

Morgan speaks around a mouth full of pie. "They're not watching you until they are."

Luther exhales heavily. "I expect you might be right. Well then, I guess I need to find another way. Or just quit my doings." He pauses. "That make you happy?"

"Don't act like making us happy is high on your list of priorities, Luther," Ava says. "You lied and you did it for yourself. Don't play the victim once you're caught in it."

Luther watches her a long moment, his eyes hooded. It seems he has more to say but decides to refrain. "Can I go now?"

"You can go," she tells him.

Luther stands and puts his hat on once again. Ava watches him, her mind working. He is nearly to the door when she calls out to him.

Luther turns. "Ma'am?"

"What's a gallon of moonshine fetch these days?"

NINE

The next morning Ava is up before the men. She drinks a cup of coffee on the front porch and eats a slice of bread with raspberry preserves while she reads a week-old copy of the *Wilkesboro Free Press*. Other than the fact that the local nine is having a good season on the baseball field, there is nothing much of an encouraging nature in the paper. She finishes her coffee and heads out for a walk.

She takes the red dirt road into Wilkesboro, retracing her steps from the day she'd returned home on the bus. That day she'd been aware of the abject poverty of the area, the paucity of hope. But of course she'd already seen it, up close and all the way from Chicago. No place in the country was immune. But today was different. She was seeing things more clearly, it seemed. She'd hardly slept the night before and that, oddly enough, had heightened her thought process instead of dimming it.

She walks in the cool of the morning, in the shade of the large pines that line the road on either side. She is wearing pants and a cotton shirt, with her hair tied back with a bandana. It is two miles to the Wilkesboro town limits, on a dusty road she'd traveled hundreds of times in her life. When they were kids, she and Morgan would ride their bicycles to the creek just outside of town, where they would swim for hours. They fished for bullheads in the same creek, taking them home on a stringer for their mother to skin and fry up. Ava's mother was handy in a thousand ways that her father was not, the practical one of the two. Jedediah's expertise existed in the ethereal and the spiritual.

Main Street in Wilkesboro is long and straight, and lined with stores and dressmakers and other commercial interests on both sides. It looks to Ava as if at least half the businesses are closed. Storefront windows have brown paper taped over them. Most show For Sale or For Rent signs. Walking past the places that were still open, Ava can see proprietors or clerks inside, sitting idly at counters, reading the newspaper or staring at the walls.

She goes into Duff's Diner and sits at the counter. She orders coffee from a young girl of fifteen or sixteen. Two elderly men sit by the front windows, one with a full, gray-streaked beard that reaches to his chest, and the other in wire-rimmed spectacles and a bowler hat. Both wear dirty overalls and are talking while watching what was happening outside on Main Street; this in spite of the fact that nothing is happening on Main Street. Or any other street, for that matter.

Ava sips her coffee as the waitress sets to cleaning the grill, getting ready for the breakfast crowd, which appears to be just Ava and the two men at the table.

"What's your name?" she asks the girl.

"Penelope Ann."

"Duff around?"

"Who's that?" Penelope Ann asks.

"Duff who owns this place," Ava says.

"Oh, him. He ain't been around for a couple years. He sold the place to Dinny Wilson."

"Where did Duff get off to?"

"I think maybe Georgia," Penelope Ann says. "Wait...maybe he died." She looks at the two men sitting by the window. "Ben, where'd old Duff go?"

"Georgia."

Penelope Ann turns back to Ava. "He went to Georgia."

"I heard," Ava says. She picks up her coffee and walks over to the two men. "Mind if I join you boys?"

"Sure," the one called Ben says. "We was just waiting for a pretty girl to come by."

"You're Ava Flagg," the other man realizes. "I didn't know you was home. Stub Parnell, Linda's father."

"Right," Ava says. "I didn't recognize you with the Methuselah beard."

Stub laughs. "Getting so a man can't even afford razor blades these days."

Ava sits down and sips her coffee.

"Home visiting the folks?" Stub asks.

"Maybe more than a visit," Ava tells him. "What about you— still on the farm?"

"Still there," Stub says. "I can still produce a good crop, if I get the rain. Try and sell it though, that's a different matter. I got two hundred bushels of corn in my crib right now from last fall. Gotta keep turning it to keep it from mildewing. And I'm growing more this year, don't ask me why."

"You never was too smart," Ben says.

"I'll not have my intelligence questioned by a man wears a spittoon on his head," Stub says. He turns to Ava. "How's things out your way? Any money these days in the molasses business?"

"Not hardly," Ava says. "Things out there are the same as everywhere, I guess. And nobody seems to have any idea of where it's going. What do you boys think—is the country broke for good?"

"Hell no," Ben says. "This here is the United States. We'll bounce back, bigger than ever. This is a minor setback."

"The Depression is a minor setback?" Stub repeats. "Did you fall out of your hay mow and hit your head again?"

"I only did that once and that was ten years ago."

"Then I woulda thought you'd have come to your senses by now," Stub says.

Ava smiles. "You guys ought to be on the radio."

Stub shakes his head. "I don't know where it's going. Roosevelt is making work for folks, sure enough, but where's that money coming from? You can't pull fifty pounds of turnips out of a five-pound sack."

"But if the government is paying people to be on the dole, they might just as well get some work out of them," Ava says.

"There's truth in that," Stub admits.

"He's a communist, you know," Ben says. "Roosevelt."

"You don't know what a communist is," Stub tells him. "Roosevelt ain't no goddamn communist. He's Teddy's cousin, for chrissakes. You gonna tell me Teddy was a communist too? Teddy who rode up San Juan Hill?"

"A communist can ride a horse up a hill," Ben points out.

Stub waves his friend off like he is a bothersome fly. At least Ava presumes they were friends, their nattering notwithstanding. She'd sat down thinking the two old boys might have some answers to the problems the nation was enduring, maybe in the form of some good old country boy common sense. It had been pretty naïve of her. Why would they know any better than all the experts in the world? Then again, why would they know any less?

"I will tell you one thing," Ben says now. "Them politicians are about the only ones out there still getting a reg'lar paycheck. Explain that to me."

"Since when is that something new?" Stub asks.

"I didn't say it was new. I'd just like somebody to explain it to me."

Ava finishes her coffee and gets to her feet. "Nice talking to you boys. I must say you have some unique perspectives on things."

"Some what?" Ben asks.

"Ways of looking at things," Ava says. "What you're telling me is that I need to become a politician to get by these days."

"Or a bank robber," Stub says. "They're making money, I hear. Crooks and politicians, take your pick, Miss Ava. As for me, I'd take a crook any day over a politician. There's something honest about a crook."

Ava walks to the door and stops to look back. "You might be onto something there, Mr. Parnell."

Ava makes a detour into Darkytown on the walk home, where she has her second conversation with Luther Briscoe in two days. She spends a couple of hours helping out in the molasses plant, where Morgan and Ezra bottle a few gallons to ship to Knoxville before passing the rest of the afternoon cleaning the vats and doing general maintenance. It is just the two of them there now; everybody else has been laid off. At one time there had been a dozen workers making Flagg molasses.

That night Ava sits alone on the front porch of the brick house watching the houses in the hollow, most lit by lanterns, a very few by electrical lights. She thinks about the hollow and the county, and the town of Wilkesboro. She thinks about the whole country. She goes over her conversation in Duff's earlier with the two old farmers, deciding they really should be on the radio. Ava would tune in.

The night grows cold and she goes into the house for a sweater and comes back. She sits bundled in an old wicker rocker until well after midnight.

Until she makes up her mind.

TEN

There is a lunchroom inside the molasses plant, twelve feet by twelve with half walls and a long plank table surrounded by a dozen mismatched wooden chairs. There's an icebox in the corner and a dartboard along the exterior wall. Decks of dog-eared cards are scattered on the table, along with ashtrays and salt and pepper shakers and a few outdated magazines.

Ava and Morgan and Ezra meet there in the early morning. Ava has already talked to Morgan over breakfast and her brother has proven to be surprisingly agreeable. Jedediah has been gone early, off to counsel a parishioner who was ailing with the cancer. Now Ava and Morgan sit at the table scarred by countless cigarette burns. They are crossways to Ezra, in more ways than one.

"It's not moral and it's not legal," Ezra is saying. "And that is the end of this conversation."

"Who says it's not moral?" Ava asks. "And hang the legal."

Ezra glares at her. "What is wrong with you these days? Is this what Chicago did to you? Did you pass your time in speakeasies there—drinking liquor and smoking cigarettes, and listening to radical nonsense?"

"Speakeasies?" Ava says. "You do realize that prohibition ended three years ago, brother."

"Not in these counties, it didn't," Ezra reminds her. "Fooling with moonshine is a crime. You can go to jail for making it and you most certainly *will* go to jail for selling it."

"Only if you get caught," Morgan says.

"Oh, you'll get caught," Ezra says. "Look in the dang newspaper. Folks getting caught every week for selling that stuff. What the local police don't find, the federal agents do. This is a harebrained idea if ever there was one. Which one of you came up with this?"

"You got a better one?" Morgan asks.

"Any idea is better than this," Ezra says. "It's time for the two of you to grow up. You're not talking about selling lemonade down at the crossroads. This is dad-blamed criminal behavior."

"Murder and rape, that's criminal behavior," Ava says. "This is supplying a need."

"Since when do people need hard liquor?" Ezra demands.

"Well, a want then," Ava says.

Ezra shakes his head. "This is beyond stupid. And not only that, but you're as green as grass, the both of you. How would you even—" He stops himself. "I don't know why we're even having this conversation. Even if you could convince me—which you *cannot*—you'd never talk Father into this in a million years."

"Talk me into what?"

It is Jedediah, standing inside the loading door. Nobody has heard him come in. His unlit pipe is in the corner of his mouth; he tucks it into his coat pocket as he approaches the lunchroom. Ezra gets to his feet to meet him. He starts to speak but Ava is quicker than him. Ava has always been quicker than him.

"Luther Briscoe has been selling moonshine over to Johnson City. *That's* where he's been going in the truck."

Jedediah considers the news in his deliberate manner. He doesn't speak for a full minute. "Well...whatever his duplicities, we will not be turning Mr. Briscoe over to the law, daughter. That would serve nobody."

"I have no intention of turning him in," Ava says. "I want to partner up with him."

"How's that?" Jedediah asks.

Now Ezra has his chance. "These two geniuses are of the opinion that the Flagg Molasses Company should go into the production and selling of hard liquor. They've come up with this scheme in spite of the legal and moral ramifications of such a dunderheaded notion. I thank the Lord you arrived when you did, Father."

Jedediah walks over but does not sit down. He glances briefly at his two sons before turning to Ava, knowing instinctively that he needs to deal with her.

"Why don't you tell me what this is about, daughter?"

"Have a look around, Father," Ava says. "Ten years ago, we'd have to go outside to have this conversation because this plant was in full production, and noisy as all get-out. Today it's so quiet I can practically *hear* Ezra stewing over there. We all know there's no money in the manufacture of molasses these days. However, there is in corn. More specifically, corn liquor."

Jedediah takes his pipe from his pocket and puts it in his mouth. He sucks thoughtfully on the stem a moment, despite the fact that the bowl is empty. "Are you suggesting that we willfully break the law, daughter?"

"That particular law is being broke all over the country each and every day," Ava tells him. "There is such a thing as a bad law."

"There is also such a thing as a bad idea, sister," Ezra says. "And this surely qualifies. Liquor has an abominable influence on man. Those who take to it in excess ignore, or even worse, abuse their families. They wallow in sin. Some move on to become dope fiends and sexual degenerates."

Morgan smiles as he props his boots on the table and clasps his hands behind his head. "You've been reading those magazines down at the drugstore again, Ezra."

Ezra glares at him. Ava goes into her purse now and pulls out the Bible that Jedediah had given her on her fifth birthday. Several pages have been bookmarked with scraps of yellow foolscap. She opens to one and reads aloud.

"'Go, eat your food with gladness, and drink your wine with a joyful heart, for it is now that God favors what you do.'" Finishing, she glances over to her father. "So advises Ecclesiastes."

Morgan grins as Ava goes to another bookmark.

"While in Psalms we find--'the Lord makes plants for man to cultivate--bringing forth food from the earth and wine that gladdens the heart of man--'"

"'And oil to make his face shine, and bread that sustains his heart,'" Jedediah finishes for her. "You were always one to do your homework, Ava."

"You can call it homework if you want," Ezra says. "I call it using the scripture for nefarious purposes."

Jedediah ignores the statement as he comes over to sit at the table. He produces his tobacco pouch and begins to fill his pipe, tamping the coarse shreds with his forefinger. He is quiet until he lights the bowl and has a rosy glow inside.

"This...*proposal* of yours," he begins, looking at Ava and Morgan. "How large of an operation would it be?"

"We don't know the answer to that yet," Morgan replies. "This plan is as fresh as this morning's biscuits."

"Would it put back to work some of the men we've laid off?"

"That's the idea," Ava says.

"Father," Ezra says sharply. "Surely you're not considering this?"

"The Lord helps those that help themselves, Ezra," Jedediah says. "There are hungry people in this hollow. Hungry and discouraged and nigh onto giving up, many of them." He looks at Ava. "What do you know about making moonshine, daughter?"

"Not the least little thing," she replies. "The first person we'd hire back would be Luther Briscoe. I spoke to him regarding this just yesterday."

"And where would you sell it?" Jedediah asks. "And how would you sell it in a fashion that does not land you in the county jail?"

"We'd have to find the markets," Ava admits. "Safe markets, not in this neck of the woods, I expect. Luther has some ideas about that." She pauses. "I'm not suggesting this would be easy,

Father. But the good Christian does not shy away from hardship."

"Nor does he court it where none theretofore exists," Jedediah reminds her.

Ava smiles. "Ah, but the hardship does exist. You said as much yourself a couple minutes ago. I didn't go looking for it."

"For crying out loud!" Ezra exclaims. "This is criminal activity. We are not considering this. We are not."

Ava ignores him, keeping her gaze fixed on her father. "Better to light a candle than to curse the darkness," she says softly.

Jedediah smiles at this. Ava has long made a habit of using his own words in discussion with him. It's hard for a man to refute his own words. He sits quietly for a time, pulling occasionally on the pipe stem. He is as calm as Ezra is not. After a while, he gets to his feet.

"I need to think on this," he says and leaves.

That night Jedediah builds a fire in the back yard, beneath the sycamore tree that his grandfather planted more than sixty years ago. He carries a chair from the porch into the yard and sits there, smoking his pipe and feeding the fire occasionally with pine limbs. Morgan has gone off to practice his music with his group and Ezra is at home with his family across the way. Ava stands in the house and watches her father. He sits there motionless, hatless in the night air, looking into the fire. A hundred yards away, Ava's mother rests in the family graveyard. Ava wonders if Jedediah is consulting with her. And with Him.

She watches for a while and then she goes into the front room and reads a paperback novel she'd picked up in a drugstore in Indianapolis on the bus ride home. The story doesn't hold her interest, but she can't blame the book. Her mind is scattered of late. Every half hour or so, she checks on Jedediah. He is still there when she finally sets the novel aside and he is still there when she heads to bed.

And he is there when she arises at dawn, staring into the fire even yet, although by now just a glowing heap of embers remain.

By the time she has the coffee boiling, he comes into the house. There are flecks of ash from the fire on his suit and even in his hair. Ava has no idea if he'd slept at all, but he looks rested and content. Her father, in general, is one of the most content people she's ever known. It is one of the things she envies most about him.

He comes in through the kitchen door and stands there, watching Ava as she slices potatoes into a frying pan. There is sow belly sizzling in a second pan. Ava glances over and tells him good morning.

"We are going to need a fairly large quantity of corn," he says.

Ava smiles. "It just so happens that Stub Parnell has two hundred bushels he would love to be shed of."

"Then let us break our fast and then go see brother Parnell," Jedediah says.

ELEVEN

Otto is in his usual seat behind home plate, flanked by Elmer and Slim. The Knoxville nine is taking a beating. It is only the top of the third inning and the score is eight to zero. Not that either Elmer or Slim care. Neither man is a fan of the game. Slim is reading a racing form, marking the bets he would make later with a bookie over on State Street, and Elmer is twisting this way and that in his seat, looking for eligible women in the bleachers. Elmer is always looking for eligible women, although not that many women are looking back. Elmer's face is pockmarked with acne scars and he has a vivid five-inch slash along his left cheek, a souvenir from a Saturday night knife fight outside a juke joint in Atlanta.

The first batter at the top of inning laces a double to left center. The outfielder bobbles the ball and the runner keeps going, sliding into third, well ahead of the throw. Second base or third doesn't matter, because the next batter hits the ball over the scoreboard in right field, landing somewhere out on Jessamine Street.

"Where did they find this rube?" Otto asks.

Slim looks up from the form, a stub of a pencil between his teeth. "What rube?"

"The so-called pitcher," Otto says. "I've seen mules could run faster than that boy can throw the pill."

Slim goes back to his nags and Otto begins to berate the

southpaw from the seats.

"You got a rubber arm!" he shouts. "My grandma could pitch better than that!"

The harassment continues off and on for a couple more innings, at which point the score has grown to thirteen to one. By then Otto has seen enough. He tells Elmer to get the car. Before leaving Otto sticks his head in the Smokies dugout and yells at the manager for being a "brainless sack of shit." The manager knows who Otto is and makes no reply.

Boone Saunders is waiting in the loading area of the Empire Hotel on Third Avenue, the back room that serves as Otto's office in the city. There is a desk there, with a half-dozen chairs, and a tiger-eye maple icebox in the corner.

Boone has his oldest boy Val with him and they've been waiting for a couple of hours by the time Otto and the others show up. Boone is not in a particularly good frame of mind. Like the baseball manager, though, he is not about to mention that to Otto.

"So what do we got?" Otto says when he walks in.

No handshakes or salutations. No apologies for being tardy. Boone and Val have been sitting on packing crates by the freight elevator while they wait, smoking and nipping from pints of busthead. They'd been wishing that Otto would show, while at the same time thinking that it might work to their advantage if he didn't, given the news they were about to share with him.

Elmer and Slim walk over to sit down in the chairs along the wall. They both lean back, tilting on the rear legs while they watch the two men across the room. Elmer lights a cigarette, then smokes, snapping his Zippo open and shut with his thumb and forefinger.

"Not a lot," Boone replies. "We got hit by the revenuers again last week. Not the stills, but they set up a roadblock at Rocky Gap and got a shipment of a hundred and twenty gallons."

"How's a thing like that happen?" Otto wants to know.

"New driver," Boone shrugs. "Kid from West Virginny. I did time with his father once and took him on as a favor. Kid figured he needed to stop off in Piney to see this skirt he's got there. Somebody saw the truck parked in the alley. Got suspicious and called the local sheriff, who got in touch with the Feds. Currying favor, no doubt. Feds set up the roadblock and grabbed the kid and the cargo both when he was leaving town. Bad luck all around."

"Christ," Otto says. He goes to the ice box and gets a bottle of beer for himself. He doesn't offer one to the Saunders boys, or to his own men either. "I trust you shot the driver?"

"He's in the hoosegow."

"Shoot him when he gets out," Otto advises.

Boone nods. He may or may not shoot the driver when he gets out. He is a dumb kid who has allowed his pecker to do his thinking for him. Boone has no qualms about killing him, but only if he can get away with it. Boone has no intention of doing a twenty-year stretch in Central Prison over a stupid kid from the backwoods.

"I promised a hundred gallons to Nashville," Otto says. "I said by the weekend."

"We're cooking this minute," Boone tells him. "We brung you twenty gallons tonight. It's in the truck."

"What am I going to do with twenty gallons when I need a hundred?" Otto asks.

"Well, that's what we brung."

Otto has a drink of beer, looking at Boone. "When do I see the rest?"

Boone glances expectantly at Val, who takes his time replying, as if he is figuring in his head. "We can have that much come Saturday. Or Sunday."

"Which is it, boy?" Otto asks.

"It's Saturday or Sunday," Val tells him. "You hard of hearing?"

Otto's face goes dark and Boone is on his feet, quick as a cat, to run interference. With that, Elmer and Slim both stand as well, watching the boss and awaiting instruction. Elmer slips his Zippo in his coat pocket and leaves his hand there.

"You'll have it Saturday," Boone says.

Otto is staring at Val though. "What did you say to me?"

"He didn't mean nothing," Boone says.

Otto tilts back the beer and empties the bottle in a long continuous gulp. Then he winds up like a pitcher and throws it at the brick wall behind where Val stands. The bottle misses Val's head by a couple of feet and explodes when it hits the brick. Foam drips down the wall and a shard of broken glass comes to rest on Val's shoulder. He brushes it off while glaring angrily at Otto, who stands there, legs spread, returning the look. Boone moves between the two and gives his son a hard look of reprimand. Even then, it takes Val a few moments to settle.

"I'm right sorry, Mr. Marx," he finally says, albeit reluctantly and without a tincture of sincerity. "I didn't mean no disrespect to you."

Otto holds the cold stare for another few moments, then smiles, as if at some private joke only he could hear, and goes to retrieve another bottle of beer. Opening it, he nods to Elmer and Slim to go unload the shipment.

"You best go on and help them boys," Boone tells Val.

Val does as he is told and follows the others outside. He's careful not to look again at Otto.

"He's a good boy," Boone says. "Gets too big for his britches sometimes and needs to be reminded of that. I was the same way at that age. I expect we all were."

"Not me," Otto says. "My britches have always fit just fine."

"I didn't mean you."

"I'm not worried about your boy, Saunders," Otto says. "I don't know him from Adam. Either he'll watch that tongue of his or he won't. If he don't, then that's something that will need to be addressed." Otto has a drink. "What I am worried about is our business arrangement. I have more markets than you can even imagine in that hillbilly head of yours. If I order a hundred gallons, I expect to get one hundred gallons—not ninety or eighty and sure as hell not twenty."

"Like I said, the revenuers—" Boone begins.

"I don't want to hear about any fucking revenuers," Otto says. "Up to you to handle that end. I don't care if you got to drive around them or over them or through them. That's your concern. My concern is the product. And if you can't deliver, then I'm just going to find somebody who can. Those hills are full of you people, all of you cooking up that good old mountain dew. What I'm saying is—you ain't even a little bit precious to me, Saunders."

Elmer and Slim come back then, lugging the crates with the jugs of busthead packed inside. Val follows moments later, with a third crate. He keeps his head down as they stack the booze by the freight elevator and head back outside for the rest.

Otto inspects the cargo, picking a jug at random and opening it for a taste.

"This the same stuff?" he asks.

"Same as always," Boone says. "Why?"

Otto shrugs. "Something different about it."

He pays Boone from a wad of bills in his jacket, after which Boone and Val leave without another word. Otto watches them out the window as they climb into Boone's Cadillac and drive off, heading south out of the city.

"Fucking hillbillies," he says before turning to Slim. "Get the gloves out of the car. I want to play some catch."

TWELVE

Even without the prospect of becoming the new owner of the wrecked coupe in the yard, Bobby lucks out getting hired on by Charley Walker. The garage is the best equipped in town and probably all of Wilkes County. Along with the gas pumps out front, there is a large shop featuring a single pole hoist and a mechanic's pit, with a five-horsepower compressor and modern pneumatic tools. There are complete socket sets and torque wrenches and acetylene torches. Bobby is used to working on cars in backyards and alleys, pulling engines with a rope draped over a tree limb or laying on his back in the dirt, swapping out transmissions or rear differentials. Walker's is high cotton compared to those yards. Not only that, but Duff's Diner is just down the block from Walker's Texaco. Bobby picks up his lunch there every day, usually a cheese-burger and French fries, along with a Coke. He's never liked to brown bag it, even when working for the railroad years ago.

The work is a snap for Bobby, mostly tune-ups or oil changes. The odd engine rebuild or brake job. Old man Walker can be on the cranky side but in general he is a good boss. He has gone from working on buckboards and spring buggies to bicycles and electric cars and now the modern stuff. He still does mechanical work himself, although he is out on the road a lot, hauling cars with the Mac wrecker or making service calls on farmers who have implements in need of repair and no way of getting them into town.

Charley keeps a tight watch on Bobby for the first few days. He knows Bobby is fresh out of jail, and not for the first time. Charley is concerned that Bobby shows up for work every day, for one thing, and that when he leaves the premises at night, no tools leave with him. He needn't have worried. There is no way Bobby is going to mess this up.

On the Wednesday of the second week, Charley returns from Fairplains, where he'd gone to install a new drive chain on a hay baler. Bobby has a Chevy stake truck up on the hoist, changing the clutch plate. Charley gets a soda from the cooler out front, then walks into the shop as Bobby is lifting the transmission back into place.

"Need a hand with that?" he asks.

Bobby hasn't heard him come in. "Sure," he says.

Charley puts his soda on the rail of the hoist and ducks under the truck to grab the tail stock of the transmission. He supports it while Bobby aligns the clutch and pressure plate to the shaft and slides the transmission into place onto the back of the engine. He then reaches for the rear cross member and slips it beneath the tail stock for support.

Charley is able to let go then. He takes his soda and leans against the workbench and watches as Bobby begins to thread the bellhousing bolts into place. When Charley finishes the pop, he puts the bottle in the crate by the door.

"Mother's waiting supper on me," he says. "You can lock up when you're done, Bobby."

"Will do."

Charley goes out the rear door, to where his truck is parked. A moment later, he returns.

"I've been thinking," he says. "The deal was you can have the coupe once you've worked it off. Which means as of right now, you don't own the vehicle. But if you've a mind to start fixing it, go on ahead."

Bobby comes out from under the truck, wiping his hands on a rag. "All right then," is all he says.

The funeral parlor owned by Edgar's father is a couple of blocks away. Most days Edgar wanders over to Walker's Texaco after getting off work to drink a pop and see what is going on. There was an afternoon funeral today so the garage is closed when he comes by but he spots movement through the front window and goes in. He is wearing his standard outfit for work—a dark blue suit with a bow tie and matching handkerchief just showing in the breast pocket of the jacket.

The '32 Ford is inside the shop. Bobby has already removed the damaged front fender and leaned it against the wall. Now he is laying on the floor beneath the car, unbolting the running board. The driver's door is open and Myrna Lee Saunders is sitting on the seat, sideways, with one foot on the running board and the other extended. She is wearing her uniform from the drugstore, a pink dress with blue trim, and the way she is sitting she is showing a fair amount of leg, although not as much as she was showing twenty minutes earlier, when she and Bobby had screwed in the front seat of the car, the cotton dress hiked up around her waist and Bobby's pants at his ankles. The tussle had been Myrna Lee's idea; Bobby was intent on tearing the car down. He hadn't protested though, not even a little bit.

None of this is apparent to Edgar as he walks in. It might have been to a more perceptive person, but that doesn't describe Edgar. And Myrna Lee, for her part, is sitting as cool as a cucumber at the moment.

"Started on her, have you?" Edgar asks, kneeling down to look at Bobby.

Bobby, working the ratchet, grunts an affirmative.

"Hello, Edgar," Myrna Lee says. "Don't you say hello?"

Edgar glances over at her, trying not to look at her legs, or at least trying not to get caught looking at her legs. "Hey Myrna Lee," he says.

"What you gawking at?" she asks.

"Nothing," he says. "I didn't know you were here."

"It's a free country, ain't it?" She laughs and reaches into her purse for a cigarette.

Edgar doesn't reply. He walks around to inspect the front fender against the wall. It had been crunched pretty badly, the steel folded back on itself. "This here is a right mess, Bobby," he says. "How do you figure to fix it?"

Bobby removes the last of the bolts and lowers the running board to the cement floor. Standing up, he carries it over to place it beside the fender.

"Who needs fenders?" he asks. "Or running boards either. That's just extra weight."

"You fixing to strip her down then?" Edgar asks.

"I am."

"That means you're fixing to race her."

"What else would I do with the car?" Bobby asks. "If I wanted a Sunday driver, I'd find a big old sedan like your Studebaker. Your daddy's Studebaker, I should say."

"Studebaker makes a good automobile," Edgar says.

"Sure, if you want to haul around a wife and a bunch of kids," Bobby says. "That is not my intention with this here coupe."

He drags a floor jack over and slides it beneath the rear axle of the car and pumps the handle until the rear wheels are off the floor. He removes the passenger wheel and then begins to unfasten the fender bolts. The rear fender isn't as badly damaged as the front, but it doesn't matter to Bobby anyway. Once it was off the car, it was staying off.

"You going to buy me a Dr Pepper, Edgar?" Myrna Lee asks then.

"I guess I could," Edgar replies. "Bobby, you want a pop?"

"No."

Edgar goes into the front of the shop and puts two nickels in the machine and takes out an RC Cola and a Dr Pepper. When he comes back, he gives the soda to Myrna Lee then wipes the workbench clean with a rag before jumping up there to sit.

"So how come you're hanging around here, Myrna Lee?" he asks.

"That's a good question," she replies, raising her voice to make sure Bobby hears. "I am *supposed* to be at the movies with a certain somebody."

"What picture are they showing?" Edgar asks.

"A new one with Barbara Stanwyck," Myrna Lee says. "I can't recall the title just now. What picture don't matter. What matters is that I'm not at the movies. I'm sitting here while that certain somebody fools around with this wrecked-up automobile."

"You saying you're not having any fun?" Bobby asks.

"No, I'm not," she says.

"*Were* you having fun a little bit ago?"

"Shut up, Bobby!"

Bobby smiles, working the ratchet.

"I'd give you a hand, Bobby, but I'm not exactly dressed for it," Edgar says.

"What would you do to help?" Bobby asks from under the car.

"Hey, I'm pretty handy with cars."

"You couldn't fix a sandwich," Bobby tells him.

"Well, I guess we all can't be wizards like you, Bobby," Edgar says. He has a drink of the soda and begins to hum a tune.

"Why do you wear that bow tie?" Myrna Lee asks.

"It's for work," Edgar says. "A man in my business has to mind his appearance."

"But you're not at work now," she says.

"You want me to take my tie off?"

She shrugs. "You can do what you like."

The tie is a clip on and now Edgar takes it off. He's had little experience with women and as a rule tries to do what is asked of him by the fairer sex. Not that there's been a lot of requests from the distaff side.

"I have an idea," Bobby says then. "Why don't you take Myrna Lee to the movies, Edgar?"

The mere thought of being that close to Myrna Lee for an entire two hours causes Edgar to break into a sweat. She saves him though.

"I don't want to go to the picture show with Edgar," Myrna Lee says.

"Why not?" Bobby asks.

"You *know* why not, Bobby Barlow."

Underneath the car, Bobby is smiling. Edgar decides he needs to change the subject.

"Hey Bobby—you know they're racing at the Hollow Saturday night? Boss Harvey says it's going to be the biggest field yet."

"Good for Boss Harvey," Bobby says. "More money in his greasy pocket."

"You gonna go watch?"

"Nope," Bobby says, sliding out from under the Ford coupe. He takes hold of the fender with both hands and pulls it away from the body. "I got no interest in spectating."

Luther takes to being in charge like a goose to a grain field. He is the only one involved with any experience in making corn liquor so Ava gives him his head. It takes them the better part of a week to set up the plant for cooking. There are vats already there from the molasses making but also required is a large amount of tubing for the condenser and a few cords of hardwood for the fire. It is decided they would build one still to start. Luther is of the opinion that any trace of molasses in the vats might spoil the mash so they boil spring water and baking soda in the tanks for an entire day before he declares them clean enough for the manufacture of what he calls panther's breath.

Morgan and Ava make a half-dozen trips in the double-T Ford truck to the Parnell farm south of Wilkesboro to pick up the corn they'd purchased. Stub doesn't ask any questions as to why someone in the molasses business would all of a sudden be interested in large quantities of corn. Ava is pretty damn sure that Stub, although not overly-educated, is capable of putting two and two together. The two of them have a brief and cryptic conversation on the subject while shoveling corn into bushel baskets.

"How's old Ben these days?" Ava asks. They are using large wooden grain shovels, filling the baskets and then lifting them into the back of the stake truck.

"Old Ben is the same," Stub replies. "Matter of fact, old Ben is pretty much exactly like young Ben was."

"A little on the dense side?" Ava suggests.

"I'd say that describes it."

"Has he ferreted out any more communists lately?"

Stan laughs. "I wouldn't be surprised. According to Ben, they're as thick as flies on a shit pile and about to take over the country."

Ava hoists a bushel up onto her knee to load it on the truck. She pauses to wipe her brow before turning back to Stan. "I don't know that I'd ever want to tell him anything that I didn't want to become common knowledge across five or six counties."

Stub is no slouch when it comes to hints, be they subtle or otherwise. "I wouldn't tell Ben if I stubbed my big toe. By day's end, he'd be telling folks I got my leg amputated."

"Fair enough," Ava says.

Back at Flagg's Hollow, they stockpile the corn inside, to avoid detection. As to not attract undue attention, they buy sugar from a dozen general stores, all from small towns and villages within twenty miles or so of home. They have an abundance of clean gallon jugs and stoppers from the molasses production.

By Monday of the second week, they are ready to begin. Luther brings his nephew, Jodie, with him that morning, and another youngster named Cal. They are both sixteen and had grown up together in Darkytown. Luther assures Ava and Morgan that the two boys have been advised of the secretive nature of the work.

"They also been advised what will happen to them if they was to tell such secrets," he says.

Luther is again in alpha dog mode and he makes a production that morning of examining the facilities in the plant, walking around with his hands behind his back, checking the vats and the corn in the bushels, the bagged sugar on pallets.

"We need a cat," he tells Ava. "All that corn and sugar, we're gonna have us a rat problem right quick."

"There's always a half dozen hanging around the house, looking for scraps," Ava says. "I'll recruit a couple."

Luther nods. "Then we're ready to make us some shine, Miss Ava."

"How long will it take?" she asks. "I mean, until we have a finished product?"

"That's the beauty of busthead," Luther says. "It ain't bourbon or rye, it don't need no aging. Person can make it one day and drink it the next. Or sell it the next. Course selling means we need some customers."

"I've been putting out some feelers," Morgan says. "It's not like selling molasses. I can't exactly put an ad in the newspaper."

"We were thinking we might have to travel a bit to find a market that is safe," Ava says.

"That would be wise," Luther says. "Don't fret none on that just now. If we make some good shine, it will sell."

"Amen to that," Morgan says.

Luther claps his hands, like a little kid just let out of school and anxious for a summer of fun. "First off, we need to pump us some water from the spring. I expect we'll need five hundred gallons just to start. And five hundred more by day's end."

The diesel pump won't start. Morgan tries it until the battery dies and then he continues to turn it over, using the hand crank. There is not as much as a sputter from the engine. Luther stands by watching, clearly annoyed. Morgan cranks the engine by hand until he is winded, then looks at Ava.

"This thing was always Ezra's department."

"Where is he?" Luther asks.

"At the house," Ava says. "Playing the part of conscientious objector."

The two teenaged boys are standing by, awaiting instructions from Luther. He looks at them and then at Ava.

"Gonna require a lot of toting, carrying a thousand gallons of water from that spring by bucket," he says.

"Wait here," Ava says.

She finds Ezra drinking coffee and reading the newspaper in the kitchen. Rebecca isn't around, nor the kids. Ava sits across from him.

"What did you do to the pump?" she asks.

Ezra keeps reading. Or pretending to anyway. "What pump?"

"Don't do that," Ava says. "So far I've put up with your pouting over this whole enterprise but I'll be damned if I'm going to let you sabotage it. So I don't care what you did to the pump. All I want is for you to come down and undo it."

Ezra puts the paper down. "When did I agree to any of this? It's being shoved down my throat."

"The family voted."

"And I voted against," Ezra says. "Maybe that excuses me from participating in your criminal activities."

"Then say so," Ava says. "I don't have time for your nonsense. If you're not going to fix that pump, then I'll hire somebody who can. He will get paid, and you will not. You can sit here and sulk."

"For crying out loud, Ava. I'm trying to do what's right."

"It's not up to you and me to decide what's right," Ava says.

"Now that is a ridiculous thing to say."

"Well, these are ridiculous times, brother. I won't bother you further. I have work to do. If the boys have to tote the water by hand, then they will tote it. This isn't some fancy of mine. This is something we're going to do, with or without you. If you think you can support Rebecca and the children by selling six or seven gallons of molasses a month, then good luck to you."

She gets up and crosses the room, pushes the screen door open and goes outside. She is down the steps and halfway across the lawn when she hears the door creak again and then he calls to her.

"Yeah?" she replies turning.

"Tell Morgan there's a valve on the fuel line needs to be open, underneath the engine," he says.

"Who put that there?" Ava asks.

Ezra turns and goes back inside. Ava smiles as she heads to the plant.

THIRTEEN

Even under Luther's tutelage, there are a lot of stops and starts. The old man is used to making liquor in a tarpaper shack in the deep woods behind his house, with a ten-gallon copper pot and makeshift tubing salvaged from a pickle factory. He has fine-tuned his little operation over the years but now he's working on a much larger scale. The most stubborn aspect of the job is getting the coils right. It takes two full days to do it, tightening the loops here, loosening them there, with Luther watching the drip-drip of the finished product with the eye of a mining assayer.

However, by week's end they have produced over forty gallons of corn liquor. Luther declares the quality to be of the highest order. Neither Ava or Morgan has much expertise in the matter, although they have certainly sampled moonshine in the past, and so they have to accept the old man's declaration as fact. After all, they had named him the master distiller, such as it is. But then, there hadn't been any competition for the job.

Late Friday the three of them sit in the lunchroom. Luther has drained off a pint of the clear liquor and placed it on the table. The two boys have gone home for the day. They'd both worked hard all week; it had taken some convincing for them to agree to defer their wages until the product begins to sell.

"Deferred wages is a damn sight better than no wages," Luther tells them.

Now he pours small amounts of the liquor into tin cups, one for each of them. They sample it while they talk. With the first sip of the raw booze, Ava coughs and almost gags. The second sip is smoother and the third smoother even yet. A fine and subtle trickster, that mountain dew.

"You can taste the honey," Luther says.

"Honey?" Ava asks.

"I always add buckwheat honey to the mash," Luther tells her. "I got me a few hives in the meadow, other side of the ridge."

"So we have bees on the payroll now," Morgan says.

"Nah, they glad to do it for old Luther."

"Good to know that something is still free in this world," Ava says.

"Well, we made us some good hooch," Luther says. "Now comes the hard part."

"I thought that *was* the hard part," Morgan says.

"No sir," Luther tells him. "Any numbskull can boil corn in a pot. Selling it is the hard part. Keeping clear of the local police, the revenuers, and any damn robbers who might get wind of it and figure that stealing from us is easier than cooking their own. Moonshining is mighty competitive."

"You make it sound like a cutthroat business," Ava remarks.

"That's what it is, Miss Ava," Luther replies. "That's exactly what it is."

"What about your skinny friend behind that hotel up in Johnson City?" Ava asks. "Is he in the market for more?"

Luther nods. "I sent word to him a few days ago. He wants twenty gallons, as soon as we can get it to him. But we need a bigger market than that, if we's figuring to make a profit."

"Isn't that the idea?" Morgan asks.

Ava stands to walk across the room to a large road map of the state pinned to the wall, the map used by the drivers who had delivered the molasses hither and yon, back when there was molasses to deliver. She taps their location with her forefinger.

"What would you say would be a safe distance from home?" she asks. "You know, without bringing attention to Flagg's Hollow?"

Luther sips moonshine from his tin cup and strokes his wiry beard as he considers the question. "The farther the better, all I knows. I expect you wouldn't want to show yourself any nearer than, say, a hundred miles. Y'all got to keep in mind that this here operation ain't exactly movable. Most stills up in the hills, they get found out and they just shunt to another location. Them backwoods is thick. Keeps the revenuers hopping. But this here molasses factory ain't on wheels."

With her thumb and forefinger Ava takes a measurement of roughly one hundred miles from the scale at the bottom of the map. Then she picks up a pencil from the chair rail and makes a circle around Wilkesboro, displaying that distance.

"Not much of any population in that circle," she says. "No point in driving a hundred miles to sell two or three gallons, is there?"

"I expect not," Luther says.

"Isn't Johnson City inside the limit?" Morgan asks.

Luther nods. "But Bones can be trusted. I know that boy since we was kids. His daddy and mine sharecropped back in Mississippi. Sharecropping—now there's a rigged game."

"Where else?" Morgan asks.

Luther drains his cup, smacking his lips. "If we are to be serious about this endeavor—Knoxville."

"Knoxville?" Morgan repeats. "Knoxville is the driest damn city in the whole south."

Luther smiles. "My point exactly."

The next morning Ava and Morgan head for Tennessee. They leave with a few sample pints of moonshine, a full tank of gas, a certain optimism—and nothing remotely resembling a plan for what they might do when they get to Knoxville. Ava hopes the optimism might trump their lack of preparedness. As hopes go, it's pretty damn iffy and as such she doesn't mention it to Morgan.

There is a fairly good road all the way, mostly two-lane blacktop. They leave Flagg's Hollow at eight o'clock and reach Knoxville shortly after noon, crossing the Tennessee River to drive into the old part of the city. They'd both been there before and were familiar enough with the streets. The city's financial outlook has improved slightly of late, with the Tennessee Valley Authority headquartering there, yet downtown there still appears to be more stores closed than open.

Without a real plan, Ava and Morgan drive around for a while before finally throwing a dart at the wall and entering the dining room of the Forrest Hotel on Clinch Avenue. The lunch crowd, if one existed, has cleared out by the time they arrive. They sit at a small table by the dirty front window and look at the one-page menu. A waiter with an overhanging gut the size of a pickle barrel stands behind the counter, giving them time, and after a while he approaches.

"What'll it be?"

"A couple of steak sandwiches," Morgan says.

"Anything to drink?"

"Root beer here," Morgan replies.

"I'll take an iced tea," Ava tells the man.

The waiter moves off to place the order. Or rather, he disappears into the kitchen, possibly to cook the food himself. It might well be a one-man operation.

"Well?" Morgan asks his sister.

Ava doesn't say anything for a moment. "Well, I guess we've been thrown in deep water. We'd better start swimming."

When the waiter brings their drinks, she begins. "Is there a manager about?"

"I expect I'm the closest thing to that," the waiter says. "What do you require?"

Morgan looks at Ava and shrugs. She reaches into her bag and produces a pint Mason jar of moonshine, which she sets on the table.

"We represent a manufacturer of fine corn liquor," she says. "We're in the area looking for new markets."

The waiter actually makes a point of taking a furtive glance around the room, as if making sure they are alone. Surely he knows this, Ava thinks. The place was deserted when they walked in. The waiter smiles and slides the jar back to her.

"You best put that back in your poke, ma'am."

"You're saying you have no interest in this?" Morgan asks.

"That's right."

"Knoxville being a dry city and all," Ava guesses.

"Wet or dry's got nothing to do with it," the waiter says. "Do you have any idea where you are?"

"Suppose you tell us where we are," Ava suggests.

"In way over your heads, that's where," the waiter says. "I'll get those sandwiches."

"It would be nice if we knew a single person here to approach," Morgan says.

They are standing outside the hotel, after their lunch. The steak was tough and the waiter silent after their initial conversation regarding their business.

"Luther didn't give you a single suggestion as to who to see here?" Morgan asks.

Ava shrugs. "Luther says he doesn't know anybody in Knoxville."

"You believe that?" Morgan says. "Luther's been around the block. He's got friends all over the place."

"Colored friends," Ava points out. "If you and I walk up to a colored man and ask if he wants to buy a few gallons of illegal liquor, he's going to run like a scalded cat. Plus, black folks are even poorer than white people these days, if that's possible. We need a buyer with deep pockets."

There is a diner on the ground floor of a red brick hotel along the river. They go inside and sit at a corner table and order coffee from the waiter, a bald man of about sixty. A slouch-shouldered man in a pork pie hat sits at the counter a few feet away, sipping on a soda. He wears a black suit, with a dingy white shirt and string tie.

When the man brings the coffee, Ava offers her pitch again. This time, wary of the stranger at the bar, she opens her purse enough for the waiter to see the Mason jar. He does not run away, as the previous waiter had. Ava takes that as a good sign. She keeps her eye on the man in the hat across the room. It is obvious he is doing his best to eavesdrop.

"And this is through Otto?" the waiter asks.

Ava looks at her brother.

"Who's Otto?" Morgan asks.

The waiter's eyebrows rise. "Where are you folks from anyway?"

"What does that matter?" Ava asks.

"It don't. But if you was smart, you'd head on back there."

They try their luck in three more places—two hotels and a greasy spoon on Broadway—and are treated little better than lepers in each instance. Nobody has the slightest interest in even discussing moonshine.

"Can't believe that nobody here is interested in corn liquor," Morgan says. "That's not what Luther had us believe."

"Or maybe," Ava says, "nobody has any interest in talking about *our* corn liquor."

They are standing outside the greasy spoon where they'd just been informed by a red-haired man with a mustache like a squirrel's tail that alcohol was not legal in the city of Knoxville. His breath stank of tobacco and whisky, the latter somewhat diminishing his argument. There is little traffic on the street. A city bus rumbles past, the passengers watching out the windows to where they stand. Ava returns their gazes, wondering just how she and Morgan appear to the good citizens of Knoxville. Do they look like bootleggers or tourists or just a couple more hillbillies down from the hills?

Turning back to Morgan, she notices the man in the porkpie hat from the Forrest Hotel standing in the mouth of an alley, rolling a cigarette. Ava has already spotted him once before, sitting on a bench in a park when she and Morgan had walked past. At the time, she'd decided it was nothing more than coincidence. She doesn't think that anymore.

"You seem to be following us, pal," she says.

The man pushes his hat up with his thumb. "I wouldn't say that."

"I would."

The man shrugs off her insistence. "Not having a whole lot of luck, are you?" he says.

Now Morgan turns to look the fellow over. Ava has a fleeting thought that the man is a cop but she dismisses it. He smells of body odor and what teeth he still possesses are the color of old foolscap; he looks too seedy even to be working undercover. Besides, what possible reason would the police have for watching them? They'd only been in town for a couple of hours and—try as they might—they hadn't broken any laws.

The man comes near now, lighting the cigarette before flicking the match into the gutter. His voice is lilting and laced with mockery. "Couple of hicks down here in the big city, trying to move a little shine. Everybody giving yous the cold shoulder and yous don't know why."

"Who the hell are you?" Morgan asks.

"I'm the one who does know why, that's who. Name's Paul Ricker but everybody calls me Petey. I was born in this town and I know every nook and cranny in it. The mayor should know as much about Knoxville as I do."

Ava considers the nonsense coming from the man. "And being the charitable type, you're going to share this information with us? I didn't know better, I'd suspect you are with the chamber of commerce."

"Oh, I love a sarcastic woman," the man named Petey says. "Even one that don't know shit from Shinola."

Morgan takes a step toward the man.

"Hold on there, bruiser," Petey says. "I might just be the man you're looking for."

Ava puts her hand on Morgan's arm to stop him. It is unlikely he intends any harm to the man anyway. Morgan has never been the violent type. Ava had more schoolyard fights than he ever did.

"We're listening," she says.

Petey draws on the smoke again. "Like I says, you're a couple of hicks that nobody knows from Adam. You might just as well have that stamped on your forehead. If you've a mind that anybody in this city is gonna buy from you and run afoul of Otto Marx, you're plumb crazy."

"Who is Otto Marx?" Morgan asks.

"Otto Marx is the big cheese when it comes to running liquor in about four states. And he's meaner than a cross-bred cur with rabies. You come around, pretending to be in the moonshine business and you don't know that?"

Ava thinks back to the barrel-bellied waiter in the Forrest Hotel. He'd asked if Otto knew what they were up to. Nobody else had mentioned the name, but they had all acted the same.

"You saying everybody in the whole damn city is afraid of this Otto?" she asks.

"I didn't say everybody," Petey replies.

"I suppose you're not," Morgan says.

"You suppose wrong," Petey says. "I'm scared shitless of the man. But Daytona Dave McGraw ain't. Daytona Dave ain't afraid of man nor beast. And at this moment he's in the market for good moonshine, if that's what you're selling."

Morgan turns to Ava. "I say this fellow is a jackass who likes to hear himself talk."

"What did you call me?" Petey demands. He flicks the cigarette butt into the street and puffs himself up, as if ready to do battle. He is no more than five foot six and wouldn't weigh a hundred and thirty pounds with his pockets full of nickels.

"I called you a jackass," Morgan repeats.

Petey holds the pose for a bit, then relaxes. "I get called worse than that afore breakfast some days," he laughs.

"What if we wanted to talk to this Daytona Dave?" Ava asks. "Where would we find him?"

"Well, you could wander around like a couple blind people, like you been doing," Petey says. "Or you could follow me."

It turns out that Daytona Dave McGraw has a warehouse in the east end of the city, a square block building hard built alongside the Southern Railway yards. To say that Daytona Dave has a warehouse isn't quite accurate; he's taken over an abandoned canning factory and claims it as his own. Dave had learned some basic electrical in jail back in Florida and he knew enough to successfully bypass the defunct meter to run free power to the building.

Daytona Dave is both fleshy and flashy, his sartorial tastes running to pinstriped suits and gold jewelry—rings and bracelets and watch fobs. He uses lemon-scented pomade on his hair and Old Spice on his smoothly shaved jowls. He'd grown up in New Jersey but had moved when he was seventeen to Florida, where he'd acquired his jailbird electrical experience, his fashion sense, such as it was, his style, and also his nickname, which he'd bestowed upon himself one night while in his cups, having decided he was in need of something more memorable than merely Dave.

There were odd pieces of furniture left behind when the canning factory went under, and Dave had gathered it together in his "office"—a large storage room near the loading dock of the shuttered plant. Now he is sitting behind a large steel desk, holding a pint jar of moonshine in his hand while he regards Ava and Morgan standing on the scarred maple floor across from him. An ornate cane with a silver inlaid head lays across the desk. Petey stands to the side, a cocksure smile on his face, as befitting the man who has put the meeting together.

"Well, well," Dave says after sampling the liquor. "That's not kerosene."

"It surely is not," Morgan tells him.

Daytona Dave takes another sip, smacking his lips like a child tasting chocolate milk for the first time. "I have to say—the two of you don't look like any moonshiners I've ever seen."

"What do looks have to do with it?" Morgan asks.

"You're right," Daytona Dave concedes. "Looks have nothing to do with it. It's about product. And this product is...um...very satisfactory. However—how do I know you made it?"

"Oh, we made it," Morgan tells him. "We make the best copperhead in Wilkes County."

"Wherever the hell that is," Dave says. "Maybe you made it and maybe somebody else made it. I don't really care, so long as you can deliver it and deliver it in quantity. All I see right now is one lonely pint jar."

Ava looks around. "I have to say, Mr. Daytona, you're kind of fussy for a man sitting in a building that is not exactly overflowing with merchandise at the moment."

Dave grins, showing gold caps. "Oh—I like you. Smart and sassy both. You're not available, are you? I might come courting."

"We'd prefer to keep this on a professional level, sir," Morgan says.

Daytona Dave regards them a moment, glancing from one to the other. "So what do we have here—husband and wife?"

"Brother and sister," Morgan tells him.

Dave smiles at Ava. "Aha—so you are unencumbered, I take it?"

"I am currently encumbered by the business of marketing fine liquor, Mr. Daytona," she replies. "We've been told that you, sir, are in the distributing end."

Dave shrugs. "All right—we'll get back to romance later. But I should warn you—I am a persistent suitor. As for these empty shelves, which you noted, I'm just getting established in this area. I'm up from Florida. I hear there's a wide-open market in Tennessee and people here quite proficient in the manufacture of corn liquor. I have cash and yes, I have distribution."

"What about this character named Otto Marx?" Morgan asks.

Daytona Dave waves away the name. "I suspect Mr. Marx has cultivated a reputation designed to intimidate people. That is—people who would be intimidated. But I'm told he's a successful man, and I have found that successful men tend to be practical men. He doesn't want trouble with me anymore than I want trouble with him. The market is large enough for both of us. I am known in the state of Florida as a man who doesn't court trouble but who—when confronted with it—puts an end to it quickly and without remorse."

Ava sees that Petey, standing beside Daytona Dave, is beginning to fidget.

Daytona Dave indicates the Mason jar. "If you can duplicate this—what did you call it—copperhead? If you can duplicate that, I'll take a weekly shipment."

"Slow down now," Morgan says. "How much do you need and what's your price?"

Dave gives it some thought. "Start me out with thirty gallons. I'm willing to go eight dollars a gallon."

"For eight dollars, you get rotgut," Ava tells him. She has no idea if this is true.

Dave flashes the lascivious grin again. "Nine."

Ava glances at Morgan quickly, then steps forward and offers her hand. "You have a deal, Mr. Daytona."

Dave takes the hand. "Do I get a kiss to seal it?"

Ava smiles. "Not for nine dollars a gallon, you don't."

Heading home after their meeting with the flamboyant Daytona Dave, Ava falls asleep in the passenger seat while Morgan drives. It will be full dark before they get back to Flagg's Hollow. They left Knoxville feeling pretty good about themselves. They'd found a buyer. It hadn't come all that easy, and maybe it wouldn't have happened at all if they hadn't encountered the foul-smelling Petey. But they had and that's all that mattered for now.

Ava wakes as they're heading through Maple Springs twenty miles west of home. She watches the mountains in the gloaming for a time, going over in her mind their meeting with Daytona Dave.

"You realize you told him where we're from?" she says.

"What?" Morgan asks.

"You told him we made the best moonshine in all of Wilkes County."

"Dang, I did do that, didn't I?" He downshifts the Nash, approaching a curve. "Well, Wilkes County is a pretty big place."

"Actually, you didn't say moonshine," Ava recalls now. "You said copperhead. Where'd you hear that?"

"From Luther," Morgan says. "He's got a passel of names for moonshine. Panther's breath, skull cracker, hooch, rotgut, mountain dew, bush whisky."

"I kinda like copperhead," Ava says.

"Me too," Morgan agrees. "As for mentioning Wilkes County, that Daytona fellow didn't know where it is anyway."

"His boy Petey might."

"That's true," Morgan says. He's quiet for a time, going back over the meeting in his mind. "I don't know about you, sister, but I wouldn't trust Petey any further than I could throw a piano."

When the two erstwhile moonshiners are gone, Daytona Dave walks out onto the loading dock, carrying his fancy cane. He has no practical need of the walking stick; he carries it for effect. Daytona had helped run a numbers game back in Daytona, under a man from the West Coast named Calabasas Chris. Calabasas had advised Dave that he needed to look sharp every day, whether he was taking an important meeting or just ducking out to the drugstore for cigars. Calabasas had holes in his socks and some days didn't have two nickels to rub together, but he always looked the part of a big-time operator. Dave had taken his advice to heart. That, and the idea for an alliterative nickname.

Now Petey comes out of the warehouse as well. The two men stand there, looking over the rail yards to the west.

"Didn't I find you a supplier?" Petey asks. "Just like I said I would."

Daytona Dave nods slightly as he takes a Havana from inside his pinstripe.

"Yessir," Petey pushes on. "This time next week, we'll be in the shine business for sure."

Dave produces a small penknife and snips the end from the cigar, then lights it with a gold-plated Zippo. Petey watches him, anxious for some sign of gratitude. Dave smokes and looks at the railroad tracks, as if something interesting might occur out there.

"If I could get my money," Petey suggests then.

"What money is that?" Dave asks.

"What was agreed to," Petey says. "You said fifty dollars for every supplier I brung you."

Daytona Dave half turns to gesture inside the old canning factory. "Do you see an ounce of liquor in this here building, boy? Cuz I don't. You'll get your money when I get some booze." He pauses to regard Petey with mock suspicion. "Is everybody in Tennessee as stupid as you?"

Petey, not being any kind of an expert on the intelligence levels of his fellow Tennesseans, has no reply for that. So he holds his tongue and moves away to sit on a wooden crate on the dock. Rolling a cigarette, he slips into a sulk and stares daggers at the man named Daytona Dave McGraw.

FOURTEEN

When Edgar stops in at the Texaco after work, he finds Bobby in the process of removing the engine from the coupe. He has the V8 hanging from a chain hoist attached to an overhead I- beam and is slowly lifting it to clear the engine compartment as Edgar walks in. All four fenders and the running boards have been removed from the car.

"What in the Sam Hill are you doing now?" Edgar asks.

Bobby pulls down on the chain, inching the engine upwards. "I'm making a banana split, Edgar. What's it look like I'm doing?"

"Charley said this here is a brand-new engine, all the way from Detroit," Edgar says. "Why would you remove a new engine, Bobby?"

Bobby gives the chain one more pull, and the engine swings free. "I'm taking it to Charlotte to my pal's machine shop. I never had a motor this good in my whole life and I'm going to make it even better. When I'm done, this coupe is going to be the fastest car in the whole goddamn state of North Carolina. You can write that down and have it notarized, Edgar."

Bobby walks around to the front of the car and pushes it backward, out from under the suspended engine. Edgar gives him a hand. When the car is clear, Bobby takes a ratchet and socket from the toolbox, and begins to remove the exhaust manifolds from the V8.

"Edgar, grab the keys off that hook by the door and back Charley's pickup in here, will you? He says I could borrow it to run to Charlotte."

After Edgar brings the truck inside, Bobby arranges a couple of scrap tires in the pickup box to set the engine on. When it's lowered into place, he chains it to the box sides to secure it and then slams shut the tailgate. He turns to Edgar.

"You want to take a ride to Charlotte?"

Edgar glances at his watch. "I better not. Mother will be expecting me for supper."

Bobby laughs. "Mother will be expecting you for supper. You're a hoot, Edgar, you know that?"

Tiger Thompson works at a machine shop on the north side of Charlotte. Tiger and Bobby met in Europe during the war. Tiger is a few years older than Bobby and was already a mechanic at that time. The Army tasked him with keeping the trucks running during the fighting at the Marne. Tiger took Bobby, who was just fifteen and as green as grass, under his wing, thinking he could keep the boy away from the front if he got him repairing army vehicles alongside himself. The military recruiters might have been fooled into believing that Bobby was old enough to enlist, but Tiger wasn't. His plan worked in theory—right up until the night they had to go behind enemy lines to rescue a patrol whose Liberty truck had broken down in no man's land. The German artillery had started up just as they arrived, probably after they'd been spotted approaching the line. Both men were hit with shrapnel. Tiger was bleeding out in a ditch when Bobby found him. Bobby applied a tourniquet and carried Tiger over five hundred yards to safety, in spite of being hit in the leg himself.

This night is a sight more peaceful than that. The two men are back working together, for the first time in years, in a shop that is set up for all kinds of machine work. Bobby has the V8 stripped bare, the block resting on an engine stand. Tiger turns the camshaft in a lathe while Bobby bores the cylinders to increase displacement. Bobby glances at a clock. It's a quarter of midnight.

"I ain't got but eight hours to get this mill together and be back in Wilkesboro for work," he says.

"No sweat," Tiger assures him. "Get that bore done and all that's left is relieving the block. Throw in the new pistons and rings, and you're ready to roll."

"Keep a total on all this," Bobby says. "I'll pay you when I can."

Tiger shakes his head to show he's not worried about it. "Oh, I almost forgot."

He goes into a back storeroom and returns with an intake manifold mounted with three carburetors. He places the intake on the workbench. "Yours," is all he says.

"Jesus, Tiger," Bobby says. "That's an Edelbrock. And Strombergs. I can't afford that."

"It's yours," Tiger insists. "I got it from a fellow down in Columbia who owes me money."

"I'll pay you for it," Bobby says.

"No," Tiger says again. "I owe you from the Marne now and forever. Besides, you want to build this engine right, or not?"

By three o'clock they have the V8 back together and resting once again in the back of Charley Walker's shop truck. Tiger opens a couple of beers to celebrate the job. He and Bobby lean their elbows on the truck box, admiring the gleaming engine.

"Remember when we were in Paris after the armistice?" Bobby says. "We went to that fancy museum--the Loover or however they called it?"

Tiger smiles and takes a drink.

"All those abstract paintings," Bobby goes on. "Nothing but a bunch of splotches and squiggly lines. And that Limey gunner—Harris, it was—telling me that a person needed to be educated to appreciate the beauty of it and such. Well, you could educate me from now until the cows come home and that wouldn't happen. I would still see nothing but splotches and squiggles. But this here flathead V8; to me, that's a thing of beauty. You gonna tell me that some Frenchie painter could create a thing like that?"

"I expect not."

Bobby looks at the clock once more. He has a three-hour drive back to Wilkesboro. He might be able to squeeze in a catnap before work. It was worth it though, no question.

"You recall that museum?" he asks.

"I seem to recall you pitching woo with the lady who ran the front desk."

Bobby smiles. "Now she was near as pretty as that engine." He drains the beer and sets the empty on the workbench. "You ought to come up and watch me race sometime, Tiger. I'm gonna turn some heads with this mill."

"All I ask is that you stay out of trouble, Bobby."

"When have I ever been in trouble?" Bobby asks.

"Only your whole damn life," Tiger replies.

FIFTEEN

Arrangements had been made to deliver the thirty gallons to Daytona Dave the following Saturday. Monday morning Luther and Morgan fire the still and begin to cook. Ava parks the two delivery trucks in the shade of a large oak tree behind the plant and then goes about the task of painting over the HOMER FLAGG & SONS lettering on the doors. She has a gallon of black paint and a two-inch brush made from hog's bristle. She finds an old milking stool to sit on while she works. The morning grows warm but it is comfortable there beneath the massive burr oak.

She is finishing the passenger door of the first truck when Jedediah walks down from the house. He stands watching her for a time, puffing on his pipe.

"I spent my whole life upholding that good name and here you're going to erase it in a matter of minutes," he says.

Ava doesn't respond while she finishes the last few strokes. Then she rises and stands back to admire her work a moment before turning to her father and kissing him on the cheek.

"People around here know who Jedediah Flagg is," she tells him. "All the paint in the world can't erase that. However, the business at hand requires a certain anonymity. I'm sure you will agree with that."

She carries the stool around to the other side of the truck to start on the driver's door. Jedediah follows her and sits down on the running board of the second truck. He takes his pipe from his pocket and raps it sharply against the fender to empty the bowl.

"I am not without doubts regarding this, daughter."

Ava smiles. "Should I call you Thomas then? Keep in mind that Thomas became a believer in the end."

"Yes, Thomas did indeed become a believer," Jedediah says. "But then he wasn't running moonshine."

"No, he was not," Ava admits. "People's woes were different in the time of Thomas. There were—oh, I don't know—locusts and floods and hellfire and brimstone and whatnot." She continues to paint as she speaks. With each stroke, another letter disappears.

"Are you mocking me?"

"Never, father."

"Nor the good book neither, I hope."

"Certainly not."

"I trust you are not," Jedediah says. "You do not want to get on my bad side. Or His neither. Now I believe I'll head into the plant and see if I can't scare up another paint brush."

Ava looks up. "You're going to help?"

"You're the one who advocated the lighting of candles, daughter."

It is decided that Luther will send his nephew Jodie to Johnson City with ten gallons of moonshine that night. The fresh paint on the truck doors is still tacky by evening but Ava reasons it is dry enough for the trip.

"The air will dry it on the way," she says to Luther.

She and Morgan watch as Luther packs the jugs beneath the truck seat, snaking an old horse blanket between the bottles to keep them from breaking. Jodie stands by, looking both eager and anxious. He's a quiet kid. Ava hasn't heard him speak more than a dozen words since he'd started working for them. He is game though and doesn't shirk from a task.

Ava thought that perhaps Luther would do the delivery, but he had nixed the idea. He was cooking mash and didn't yet trust

Morgan or Ava to oversee it while he was gone. Ava then suggested that she and Morgan deliver the liquor.

"Bones is on the nervous side," Luther had said. "He might get antsy, seeing white folks showing up to sell him shine. Keep in mind that the revenuers is all white."

So it was decided that Jodie would go. He'd met the man called Bones once, when Bones had been in Flagg's Hollow, visiting Luther.

"He be waiting on you around back the hotel," Luther says to the boy now. "With the cash. Take the old road through the gap on the way, stay offa the macadam. No point in drawing attention you don't need."

Jodie squints as he takes in the information, committing it to memory.

Luther replaces the seat in the truck, making sure it clears the jugs beneath without snapping the bottle necks. He looks at Jodie.

"Now don't be driving like a damn fool, boy," he says. "You transporting precious cargo here. Bones is interested in a weekly shipment and maybe even more than ten jugs. There's thirsty people down in Johnson City."

It's still daylight when Jodie drives out of the yard, bent on delivering the first shipment—albeit a small shipment—from the Flagg moonshine company. He follows the county road northwest towards Maple Springs. The tired Model T has a top speed of around twenty-five miles an hour and it's full dark by the time he turns onto the old pike.

And the old pike is where Boone Saunders and his boy Val begin to follow him. Boone is behind the wheel of the Cadillac sedan. They are heading home when they spot Jodie, taking a leak in the woods alongside the road, the old truck parked a few yards away. When Jodie sees them, he ducks his head beneath the gleam of the Caddy's headlights and scurries back to the truck. Boone slows down and pulls over.

"What?" Val asks.

"You see that?" Boone asks.

"See what?"

"That's a suspicious-looking nigger," Boone says.

"Ain't they all?" Val asks.

"Yeah, but we'd best investigate this one," Boone says. "Way he ducked his head; that boy is up to something."

He makes a U-turn and catches up to Jodie in minutes, roaring up on the truck's tail, flashing his lights from low beam to high before slamming the heavy Cadillac into the rear bumper.

Inside the truck, Jodie is gripped by primal fear. The road is narrow and winding, more mud than gravel. Jodie is not an experienced driver under the best conditions. The Caddy rams into the truck three more times before pulling out to come alongside. Jodie accelerates but the old Ford is no match for the big sedan. Boone runs along beside the truck for a bit and then sharply pulls out in front, veering to the right and forcing the Ford into the ditch. The truck smashes into a tree, crunching the fender and hood. Steam pours from the radiator. Jodie is flung forward, his head crashing into the windshield, shattering the glass into spiderwebs.

Boone parks the Caddy fifty feet away and he and Val get out to walk over to the truck. Jodie is dazed from the crash; blood runs down his forehead and into his eyes. Boone opens the door and grabs the youngster by the collar, flings him out of the truck and into the muddy ditch.

"What are you up to, boy?"

"Nothin'." Jodie's voice is thin with fear. He gets to his feet but remains in the ditch, water up to his ankles.

"Jesus, you're still pulling on your mama's tit. Where'd you get a truck like this?"

Jodie says nothing else. He's too frightened to speak and doesn't know what to say anyway. Boone moves away from him to look inside the truck.

"Val, swing them headlights around so I can see."

Val gets into the Cadillac and turns it around on the road.

"You didn't make no answer, boy," Boone says. "You hidin' something? You didn't steal this truck, did you?"

Again Jodie doesn't reply, nor does Boone expect him to.

As the Caddy's headlights swing around to illuminate the scene, Boone leans inside the truck for a look. After a moment he lifts the seat. Val gets out of the Caddy and approaches.

"Well, lookit here," Boone says. "We got us a bona fide bootlegger, Val. One, two, three, four, five—looks like ten gallons of what appears to be mountain busthead." Boone gives Jodie the eye. "Where you from, nigger? You been cooking up in these hills?"

"No, sir."

"Well, somebody has been cooking," Boone says. "I doubt you got the smarts. That means you're just the delivery boy. Where you taking this?"

"No place, sir."

Boone's eyebrows rise. "No place? You're just driving around the county in a stolen truck with ten gallons of mountain dew under the seat. That's your story?"

"I didn't steal no truck," Jodie says. "And that stuff—well, I didn't even know it was under there, sir."

"You're a black liar," Val says.

"No, I tend to agree with the boy," Boone says. "He says this ain't his fucking shine. So if he don't own it, he ain't got nothing to say about me taking it."

Boone reaches in and retrieves one of the jugs. He uncorks it and has a drink. "Well now," he says, handing it to Val. "That's what I might call above average hooch."

Val has a small drink and then a bigger one. "Where'd you get this, boy?"

"Done told you—I didn't even know it was there," Jodie says.

Boone walks to the Caddy and opens the trunk. "One thing I hate is a goddamn lying nigger thinks he can run shine in my backyard." He produces two stout blood-stained lengths of oak and tosses one to Val. "You take the truck, I'll take the liar."

SIXTEEN

Ava goes into town first thing the next morning, driving Morgan's coupe. First off, she stops at Doc Haskell's and asks that he go out to Flagg's Hollow to administer to Jodie. Luther and Morgan had brought the boy home late the night before. They'd gone looking for him when Jodie was several hours late returning. They'd found him in the damaged truck. He hadn't known what to do but decided he should stay with the vehicle. He'd lost the liquor; he didn't want to lose the truck as well.

Leaving Doc Haskell's, Ava heads over to Charley Walker's Texaco garage. She parks in front and as she's getting out of the car, Bobby Barlow walks out of the shop, wiping his hands on a rag. He wears work clothes and a dirty fedora, brim up.

"How many?" he asks, indicating the glass pumps.

"What?" she asks and then realizes. "Oh, I'm not here for gasoline."

"You're Ava Flagg," Bobby says.

"I am."

"Bobby Barlow."

"I know who you are. Is Mister Walker around?"

"Not just now," Bobby says. "Went over to Stanton to collect a grain truck."

As he speaks, a phone begins to ring inside. Bobby goes to

answer it, and Ava follows. The phone is by the counter in the front of the shop, beside the cash register. There are batteries on display along the wall, as well as fan belts and wiper blades and cans of motor oil.

"Walker's Texaco," Bobby says into the receiver.

Ava wanders through the front shop and into the double bay behind. There's a Chevy sedan on the hoist, with the front wheels off. Bobby's coupe sits to the side, stripped down, the fresh engine now back in the car. Ava goes over for a look at the vehicle as he talks on the phone.

"Just the oil and lube then? How are the brakes?"

Ava walks around the coupe, has a look inside. There's a large gauge of some kind mounted on the steering column, with RPM on it.

"We can pull the wheels and have a look," Bobby says. "No charge for that. All right then, see you first thing in the morning."

He hangs up the phone and walks back into the bay where Ava stands waiting.

"I need Mister Walker to tow a truck home from Hickory Creek for me."

"Break down, did it?" Bobby asks.

"Something like that," Ava says. "When will he be back?"

"Any time," Bobby says. "You want to wait?"

Ava looks around the dirty garage. "I guess I can wait."

"There's chairs out front," Bobby suggests.

Ava looks at the coupe again. "Why are there no fenders?"

"That's extra weight," Bobby says. "I'm building this car to race. The lighter the better. That engine is the fastest V8 this county has ever seen. Want to have a look?"

"Not particularly," Ava said. "I'll wait out front."

Doc Haskell sets Jodie's broken left arm and then uses more than fifty stitches to close up the wounds inflicted by the truck windshield and Boone Saunders, and his shillelagh of white oak. Morgan pays the doctor when he's finished. He doesn't ask any questions about the origin of Jodie's injuries. Doc Haskell has lived in Wilkes County his entire life and he knows when to ask, and when to keep quiet.

When Charley Walker tows the wrecked truck in later that day, Ava and Morgan are there waiting. Luther walks over from Darkytown when he sees the wrecker pull into the yard. The three inspect the truck as Charley unhooks the chains. The headlights and door glass are smashed and every square inch of the fenders and hood are bashed in. The moonshine is gone, of course. The seats and dash are streaked with dried blood from Jodie's wounds.

Ava pays Charley three dollars for the tow and he fires up the big Mac wrecker and heads for town, just as Jedediah walks down from the big house. He stands looking at the double-T Ford for a time, his hands behind his back.

"And we suspect Boone Saunders is behind this?" Jedediah asks.

"More than suspect," Morgan replies. "He bragged on who he was to Jodie."

"That's bold," Jedediah says. "Speaking his name like that. Proud of his sinful ways. What kind of man boasts of his evil doings?"

"Maybe telling his name is bold," Ava says, "but beating that boy is pure cowardice in my books." She pauses. "Good thing we painted over that lettering, else Boone and his ilk would no doubt be on our doorstep by now."

"Are we sure the youngster didn't tell him?" Jedediah asks.

"He says no," Luther says. "And I believe him. He ain't but a sapling but the boy has backbone." He glances at Ava "My only question is—are we still in business?"

"We are definitely still in business," Ava tells him. "Why wouldn't we be?"

"Just making certain," Luther says and he turns and goes into the plant.

Moments later, Ezra walks over from his house to view the damage. His contributions to the cooking of moonshine have been minimal at best, confining himself to whatever odd jobs need doing around the plant, while maintaining a superior yet petulant attitude in the process.

"Well, well," he says now. "It looks like the chickens have come home to roost."

"You know what you can do with your chickens," Ava snaps.

"Daughter," Jedediah warns.

Ava glances briefly at her father before turning back to Ezra. "When you're done gloating, you can fire up that pump. This ain't a holiday."

Ezra gestures to the wrecked truck. "So your intention is to just ignore this? Pretend it never happened. Or are we treating it as an act of God?"

"It's an act of Boone Saunders," Morgan tells him. "A damn far piece from God."

"But God was watching," Ezra pushes. "And did nothing to intervene. What does that tell you about His view on these activities?"

"Brother, I don't have the inclination right now to argue with you on God's views on what we're doing," Ava says. "Seems to me that God has long had a habit of watching atrocities and doing nothing. So what is your point?"

"That will suffice," Jedediah interjects sternly. "God answers all prayers in time. We do not know his thinking. It is not our task to try to know it."

"What precisely is our task these days, father?" Ezra asks.

Jedediah looks at Ava a moment before making his reply.

"To carry on," he says.

"Try it again," Bobby says.

He's leaning over the engine in the coupe, screwdriver in his right hand, the gas pedal linkage in his left. He has just adjusted the mixture on the middle carburetor. Edgar is behind the wheel. He hits the starter button with his left foot and then pumps the gas.

"Whoa!" Bobby yells, looking up through the windshield. "I told you to stay off the goddamn gas pedal. I got the linkage here."

"Sorry!"

"Again," Bobby says.

Edgar hits the starter switch and the engine roars to life, coughs and misses, then stalls. Bobby gives the mixture screws on the carb a quarter turn.

"I still say it's the timing," Edgar tells him.

"You don't know jack shit," Bobby says. "She's running rich."

"I'd check the timing," Edgar replies.

"I'm sure you would," Bobby tells him. "That's why you're in there and I'm out here. Hit it again."

Edgar bumps the starter and the V8 immediately coughs to life. This time it keeps running, albeit roughly. Bobby turns the mixture screw and the engine levels out. He moves to adjust the other two carbs and the engine smooths, falling into a low idle with a thump-thump-thump. Bobby glances at Edgar, nods his head, satisfied.

"She's still a little rough," Edgar points out.

"That's the cam does that," Bobby says. "It's your giddy-up and go, Edgar. It all starts with the camshaft. You ought to be taking notes, boy."

"I work at my father's funeral parlor," Edgar replies. "Not sure that I need to know about camshafts and carburetors and all like that."

"You never know, you might take a notion to juice up that old hearse," Bobby says. "Hell, you could even advertise. *We'll get you to the graveyard in no time flat.*"

"Very funny, Bobby."

Bobby walks over to open the bay door, then returns and tells Edgar to push over so he can get behind the wheel. He slips the shifter into first gear and eases out the clutch. They roll out onto Main Street, heading north. Bobby idles along for a hundred feet and then shifts into second, barely touching the gas pedal. He finds third gear as they go through the intersection at State, still poking along. Edgar, in the passenger seat, gets antsy.

"Well?" he finally asks.

Bobby lights a cigarette. "Well what?"

"You gonna punch this thing or not?"

"Edgar, Edgar," Bobby says, exhaling. "You ever been with a girl?"

"I've been with lots of girls."

"Sure you have," Bobby says. "Except they've all been named your right hand."

"You can go straight to hell."

"Why are people always telling me to go *straight* to hell?" Bobby asks. "Maybe I'd like to take a few detours along the way."

"I'm certain that's exactly what you've been doing."

Bobby laughs as he slows down, turning left on Cherry Street. "Thing is, Edgar—when you're with a girl for the first time, you don't go from standing still to ninety in five seconds. Same with a new engine. You got to take it slow. It's a matter of lubrication, of breaking things in. The rings have got to seat. And when we get back to the garage, I'll torque those heads again. You can ruin a fresh-built engine by pounding hell out of it."

"How long do you intend to baby her?"

Bobby gives it some thought. "I'll put a good two hundred miles on this mill before I even think of jumping on it." He pulls on the smoke. "But when I do—it's gonna be Katie-bar-the- door, Edgar my boy."

They're out of the town now, driving the gravel road that crosses the wooden bridge over Cub Creek. A few miles along, Bobby takes a left on a dirt road running west.

"Where we going?" Edgar asks.

"Thought we might stop and see what Myrna Lee is up to," Bobby says. "Maybe she'll fix us some lunch."

Bobby downshifts into second gear as they climb a steep hill. When they get to the crest, he has a look ahead and then rolls to a stop. The Saunders farm sits in the valley below, fifty rocky acres surrounded by scrub and brush. There's a ramshackle frame house, with a bank barn and chicken coop behind. The blades of a windmill turn lazily and uselessly, as the drive rod to the pump is missing. There's a Cadillac sedan parked by the house. Bobby snorts as he tosses the cigarette butt out the window.

"What?" Edgar asks.

"That's Boone's car," Bobby says.

"The old man?"

"Yeah," Bobby says. "He don't have much use for me and I don't have any for him. I guarantee he won't like me coming around to see Myrna Lee. I didn't figure him to be here."

"Well, it's his farm, ain't it?" Edgar asks.

Bobby nods. "But he's usually up in the hills somewheres, cooking shine and staying one step ahead of the feds. Or trying to; he's done a few stretches in jail for running it. Although not as much as he should have. Story is he's killed upward of six men."

As they watch, the door to the house opens and Val Saunders walks out. He goes to the trunk of the Cadillac and retrieves a satchel before going back inside.

"That's Val," Bobby says. "He's the oldest and a right sonofabitch too. About as dumb as a fence post but just as mean as the old man. I wouldn't trust him if he told me that birds could fly."

"There's another brother, right?" Edgar asks.

"Two," Bobby says. "The middle one, Leon, got killed in a quarry accident, must be fifteen years ago now. Jake is the youngest. He's a square shooter, him and I go back a ways."

"I thought he was doing time."

"He is."

"And you call him a square shooter," Edgar says.

"He's always been square with me," Bobby says. "If he wants to hang a little paper in these tough times, I say more power to him. Only problem is, he keeps getting caught. But Jake isn't a patch on Val and Boone. They'd kill you as soon as they look at you."

"Doesn't that make you nervous then—courting Myrna Lee?" Edgar asked.

Bobby laughs as he puts the coupe in reverse and turns around. "I wouldn't call it courting, what we're doing. We're just having a little fun."

"You for certain, she sees it that way?

"Why wouldn't she?" Bobby asks.

"You know," Edgar says. "Women."

"What do you know about women?"

Edgar, who doesn't know a hell of a lot about the distaff side, is silent for a time. "What about Boone—you figure he'd see it that way?"

"I'm sure he would not," Bobby says. "Which is why we're currently heading back to town, Edgar."

SEVENTEEN

It is decided that Morgan and Luther will deliver the shipment to Daytona Dave McGraw in Knoxville. At least it is decided by Morgan and Luther. They don't tell Ava until the truck is being loaded Saturday afternoon. Morgan had driven to Stub Parnell's farm that morning to pick up a half-dozen bales of wheat straw, which he and Luther break open and use to pack around the gallon jugs of moonshine in the back of the truck. Once the liquor is properly buffered, they cover it with a tarp and then proceed to pile a number of items on top—two old tires, a bed spring, broken rocking chair and a wringer washing machine.

Ava had gone into Wilkesboro to the market earlier, and returned as the two men were tying the load down. She parked Morgan's coupe alongside the truck and got out to take in the scene.

"People are going to figure us for a bunch of Okies, heading to California," she says.

"That's the general idea," Morgan says. He hesitates a long moment, not eager to tell the rest. "Not us though, sister. You aren't coming along."

"I most certainly am," she tells him.

Morgan nods toward Luther, who's tying a clove hitch in the rope to secure the load. "Luther and me are going."

"And why is that?" Ava demands.

"This here is my shine, Miss Ava," Luther says. "If this Daytona man is a sure enough customer, he might maybe have questions about the manufacture, and the like. I have them answers. The making of good busthead is an art. And, all due respect, I am the artist."

Finishing, Luther nods to her defiantly and goes into the plant to retrieve more rope. Ava suspects that the old man has been practicing his little speech. Morgan may have even helped him with it.

"I'm not sure he's telling you everything," Morgan says when Luther is inside. "He's pretty broken up about what happened to Jodie. He blames himself for getting the boy involved in the first place. So he figures he needs to be the one to go this time."

"If he'd gone last time, it would be him with the broken arm and stitches. Or does he think the outcome would have been different?"

"I expect not," Morgan says. "But he's still remorseful about the whole thing."

Ava considers it a moment. "Then we'll all go."

"You may have noticed that Luther isn't exactly skinny," Morgan says. "There's barely enough room for the two of us in that truck. And it's no ten-minute drive, here to Knoxville."

Ava looks away, unhappy. "It's because I'm a girl, isn't it?"

"I quit thinking of you as a girl when you broke my nose when we were ten years old," Morgan says. "We don't have the room, simple as that. You and Cal can get started on that next run of mash."

Luther comes out of the plant in time to hear the last of this. "Oh, I don't know about that."

"About what?" Ava demands.

"You starting the mash," he says. "I'd best be here for that."

"You can't be everywhere at once, Mr. Briscoe," Ava informs him. "And I believe I can put corn and water in a pot and light a fire underneath, thank you very much." She turns on her heel and marches into the warehouse.

"You don't never hand over your load before you gets paid," Luther says. "All you're doing there is setting yourself up for trouble. They'll take the cargo and then say, 'oh, we be paying you later.' Well, later turns into never and where you at then?"

They are entering Knoxville, with Morgan behind the wheel. It's growing dark. They had a flat tire twenty miles shy of the city and had to remove the tube and patch it before going on. Now Morgan is watching the street signs, trying to remember the route to the rail yards.

"Where this place anyway?" Luther asks.

"Right along the railway tracks," Morgan says.

"And where are they?"

"I'm looking," Morgan says. "Somewheres off to the east, if I recall."

Farther on, they crest a long incline and see the rail yards in the distance. A few minutes later, they pull up to the old canning factory. There are dirty windows in the big wooden doors of the loading dock, through which faint electric lights can be seen inside. Two cars--a large black Lincoln and a canary yellow Packard—are parked alongside the building.

Morgan rolls the truck to a stop fifty yards short of the steps leading up to the dock. They sit there for a few moments, waiting for somebody to appear. Finally Morgan gets out, takes a couple of steps toward the building before stopping.

"Hello!"

There's no response. Morgan waits a bit before shouting again. Luther climbs out of the cab.

"You sure this is the place?"

"I was just here last week," Morgan tells him. He takes a couple more steps toward the dock. "Hello, Daytona Dave!"

Silence. Morgan glances over at Luther and shrugs.

"I best go knock on the—"

At that precise moment the warehouse doors explode open, glass shattering, hinges ripping from the jambs. Daytona Dave is flung forward onto the rough planking, landing face first. He is bleeding heavily, his face a mess, his pinstriped jacket torn.

Otto Marx steps out through the shattered doorway, followed

closely by Slim and Elmer, all three men in their shirtsleeves; presumably they had removed their jackets in order to give Daytona Dave a proper beating. Otto carries Dave's silver-tipped cane in his right hand and now he steps over to Dave's inert form and begins to thrash him with it. Dave throws his hands over his head in defense and scrambles to the edge of the dock and drops to the gravel there, landing with a thud. Otto leans down to speak to him.

"You get to running, boy, and don't you stop 'til you smell them orange blossoms back there in Tallahassee. You hear me?"

Daytona Dave has never been to Tallahassee but he sees no upshot in telling Otto Marx that. He manages to get to his feet and begins to stumble across the railway tracks, falling twice, and getting up. Soon he's lost in the gloaming.

Watching the assault, or at least the tail end of it, neither Morgan nor Luther have moved a muscle. Now Morgan glances at Luther.

"We need to get out of here," Luther whispers, turning for the truck.

Morgan needs no convincing. He follows Luther to the idling truck at a run, jumps in and swings a wide U-turn and guns the engine. Luther clings to the dashboard as they bounce over the potholes and ruts in the lane leading to the street.

Otto watches the retreat from the loading dock, leaning on Daytona Dave's cane. He glances over at the other two men.

"Get after 'em."

The two are in no particular hurry as they go down the steps and walk over to the Packard parked a few yards away. They climb in, with Slim behind the wheel, and drive off after the truck.

Otto watches as he fishes a cigar from his vest pocket. He lights it, then turns toward the interior of the building. "Come on out, sonny. Looks like you're with me now."

Petey emerges from the dim warehouse, stepping carefully, as wary as any Judas ought to be. Puffing on the Havana, Otto pulls his watch from his pocket and looks at the hour.

"You like baseball, sonny?" he asks.

Petey shrugs his thin shoulders. He's unnerved by the beating Daytona Dave received, even if he was the one who engineered it. He's determined not to set himself up for more of the same.

"The Smokies ain't got nothing this year," he says.

"That's about to change," Otto predicts.

"How do you figure?"

"I'll tell you how I figure," Otto says smiling. "I just bought the team."

A mile away Morgan has the old Ford running flat out. Unfortunately, flat out is thirty miles an hour. Within minutes he sees the headlights of the Packard in the mirror. Luther twists in his seat to have a look.

"Floor that gas pedal, Morgan!"

"It's floored, goddamn it!"

Luther begins to rock frantically back and forth in the seat, as if that will make the truck go faster. The Packard draws closer. Luther looks back again, sees the approaching headlights, like a freight train bearing down on them.

"Maybe it ain't them," he says.

"It's them," Morgan replies. He's clutching the steering wheel so tightly his knuckles are white. Sweat runs down his armpits.

Luther glances out the side window and then points. "Up there!"

There's a narrow lane leading off the road to the left, through a copse of large white pine trees. Morgan slows the truck, then cranks the steering wheel sharply to veer onto the path. The truck tips up on two wheels, almost turns over, and then slams back down. Morgan bounces across the cab into Luther then slides desperately back behind the wheel and hits the gas again.

They have no chance of losing the Packard. The sedan makes the turn and seconds later roars up beside them and slams into the truck, forcing it from the road and into the pines. The front tire of the truck hits a stump and stops there, the wheel up in the air, the rear tire spinning in the dirt.

"Oh, lord," Morgan says.

Slim and Elmer get out of the yellow sedan and walk over. Slim pulls a .45 semi-automatic from his belt as he opens the driver's door.

"Get out of there," he says, tapping the gun barrel on the truck's roof. "The both of you."

Elmer stands looking at the assortment of cargo in the back of the truck.

"What's all this junk?" he asks.

Slim looks over. "Camouflage is my guess."

Luther, standing in the half-darkness on the other side of the truck, begins to inch away, getting ready for flight. When Slim notices, he casually pumps three rounds from the .45 into the door of the truck.

"Hold tight, fat boy, or you'll get the same."

Luther holds tight.

Elmer takes a clasp knife from his pocket and cuts the ropes securing the scrap in the truck. He tosses aside the bed springs and tires and the rest before pulling back the tarp to reveal the moonshine beneath. He reaches for a jug, uncorks it and has a drink. He shrugs then smashes the jug against a tree trunk before turning to Slim. He indicates Morgan and Luther, standing nervously in the Packard's headlights. Luther shakes like tall grass in the wind.

"What are we supposed to do with them?"

Slim shrugs. "Kill 'em, I guess. Otto never really said."

Elmer gives it some thought, then pulls a snub-nosed Smith & Wesson from his coat and points the barrel at Luther. "Maybe just kill this one. Otto don't care for an uppity nigger."

"No!" Morgan shouts.

"You kill one, you gotta kill 'em both," Slim reasons, waving the .45 in Morgan's direction. "Can't be leaving the other one to tell tales."

"What did we do?" Morgan pleads. "What did we do?"

"You infringed, son," Slim tells him. "Can't have that."

"We didn't know," Morgan protests. "We're not even from here."

"We ain't from here, sir," Luther repeats, his voice thin.

"Don't matter where you're from," Slim explains. "Infringement is infringement."

"Please," Morgan says.

"Please, sir," Luther adds. He drops to his knees. "We ain't from here."

Slim looks over at Elmer. "Otto never said nothing. In a big damn hurry to get to the ball game."

Elmer takes a moment to think it over. "All right. The two of you get them jugs out the back of the truck and smash 'em against those trees. Do it now!"

Morgan and Luther hurry to do what they're told. Elmer puts the revolver in his hip pocket and walks over to stand beside Slim, who still holds the .45 in his hand. Morgan climbs into the truck and hands over a jug to Luther, who lifts it above his head and throws it against a tree trunk. The jug doesn't break and he's obliged to do it again, shattering it this time.

"Stuff any good?" Slim asks as he watches.

"It is," Elmer replies. "Better than most even."

Morgan keeps handing over the jugs for Luther to break.

"I expect Otto wouldn't like it, if he knew we was busting up good merchandise," Slim says. "Doesn't make a lot of sense."

"No, it don't," Elmer agrees. He looks over at Luther. "Hey you, fat boy. Stop breaking them jugs and start toting them over to that Packard."

Morgan and Luther have no reason to argue and enough sense not to try. They carry the rest of the moonshine to the Packard sedan and stow it in the trunk and back seat. When they're done, they retreat toward the truck, silently praying they'll be allowed to drive away.

"All right," Slim says. "Now you boys need to get out of the city. We ain't going to kill you because we ain't been told to. Count this as your lucky day. But I can tell you that next time will be a different story."

"Next time you infringe on Otto," Elmer clarifies.

"Won't be no next time," Morgan assures them.

"No next time, sir," Luther says.

"You see to it," Slim says. He tucks the .45 back in his belt and turns to Elmer. "Let's get the hell out of here. These damn pikers are a pain in the ass."

The two get into the Packard and turn around in the narrow lane and drive off. Morgan and Luther stand side by side, watching, relief pouring through their veins.

"Morgan," Luther says, his voice weak.

"Yeah?"

"I may have messed myself."

EIGHTEEN

Ava and Morgan sit in the lunchroom of the plant. It is early morning and just the two of them there. Morgan had roused Ava when they'd returned from Knoxville the night before, taking care not to awaken Jedediah. She had waited until morning to have a look at the damaged truck. It wasn't nearly as bad as the other Ford; at least this one they'd been able to drive home. Now she and Morgan sit at the rough pine table, drinking coffee.

"I'd hate like hell to think that Ezra was right," Morgan says.

"Right about what?" Ava demands.

"This whole damn venture."

"The way I see it, there's nothing wrong with the venture," Ava says. "What we have is a marketing problem. And obviously a transport problem. And that all boils down to the fact that we don't know what we're doing. We sent a boy into Boone Saunders's territory with a shipment of bootleg hooch. That wasn't smart. And then we ran afoul of this Otto character. Hell, we'd even been warned about him."

"We don't know it was this Otto."

"You said the hoodlums called him by name."

"Who it was doesn't matter," Morgan says. "Where do we go from here? We're floundering, sister."

"There's a learning curve to every endeavor, Morgan."

"Most learning curves don't result in calling Doc Haskell in to set broken bones and stitch up wounds," Morgan reminds her. "That boy Jodie looks like he fought at Chickamauga. And I suspect that Daytona Dave doesn't look a whole lot better today."

"Ah, my potential swain," Ava smiles. "How did I ever let him slip away?"

"This isn't the time for jokes." Morgan glances out the window to see Luther approaching along the dusty road. "Well now, Luther is going to want to cook some mash. What's the point of making moonshine if we're just going to hand it over to these evil bastards?"

"We're not giving up this easy," Ava tells him. "You and Luther get to cooking. I need to think on the rest."

Bobby reaches above his head and grabs onto the iron headboard with both hands. He tilts his head back and closes his eyes, smiling. Straddling him, Myrna Lee has the palm of one hand flat on Bobby's chest and the other on her forehead. Her mouth is open and she's making little rhythmic chugging sounds in her throat, like a steam locomotive making a steep grade.

Bobby arches his hips as he ejaculates and this spurs her on. When she orgasms, she releases a sound like a screech owl and then collapses on his chest, her breath coming in great gulps. It takes a few moments for her to settle and then she rolls off him, hooks one leg over his and throws her arm across his waist.

"You sonofabitch," she says.

"I do something wrong?" Bobby asks.

Myrna Lee moans. "No, you do everything just right."

"Then why you cursing me?"

"I don't rightly know," she says. "Makes me mad."

Bobby smiles as he reaches for his cigarettes on the nightstand, lights one up. "Doing everything right makes you mad?"

"I can't explain it," she says. "Just leave it alone, okay. Gimme a drag on that."

Bobby hands the smoke over, taking a quick look at his watch as he does. Racing at the Hollow starts in about an hour. The engine

in the coupe is broken in and Bobby is anxious to give it a try. He
can make the race on time but he's low on gas. He's flat broke again
having spent his wages getting the coupe ready to run. And Boss
Harvey isn't about to extend Bobby any credit.

Myrna Lee blows smoke above her head and hands him back
the cigarette before reaching past him to turn on the radio. The
tubes buzz and warm and then the Carter Family emerges, singing
"Will the Circle Be Unbroken." Myrna Lee joins in.

By now Bobby is too familiar with what Myrna Lee considers
to be her great talents as a singer. He's getting antsy to go, and her
caterwauling makes him more so. He turns the volume down as he
gets out of bed and reaches for his pants.

"I gotta run, baby."

"Noo."

"Told you, I'm due at the Hollow."

"Hang the Hollow," she says. "Stay with me a while. Daddy's
up at cousin Cyril's cooking. They'll open a jar and get into some
jacks or better, and he won't be back around here for days."

Bobby buttons his shirt and glances out the window. His
coupe is parked between the house and barn. Boone Saunders has
a gas tank by the machine shed, gravity-fed, up on stilts. Of course
he'd have his own tank. A man running as much shine as Boone,
couldn't be depending on the local gas stations, especially when
the transporting was mainly at night.

Myrna Lee reaches her left foot out and runs it up Bobby's
thigh. "You gonna tell me you like that dirty old track better than
you do this?"

"Why can't I like 'em both?" Bobby asks. "Hey baby, you got a
couple bucks you can lend me? I need gas money."

"You're a bastard, Bobby Barlow," Myrna Lee pouts. "Leave
me for that damn track and then ask me for money to get you
there."

"Pay you back come next week," Bobby says. "Or maybe
tonight, if I win."

She sulks a little longer before reaching into the nightstand.

"You know, I been saving my money to go to Raleigh. Give me a minute to put something on. I'll walk you down."

"No," Bobby says quickly, shoving the two bucks in his pants. "You stay right there. No need to get up. I like seeing you in bed like that, naked beneath them sheets. All sexy and cool, laying back, your hair spread out. You look like a movie star, I swear."

"Stop it," she tells him. "You already got your money, so never mind the blarney."

Bobby sits on the edge of the bed to pull his boots on. She watches him a moment.

"Which movie star?" she asks.

"Oh, I have to say Jean Harlow," Bobby says. "Maybe a little Clara Bow. But the fact is, you're prettier than both of them put together."

"Silver-tongued devil, that's what you are."

Bobby leans over and kisses her on the mouth while his hand slides beneath the sheet. "Ooh, I am coming back for more of that. That is sweeter than honey."

He goes down the stairs quickly, hoping she doesn't follow. Crossing the yard to the coupe, he stops to look at the bedroom window upstairs, then glances at the fuel tank, his mind working. He doesn't want to start the car and draw attention to what he's doing. He reaches inside, puts the shifter in neutral, and pushes the coupe the short distance to the tank. Keeping watch on the house, he quickly cranks a few gallons into the tank.

He jumps in and fires up the V8. The headers roar as he floors it, fishtailing out of the yard. Out on the dirt road, he lights a cigarette and reaches under the seat for a pint. Easing the coupe into third gear, he has a drink and heads for the races at the Hollow.

NINETEEN

It's a warm night with no threat of rain. There's a sizeable crowd gathered at the makeshift track, fifty or sixty spectators milling about, some sitting in the temporary bleachers that Boss Harvey has borrowed from the fairgrounds in Wilkesboro. Boss Harvey's brother-in-law is the reeve of Wilkes County and it was he who arranged the loan. There's a booth beneath the seats, selling hot dogs and soda. Bubble gum is two cents and licorice a nickel. Boss Harvey doesn't miss a trick.

The crowd is anxious for action of any kind. It's Saturday night and Mason jars of moonshine are being passed about in plain sight. No revenuers here. Boss Harvey is over at the entrance to the track. Admission has been raised to twenty-five cents and Boss tells the gatekeeper Sue Ann Tibbles, who weighs two hundred and forty pounds and happens to be his sister, to make sure nobody sneaks in under the fence. It seems unlikely; if there is anybody who scares the local boys more than Boss Harvey, it's Sue Ann Tibbles.

Leaving the gate, Boss walks toward the starting line, striding in his coveralls and heavy Wellington boots. He has a cigar stub the size of a pine cone clenched unlit between his teeth.

"Where in the hell is that twerp Edgar?" he demands. "Night coming on, we need to get this thing rolling."

Edgar emerges out of a cluster of men. "We got to get the cows off the track," he tells Boss.

"Cows? What cows are you talking about?"

Edgar points to the far end of the track. In the coming dusk, there are a half-dozen Herefords, grazing in the infield.

"Why in the hell do we got cows on the goddamn racetrack?" Boss Harvey shouts.

"Being cows, they might not know it's a racetrack," Edgar says. "They might be of the opinion it is still a hay field."

"Never mind your lip," Boss Harvey says. "Get 'em the hell out of there!"

"I was just fixing to do that," Edgar explains and he goes back to the men he'd been talking to. He gets a couple to join him and they go trotting off to see to the cattle.

Bobby Barlow arrives as Edgar and the others are chasing the uncooperative Herefords around the field. Rolling up to the gate, he tells Sue Ann that he's there to race, excusing him from the admission fee, and then idles the coupe over to the rest of the cars at the starting line. Boss Harvey spots him and makes a beeline over.

"Hold on, peckerwood," he says. "Two-dollar entry fee, and no—I ain't taking your goddamn IOU."

Bobby gets out of the coupe. "You getting smarter, Boss? I can remember when you couldn't spell IOU."

A few of the boys get a laugh out of that, which does nothing to improve Boss Harvey's attitude toward Bobby. He reaches out and grabs Bobby by the collar.

"Never mind your wisecracks, gasbag," he says. "Pay up or get the hell out."

Bobby brushes the hand away, then takes the two dollars from his pants and stuffs it in Boss Harvey's breast pocket. "Boss—if I want any shit out of you, I'll squeeze your head."

From her vantage point on the grassy knoll above the track, Ava watches the exchange between Bobby and Boss Harvey. She had arrived a half hour earlier, paid her admission and walked along the fence to where she now sits, avoiding the boisterous crowd. She isn't quite sure what she is looking for but she has decided that the answer to at least one of her problems might be somewhere on these premises. She could be wrong, as she has been somewhat frequently, of late.

Boss Harvey stares Bobby Barlow down as he walks over to join the other drivers gathered around their cars. Boss calls a youngster over and speaks to him, whereupon the kid gets on a bicycle and rides out through the gate, pedaling back toward town as fast as his legs can manage. When he's gone Boss turns, hands on his hips, and glares down the track where Edgar and the others are still chasing the half-feral cattle.

Bobby and the other drivers are waiting. A quart jar makes the rounds. Ava smiles. Maybe she merely needs to set up a booth here at the track. She could sell Flagg copperhead by the pint or the jug. That would solve both her marketing problems and the transportation woes too. Of course, as a plan it isn't feasible. It is a little too close to home for that.

It takes a while but Edgar and his fellow wranglers finally manage to chase the Herefords into the adjoining field, from whence they came. Edgar props a fallen gate back into place and then marches back along the track like a returning hero. Boss Harvey produces the starter's flag—a blue bandana on a stick—from his hip pocket and waves the cars into position, making a point of putting Bobby at the very back of the pack. Seconds later he drops the flag and the cars surge forward as one, exhausts roaring, tires spinning as they fly down the track.

The race is twenty laps. Within minutes the air is laden with dust, the smell of exhaust fumes and burning oil, the scream of smoking clutch plates. As usual, half of the drivers are green teenagers driving family sedans and pickup trucks, and they careen all over the track. One car goes into a corner too quickly, and flips over. Another blows its engine and coasts into the infield.

Boss Harvey positioned Bobby at the back of the pack to handicap his chances. He could have started Bobby in another county and it wouldn't have mattered. The stripped-down coupe is twice as fast as the other vehicles in the race, and Bobby is ten times the driver. He picks his way easily through the crowded field, drifting through the corners and roaring past everybody in the straights.

Ava watches from the hill, the noise and fumes an affront to her senses. She has no interest in any of the cars or trucks and doesn't care who wins. But the driving itself intrigues her. Not the teenager drivers; most of them end up in the ditch, or on their roof. The Flaggs have already tried men who can do that. It's the few skilled drivers that she watches, how they slide through a turn and accelerate into a straight, how they overtake another car on the inside, with inches to spare. Ava hadn't noticed any of this the first time she'd been here with Morgan. Things have changed since then. Perhaps Ava herself has changed since then.

Edgar stands alongside Boss Harvey near the finish line. Sometime in the middle of the race, a Wilkes County police car arrives and Chief Truscott Parr and his deputy Danny Watson get out to watch. Apparently everybody in Wilkes County is a fan of stock car racing. Ava wonders who exactly is minding the store back in town. Not that Wilkesboro has ever been a hot bed of criminal activity, and is even less so now, when nobody has anything worth stealing. She notices that the pints of liquor being freely passed about now disappear. Chief Parr is known as a hard case on the making and distributing of moonshine.

By the end of the race, Bobby has lapped the entire field once, and some cars twice. He coasts over the finish line. Boss Harvey waves a red bandana now, indicating that Bobby is the winner. Bobby rolls to a stop a few yards away, where's he's immediately surrounded by a small crowd, mostly kids still in their teens. They clap him on the back as he gets out of the car and cluster around to admire the engine in the coupe.

Boss Harvey approaches Bobby and hands him the twenty-dollar purse. Boss's attitude has changed for some reason. He smiles at Bobby and shakes his hand.

"Nice job out there, son," Boss says.

Bobby makes a showing of counting the money under Boss Harvey's eye. "It was a pleasure, Boss."

"A pleasure to watch too."

Bobby looks warily at the big man. "You're getting real sociable in your old age, Boss."

"Don't get used to it, boy," Boss Harvey says.

With that, Truscott Parr comes up behind Bobby and clubs him senseless with a billy club. Bobby drops in a heap, rolls over on his back and lays still. On the hill, Ava is not quite certain what she just witnessed. Or why it occurred. She gets to her feet and watches while Parr and the deputy grab Bobby beneath the arms and drag him to the police car.

Next morning, Bobby lays on the hard cot in the Wilkesboro jail, adjacent to the police station. He's been awake since six o'clock. There's a goose egg on the back of his skull where Truscott Parr's nightstick landed and scrapes on his chin from where he landed in the dirt. He has a pounding headache.

At around nine, he hears somebody moving around in the front of the station. There are the sounds of drawers being opened and closed and keys rattling. Then Truscott Parr appears in the doorway to the lock-up.

"Wake up!"

Bobby puts his eye on the man. "I'm awake."

"Then get up."

"Can't be court this morning," Bobby says. "It's Sunday."

"That's right, genius," Parr says. "At least you know what day it is. Come on, you and me are going for a walk."

"When you going to tell me why I'm even here, Parr? I know my rights. You can't arrest me and hold me for no reason."

"Around here, I can do what I want." Parr unlocks the cell door. "Get on out of there."

Bobby gets to his feet and when he does, his headache worsens. The man who caused it stands ten feet away, smirking.

"I want to know why I'm here," Bobby says again.

"I'll tell you when I'm good and ready," Chief Parr says. "First we need to have us a conversation. Now come on."

Bobby steps out of the cell. "Where we going?"

"Follow me and shut up," Parr says. "And if you got any notions of running, forget it. You'll earn yourself another whack from my nightstick."

"I wasn't running the first time, dipshit."

Parr lets the comment slide. He leads Bobby outside and around back of the station. Bobby's coupe sits there in the alley, parked alongside a Wilkes County police car, a Chevrolet sedan. Bobby turns on Parr.

"Who said you could drive my car?"

"Deputy Watson drove your car and we don't need your goddamn permission, gasbag," Parr says. "I'll drive it off a cliff if it pleases me."

Bobby walks around the coupe, making sure it hasn't been damaged.

"I want you to tell me how come this rattletrap is so damn fast," Parr says. "It's the fastest car in the county and you ain't exactly the smartest person in the county so why in the hell is it so fast?"

"That's the conversation?" Bobby asks.

"That's the conversation," Parr says. "I got moonshiners coming out the goddamn woodwork and my Chevy sedans can't hold a candle to them jacked-up cars they drive. So you tell me how you do it."

Bobby drops down to have a look underneath the car, concerned that the deputy might have damaged something driving it out of the field. On one hand, he has no desire to tell Truscott Parr anything. But then he doesn't appreciate the chief calling his intelligence into question.

He straightens up. "I can tell you why I got the fastest car this side of hell—but it ain't going to do you any good. You can't do what I do. You don't have the brains and you don't have the skills."

"Let me worry about what skills I got or don't got, punk," Parr says. "Tell it."

Bobby is still deciding. Parr glares defiantly at him, and Bobby returns the look. The police chief has a flushed face and yellow horse teeth. His breathing is shallow and quick. He is a few years older than Bobby and has been chief for a decade or more. Bobby had never much cared for the man, and that was before Parr had sneaked up and clubbed him senseless for—so far as Bobby had been told—no reason in the world.

"I'll tell you, Parr," Bobby decides. "I got a buddy works in a machine shop over to Charlotte. Tiger Thompson—him and I was in France back in '18. Remind me—what branch of the service were you in?"

"I couldn't go," Parr says defensively. "Dislocated my shoulder back on the farm and it never did heal right."

"Ain't that a shame," Bobby says. "It's a wonder you can still swing a billy club like you do. I guess it helps when the guy you're swinging at is looking the other way."

"What about the goddamn car?" Parr demanded.

"I'm getting to it," Bobby says. "Well, my pal Tiger has the run of the shop after hours. Him and me used to juice those army trucks in France. You know--when we were over there fighting the Kaiser. Serving our country."

"Keep it up, shithead."

"About three weeks ago I took that engine there over to Charlotte, and him and me bored it and stroked it. Relieved the block and beefed the cam. Put on an Eldelbrock intake manifold with three Stromberg carbs. Brought the engine home and put her back in the coupe, in front of a bulletproof Cadillac transmission. Welded up the spider gears in the rear end so she's solid posi-track."

As Bobby's talking, Parr walks over to look at the engine in question. Bobby reaches inside the coupe and finds his cigarettes. He lights one as he turns back to Parr.

"You're like a monkey looking at the inside of a watch," Bobby laughs. "But now you know what makes my car so fast, although I suspect I might just as well been speaking Chinese just then. What are you going to do with the information?"

"I'll just tell you what," Parr says. "Today you are going to sign this car over to the Wilkes County Police Department. Then we're going to take it over to Buck's Garage and have him put the fenders back on and give it a paint job and turn it into an official police car."

Bobby stares at the chief in disbelief. "You figure I'm just going to give you my car? You figure I'm going to give you my pride and joy so's you can chase down a bunch of damn moonshiners? Why in the name of Christ would I do that?"

"I'll tell you why," Parr says. "After you sign over this car, I'm going to tell the authorities over in Stony Point that you were right here in town the day they're claiming you and that skirt robbed that gas station."

Bobby falls silent. He'd almost forgotten about the incident, even though it had been less than two months ago. They'd driven off with seven dollars and change and a carton of Luckies.

"Cat got your tongue all of a sudden?" Parr asks. "Maybe you don't remember that gal, name of Luanne Dixon. She remembers you. She told the Stony Point police it was all your idea. Is that right, Barlow? Did you lead that poor girl down the garden path? Most judges I know have little regard for men who lead innocent girls down the garden path."

Luanne is about as innocent as Ma Barker, Bobby thinks. "I don't know what you're talking about."

"Yes, you do," Parr says. "And there's more I can talk about. The First National Bank over to Lenoir was robbed two weeks ago. A gal looking a lot like this Luanne went to the bank manager's house and held a gun on the man's wife while her partner—a man about your age, I'm told—went to the bank and told the man to call home. They got away with over three thousand dollars."

Well shit, Bobby thinks. It sounds as if Luanne found another sucker to go along with her grand schemes, although it did not appear as if they had gotten her out to Hollywood and movie stardom yet.

"That's got nothing to do with me," Bobby tells the chief.

"We'll see about that," Parr says. "That girl Luanne sang about the gas station job; she just might sing about this one too, once they explain to her what her future might look like if she don't. Gas stations are small potatoes, but the state of North Carolina takes a dim view of folks holding up banks. Not only that but it seems to me that you recently got out of jail for stealing automobiles. I can't see that working in your favor neither."

"You say the bank was two weeks ago?" Bobby says. "I've been working for Charley Walker's Texaco for nigh on a month. I been there every damn day."

"Oh, I have given that some thought, you best believe," Parr says. "I figure you'd think you had a perfect alibi. But everybody knows that old Walker is gone half the time, out fixing farm implements or whatever. What's to stop you from closing up shop for a couple hours, driving over to Lenoir to do a little bank robbing and then be back here in time for supper? Especially in this hopped-up car you're so proud of."

Bobby pulls on the cigarette. "You can invent all the stories you want. There's no way anybody can put me in Lenoir that day. You know why? Because I wasn't there."

"You wasn't there unless this Luanne woman says different," Parr tells him. "That poor innocent gal. So, we'd better get the paperwork signed over on this car and then you won't have to worry about it. What do you say?"

"What do I say about signing my coupe over to you?" Bobby asks. "I say kiss my ass."

Parr's red face gets redder but he holds his temper. "All right, we'll just put you back in that cell for a few days and let you think about it."

"You can't hold me with no charges," Bobby reminds him.

"Oh, I forgot to mention," Parr says. "I just this minute decided to cooperate with the Stony Point department and charge you with the gas station job. Now what do you say?"

"I already said it," Bobby tells him. "You can kiss my ass."

TWENTY

Deputy Watson is Truscott Parr's cousin, the dimmest in a family of notable dimwits. Parr hired him after being harangued by his widowed aunt for months, finally deciding that having an incompetent deputy hanging around the station was less bothersome than listening to a meddlesome relative on the telephone three or four times a week.

Watson is at the station alone on Monday morning, drinking coffee while cleaning his fingernails with a jackknife and reading the *Police Gazette*. He's at a desk by the front windows, his feet up, hat tilted back. When Ava Flagg walks in, he tosses the magazine aside and jumps to his feet.

"Miss Ava Flagg," he says.

"Hello, Turtle," Ava says.

Deputy Watson cringes. He's been called Turtle since grade school, a nod to his plodding manner, in spite of his protests against the moniker. He stares at Ava; she wears a felt hat and a summer dress that shows her legs. She looks like an angel.

"What brings you down here, Miss Ava? Has there been some malfeasance in your neck of the woods?" Deputy Watson had moments before been reading in the *Gazette* of some instances of malfeasance. He has a habit of appropriating.

"I hear you have Bobby Barlow locked up back there," Ava says.

"He's here," Watson says. "The chief and I picked him up Saturday night on a robbery charge."

"You didn't exactly pick him up," Ava says. "I was there watching."

"You was there?" Watson asks. "At the races?"

Ava nods. "What's the bail?"

"I didn't know you was a fan of the car races," Watson says. "Might I accompany you there sometime?"

"You may not," Ava says. "What's the bail on Barlow?"

Watson's face falls at the rejection but he nonetheless begins to rummage under the counter for the paperwork. "Not altogether certain what the chief done with it."

"What's the charge again?" Ava asked.

"Him and this woman are supposed to have robbed a gas station over to Stony Point, a month or two ago. They didn't get but a few dollars." Watson continues to look through the paperwork.

"I wouldn't expect too high a bail for a minor crime such as that," Ava says.

Deputy Watson gives up on the counter search and heads for a rolltop desk in the corner where he begins to open and close drawers. Ava presses him.

"What would you say a typical bail would be in a situation like this, Deputy?"

"Well, Chief Parr sets the bails."

"I didn't ask you who set them," Ava says. "Looks to me like the Chief has left you in charge here today. Which means he trusts you to handle whatever needs handling. Wouldn't you agree, Deputy?"

"Oh, I can handle the job," Watson assures her.

"I admire a man with confidence." Ava pulls out all stops now. "I might even have a change of heart and attend the car races with a man like that."

That particular lie has the desired effect. Watson's search for the paperwork comes to an immediate halt and he approaches the counter where Ava stands.

"Chief Parr is the justice of the peace, and so he is the one to set bail," he says. "But since he has left me in charge, I see no reason why I can't do it." He pauses, doing some figures in his head. "For a seven-dollar robbery, I suspect two hundred dollars would be a fair bail."

Ava flinches. She'd been burning her own money and family money since they'd started cooking moonshine. There had been corn to buy, and sugar and yeast. A doctor for Jodie and money for the tow truck. A lot of cash going out and not an Indian head nickel coming in. Ava has a hundred and twenty-three dollars in her pocket at the moment, the last of her savings.

"That's sounds a might high for robbing a gas station," she tells the deputy. "For a seven-dollar robbery, I figure fifty dollars is about right."

Deputy Watson, flush with thoughts of escorting Ava to the races some night in the near future, is amenable to that figure. Ava pressures him to get something down on paper, eager to get it done before Chief Parr shows up. Watson manages to find the proper form and Ava helps him fill it out after she notices him having trouble spelling the name Bobby. When it's done, she counts the money out onto the counter. The deputy carries it over and deposits it in a wall safe, then returns to stand before Ava, grinning like a lovesick schoolboy.

"Well?" she says.

"What?"

"You going to fetch the man?"

"Oh, right," Watson says.

Moments later he leads the prisoner out from the back. Bobby stops short when he sees Ava.

"*You* paid my bail?"

"Let's go," Ava says.

Bobby regards her quizzically for another moment, then turns to Deputy Watson. "Give me the keys to my car."

"I don't know," Watson says. "The vehicle has been...what do you call it...pounded?"

"Impounded," Ava says.

Bobby steps closer to the deputy. "Give me the keys, Watson."

"I best wait for the Chief on that."

"Give him the goddamn keys, Turtle," Ava snaps.

Watson goes back to the rolltop and produces the keys and hands them to Bobby before turning to Ava.

"I will see you soon, Miss Ava," the deputy says. "When would you like to go to the races?"

"I think we should wait," Ava says.

Watson hesitates. "Well…wait until when?"

"I don't know…'til hell freezes over?"

Outside she and Bobby walk around the building. It had rained overnight and there are puddles on the street and sidewalk. Ava sidesteps the deepest holes, striding along with purpose, not speaking. Bobby follows her.

"What in the hell is going on here?" he asks. "Why would you post my bail? You're not sweet on me, Ava Flagg?"

"Hardly."

Bobby smiles. For the first time in two days, his headache has disappeared. "Don't seem to me like you're too sweet on the deputy neither."

Ava snorts in response. They round the corner of the building. Morgan's Nash is parked in the alley, alongside Bobby's coupe.

"Get in your car and follow me," Ava says.

"Follow you where?"

"Flagg's Hollow," Ava says. "You're coming to work for my family."

Bobby stops walking. "Hold on now, girl. I appreciate the bail money and I swear I will pay you back but I got no desire to go into the molasses business."

"Just do as I say," Ava tells him.

"Why?"

"Because five minutes ago you were locked up and now you're not."

Bobby follows her. Whether it is from obedience or curiosity or the fact that someone who looks like Ava Flagg has instructed him to do so, he can't say.

But he follows her.

Morgan and Luther are working in the plant. They have a large vat of mash cooking and another vat in the distilling stage. The youngster Cal is monitoring the drip-drip of the finished product into the jugs.

Ava and Bobby enter though the side door. Ava gives Bobby the lead and purposefully hangs back to allow him to take in the situation, a picture being worth a thousand words, as she's been told. Bobby has a long look around as he lights a cigarette. Closing his Zippo with a snap, he turns to Ava and smiles.

"Seems like you Flaggs have moved on from molasses."

"Can't get nothing past you."

Morgan approaches, wiping his hands on a towel. "Hello, Bobby. I hear you're coming to work for us."

"You heard wrong," Bobby says. "I know how to drink liquor but the only time I ever made it I near poisoned half the 2nd division."

"Who said anything about *you* making liquor?" Morgan asks. "Come on."

He goes out the back door, with Ava at his heels. Bobby follows again. Following Flaggs seems to be the order of the day. Behind the building, the two damaged double-T Fords are parked. Bobby looks at the vehicles a long moment and then at Ava and Morgan, who are watching him silently.

"So what's the lowdown here?" Bobby asks. "You bailed me out of jail so I could fix these old trucks?"

"Not exactly," Morgan says. "We have come to realize that these old trucks are not the solution to our problems."

"And what problems are you referring to?" Bobby asks. "Seems as you both take your own sweet time to get the cow into the barn."

Morgan nods toward the plant. "We've obviously gone into

the moonshine business. You are the first outsider to know about it and we're counting on you to keep it quiet. Right now we can produce good quality busthead in suitable quantities. Problem is— so far we've been losing most of it."

"Losing it how?"

"To our competitors and other sundry thieves," Morgan says. "They're a damn sight meaner than us and the cars they drive are a damn sight faster. So we're outgunned from every direction."

Ava indicates the worst of the trucks. "Boone Saunders's boys run this one off the road near Hickory Creek a week ago. The colored boy driving looks worse than the truck. Broken arm and fifty-some stitches in his head."

Hearing the name Saunders, Bobby reacts. He takes a moment. "Boone's men take the booze?"

"Of course they took the booze," Ava said. "Do you know anything about the man?"

"I know a little," Bobby admits. "I know enough I wouldn't send a colored boy to bootleg in Boone's backyard."

"In hindsight, we're all geniuses," Ava tells him.

Bobby is only half listening. He's looking past her now, to where Jedediah stands. He must have come around the corner of the building while they were talking. He wears his broad-brimmed Sunday hat and has the stem of his pipe clenched in his teeth. He watches Bobby openly, as if taking his measure.

"Now here comes the parson," Bobby says. "Don't tell me y'all brought me here to save my soul."

Jedediah takes the pipe from his mouth and approaches. "I don't believe we're equipped to take on a chore that size."

Bobby laughs. "At least somebody in the family has a sense of humor."

"We haven't had much to laugh about of late," Morgan says.

"That's where you come in," Ava tells Bobby. "It's pretty obvious that these tired trucks are not up to the job. We're lucky to get twenty-five miles an hour out of them."

Bobby comes slowly to his conclusions. "Now we're getting

down to it. You wouldn't be of a mind to suggest that I give you my coupe, for getting me out of jail? Truscott Parr told me the very same thing just yesterday. I told him what he could do with that offer. As a gentleman I will rephrase it for you, Miss Ava—but suffice it to say you're not getting my car."

"We don't want your car," Ava says.

"Good thing, cuz like I said, you're not getting it." Bobby pauses a moment, trying to figure the angles. "What then?"

"Your skills," Morgan says. "We need you to build us a delivery vehicle every bit as fast as that Ford of yours. With springs and shock absorbers and whatnot that can handle these mountain roads at high speeds."

Jedediah has been hanging back but now he comes near. "Whatever talents the Lord deprived you of in the common sense department, He made up for in the mechanical gifts He bestowed on you."

"You insult me and praise me all in one sentence," Bobby says. "So you figure this is the Lord's work, do you, Parson—selling mountain dew?"

"He moves in mysterious ways," Jedediah replies.

"We have heard that your employment at Charley Walker's garage is about to come to an end," Ava mentions.

Bobby nods. "Yeah. Bill Charters started back today. Sounds as if you Flaggs have me under surveillance."

"It's a small town," Morgan reminds him. "Can we assume you are currently seeking employment?"

"Not so sure about that," Bobby says. "I consider myself a race-car driver these days." He pauses a moment. "Not a bootlegger."

"You getting rich racing against those silly farm boys over at Boss Harvey's pasture, are you?" Ava asks.

"Not so you'd notice," Bobby admits.

Ava shrugs. "I suppose you could always supplement your income by robbing more gas stations. But isn't that what landed you in the jailhouse to begin with?"

Bobby, knowing full well that she's the cat to his mouse, makes no reply to this.

"Then again, you're not in the jailhouse at this particular moment," Ava points out. "But I suppose you could be again. I suspect Truscott Parr isn't going to be too happy when he hears how I convinced that puddn'head Turtle Watson to set bail. I suspect Truscott Parr might be more than happy to offer me a refund and take you back into his loving arms."

As threats go, this one isn't even remotely veiled.

"You've got some hard bark on you for a woman," Bobby tells Ava.

"These days a woman needs a hard bark," Ava replies.

TWENTY-ONE

The Smokies are down to the Tigers by six runs in the ninth inning when manager Hobbs goes out to lift his pitcher from the game. The hook is expected. The rookie right-hander had just given up a walk, a homer and a double. Pulling him from the game is an act of mercy and certainly no surprise.

But the pitcher that Hobbs now waves in from the bullpen is.

Otto Marx, wearing a brand-new uniform, cleats and hat, trots across the outfield like he is an old hand at it. He has a plug of tobacco in his cheek (although he doesn't care for the taste) and a new Rawlings glove. As he runs, he tips his hat grandly to the scant crowd, as if responding to cheers that aren't actually there.

Manager Hobbs meets him on the mound and hands over the ball. Manager Hobbs isn't bringing Otto out of the bullpen as a result of some shrewd tactical thinking. He is bringing Otto in to pitch because Otto now owns the team and fancies himself a bona fide player. Manager Hobbs knows he will be looking for a new job if he opposes the notion. Jobs in the world of minor-league baseball are just as scarce as everywhere else.

The third baseman Piotrowski is up for the Tigers. The first pitch Otto throws flies over the catcher's head and into the screen behind. The second goes behind Piotrowski and the third hits the ground fifteen feet in front of home plate. The fourth pitch is finally a soft looping strike and Piotrowski hits it over the fence in center field for a two-run homer. Otto glares at the hitter all the way around the bases.

The players in the Tiger's dugout are having a lot of fun at Otto's expense, catcalling him, referring to him as an old woman and asking him if he can throw any better with his other arm. Like most bullies, Otto is insecure about any number of things. His pitching abilities just might top the list. The players in the Tigers dugout don't know that. The players in the Tigers dugout don't know who they are dealing with.

Hours after the game, Slim and Elmer find third baseman Piotrowski drinking beer in an underground bar downtown. They take him into the alley and beat him up beneath the faint light from the street lamp out front. They break his collar bone and advise him that, when he is healed, he shouldn't hit any more home runs off Otto Marx. Wincing through the pain while lying in the urine-soaked dirt outside the speakeasy, Piotrowski is agreeable to such an arrangement, even if he has no idea who Otto Marx is.

After their negotiation with the now remorseful Piotrowski, Elmer and Slim go back to the Empire Hotel, where they find Otto in his storeroom office. Using a garbage can lid for home plate, he is standing sixty feet away, throwing baseballs against the brick wall. Otto is still in his Smokies uniform, right down to his cleats, although he now has a lit cigar in his mouth. When the men come in, he glances at them but doesn't say anything, just keeps flinging balls at the wall.

"We talked to that Piotrowski fellow," Elmer says.

Otto pauses for a moment.

"Who is that?" Otto says.

"Him what hit the home run offa you."

"Oh, that hump," Oto says. "Was that his name? Did you explain things to him?"

Elmer, lighting a cigarette, nods. Otto reaches into the bushel basket at his feet for another ball and begins to throw again, one after another.

"Why the hell can't I make my curve ball curve?" he demands.

Elmer and Slim look at one another, pretty sure that the question doesn't beg an answer. Even if it did, neither of them could come up with one. They are thugs, not baseball analysts. Otto retrieves another ball. He places two fingers along the seams and shows the grip to Slim.

"You see that?" he asks. "That's the grip. And when I release it, I put spin on it—like this. And the ball goes sideways and down." Otto fires the ball. It goes dead straight, smacking into the brick wall with a dull thud. "Goddamn it! Why don't that thing curve?"

"I might have an idea," Slim says carefully.

"What idea?"

"That old guy with the team," Slim says. "With the side whiskers. They call him Spit Fletcher and he's some kind of coach, I believe. They say he was with the White Sox way back when. They say he even pitched against Ruth and Gehrig."

"He pitched against the Bambino?" Otto asks. Babe Ruth is Otto's hero. They are about the same size and enjoy many of the same pursuits. That Otto wasn't a patch on the great slugger when it came to the game of baseball was of little consequence.

"So they say."

Otto considers it. "What's that got to do with me?"

Slim shrugs. "I just figure a mug who pitched against them guys would know how to make the ball curve. And maybe he could teach you, boss."

Otto has picked up another ball and now he turns it over in his hand, searching for the grip. "That's a good idea. Especially since this Spit character is now working for me. He can't tell me no."

Slim glances over at Elmer. Saying no to Otto didn't seem to be an option for anybody, whether they were working for him or not.

"Tomorrow you're going to point this mug out to me," Otto says. "I can't wait to get back on that mound. I have no doubt that I'll be the star pitcher once I get my curve ball working."

"Sure you will," Elmer said. He's sitting in a chair now, tilted against the wall. "All it takes is practice."

Otto throws one more ball against the wall, and then quits it. He'll wait until he gets his lesson from Spit Fletcher. He crosses the room and retrieves a Mason jar of moonshine from the ice box. He opens it and takes a couple small sips, savoring it, before glancing over at the other two.

"What did we find out about this stuff?" he asks.

Elmer and Slim exchange looks again. This time it seems as if a response will be required.

"What do you mean, boss?" Elmer asks.

"This here liquor is head and shoulders over that piss Boone Saunders has been bringing of late," Otto says. "You boys were supposed to find out where it came from. And who made it." He pauses while he has another sip. "And how I go about getting them to work for old Otto."

This is the first that Elmer and Slim have heard the request, but they won't tell Otto that. There's no upside to telling Otto he's wrong.

"We're looking into that," Slim says vaguely. "Trying to track these characters down. I don't believe they hail from Knoxville."

"The hail from someplace called Wilkes County," Otto says. "That's where they hail from." He has one more sip then kneels to put the jar back in the icebox. Elmer looks at Slim and shrugs his shoulders.

"Where did you hear that?" he asks. "About Wilkes County."

"That boy Petey," Otto says. "He heard it from them that was making it. When they come courting that pretender from Florida."

"Where is Petey?" Slim asks. "Looks like we need to talk to him."

Otto shakes his head. "We were out on my boat a couple of nights ago. He got on my nerves and I threw him in the river."

"Drowned, did he?" Elmer asks.

"Dunno," Otto says. "He was still bobbing around out there last I seen him." He straightens and flicks the ash from his cigar.

"Where is this Wilkes County anyway? Can't be too far. Those hill-billies drove here in the rattletrap truck of theirs."

"Only Wilkes County I ever heard of was in North Carolina, a far piece from here," Slim says. "Little town there called Wilkesboro. But shit, there's more stills in North Carolina than there's stars in the sky."

"I'm only interested in the one what made that particular run," Otto says.

"You know that Boone Saunders is from down there some-place," Elmer said. "Why not ask him? He's a man keeps his ear to the ground."

Otto shakes his head. "Boone gets wind of this and he'll sniff these pikers out on his own. They'll sell to him and he'll sell to me at his profit. I want to eliminate the middleman. We find out who made that good shine, I can foresee the day when we don't need Boone nor that bozo kid of his neither."

"What else did Petey say before you threw him in the drink?" Elmer asks.

Otto laughs. "He said 'I can't swim.'"

They all three get a chuckle out of that.

"Maybe we ought to try and find him," Slim says. "You know, in the event he wasn't drowned. He might have more information."

Otto shakes his head. "All he knew was Wilkes County. Which is where you boys are heading, I suspect."

At first Bobby isn't thrilled about going to work for the Flagg family. They haven't left him much choice though. It was either work for them or get thrown back in jail, where Truscott Parr was doing his level best to get him convicted on the gas station job and maybe even the bank robbery in Lenoir, even though Bobby hadn't been within fifty miles of the place at the time. Of course, Bobby still had the option of signing over his coupe to the Wilkes County police. To Bobby, that wasn't an option at all. He will work for the Flaggs.

Surprisingly, once the feeling that he is being coerced against his will settles some, Bobby takes another view of the situation. In short, the Flaggs are asking him to build them a race car, albeit one that would be used for transporting liquor, not racing. An argument could be made that they were pretty much offering Bobby his dream job. Find a car and make it fast. And get paid for doing it.

It is soon apparent that the getting paid part was going to be tricky, at least in the short term. After the initial meeting at Flagg's Hollow, Bobby is gone for a couple days, looking for what he would need for the job. Returning on the Wednesday, he finds Ava in the plant with the men, cooking even more mash. There's over a hundred jugs lining the shelves of the place, the same shelves that had once held dozens of gallons of molasses.

Ava is inside an empty vat, scrubbing it clean, when Bobby walks in. Morgan is shelling corn, while Luther and the youngster Cal strain mash through a screen. When Bobby calls hello, Ava climbs out of the vat and walks over. She wears coveralls and has her hair tied in a kerchief.

"You're hands on, Miss Ava," Bobby says.

"What did you find?" she asks.

"So much for small talk," Bobby says.

"You want small talk, go to a church social. What did you find?"

Bobby smiles at the attitude. "Mechanic I know, George Jansen over to Yadkin County, has a Ford sedan in the yard there. Got hit by a dump truck last year, smashed the rear end all to hell. George pulled the engine and transmission and used them elsewhere. We can have the car for twenty bucks. The frame needs straightening. I can pound out the dents and replace the broken glass, good enough to run her anyway. We ain't looking to win a beauty contest here, I suspect. Matter of fact, the uglier the better, if it's discretion you're after."

"What about a motor?"

"It ain't a motor, it's an engine."

"Potato, potahto," Ava says. "What about it?"

"My pal Tiger down in Charlotte has a line on a V8," Bobby

says. "She's got some miles on her and will need a rebuild. Not to mention the work we'll have to do to get the horsepower we're going to need."

"How much?"

"Ten dollars for the engine, only because it's tired," Bobby says. "But it's going to take at least a hundred more than that to get it up to snuff. And we'll need a transmission too, something tough. Those stock Ford gears won't hold up to a race engine. And we'll need to beef the springs, if it's your intention to transport in quantity. And I assume it is."

Ava falls silent, considering the expense. While Bobby waits for a response, he has a long look around the building. The odor of mash cooking hangs in the air, not unpleasantly. The two colored men straining the liquid into barrels have paid Bobby no mind since he arrived. He recognizes Luther from seeing him around town over the years but can't recall his name.

"I assume these men you're talking to—they need to be paid up front?" Ava asks.

"All due respect, Miss Ava, these men don't know you from a bale of cotton," Bobby tells her. "Would you take a stranger's note?"

"I expect not," she admits. "But wouldn't they take yours? You being pals and all?"

"They might," Bobby replies. "But I ain't asking them. This is your merry-go-round, not mine."

Ava exhales, thinking. "Thing is, money is tight right now. Well, money is tight in general and then we put everything we had into getting this up and running."

"You're broke?" Bobby asks.

"As close as damn is to swearing," Ava says. "Spent my last fifty dollars bailing an over-aged juvenile delinquent out of jail."

"That's pretty funny," Bobby says. "Nearly as funny as you asking me to build you a moonshine runner, and then telling me you got no money to pay for it."

"We will have the money," Ava says. "Once we get our product to market. At this moment though, I am not particularly flush with cash. I was hoping there might be some sort of contingency plan we could work out. You're saying there's no chance these friends of yours would extend me a little credit?"

Bobby shakes his head but only because he already has a better idea. "You say you're not flush with cash, but you ain't exactly lacking in currency."

"What do you mean?"

Bobby indicates the jugs of moonshine on the shelves. "There's your bankroll right there, lady. Surprised you haven't come to that conclusion yourself, smart city girl like you."

Ava decides to let the city girl remark slide. "You're talking barter?"

"That I am."

"And these men would be open to that?"

"I haven't asked them," Bobby says. "I have been operating under the assumption that you would deal in cash. Apparently, that is not the case."

"Do I need to mention the bail money again?"

Bobby laughs. "You only got the one arrow but you do like to let it fly, don't you?" He pauses. "So tell me—what's a gallon of shine going for these days?"

"It varies," Ava says. "Anywhere from five to ten dollars, depending on the quality and the size of the order."

"Then I need to ask—how's the quality?"

"Top shelf," Ava tells him.

"Says you."

Ava turns and walks across the room to take down a gallon jug from the shelf. Returning, she hands it to Bobby. He takes a swig, rinses it briefly in his mouth and then swallows. He has another drink before putting the stopper back in the jug.

"Hell, yeah," is all he says.

"You didn't answer my question," Ava says. "Would these friends of yours be open to barter?"

Bobby Barlow smiles. "Does a possum have a pouch?"

TWENTY-TWO

It takes some traveling, and some horse trading, but for the total cost of twenty-seven gallons of moonshine, Bobby is able to acquire pretty much everything he needs. Under darkness, he and Morgan tow the sedan from Yadkin County to Flagg's Hollow, where they park it inside the plant. Down in Charlotte, Tiger is rebuilding the V8, beefing the engine as they had done Bobby's a couple weeks earlier. While Bobby waits on Tiger, he borrows acetylene and oxygen tanks from his Uncle Stan and goes about straightening the frame on the sedan, heating it, and stretching it back into position with chain falls and come-alongs. Uncle Stan accepts a gallon of hooch for the loan of the tanks and asks not a single question.

Bobby pounds the dents out of the sedan's rear fenders and trunk lid, then paints the damaged areas from the same gallon of black that Ava used on the truck doors. The cosmetic work is simple enough and doesn't require any finesse. The matter of reinforcing the suspension is more complicated. Bobby studies on it for a while.

"We can't load the car down with the original springs," Bobby tells Morgan. "For one thing, they won't carry the weight. You get on those rough country roads you could break a leaf or two. For another, the cops or the Feds see a car sitting down on its rear axle, they're gonna know it's carrying a load of something.

And in these parts, they're gonna know what that something is."

The two of them are sitting in the plant, looking at the battered sedan across the floor while drinking coffee and eating sandwiches Ava had made for lunch. Across the factory, the cooking continues, with Luther and young Cal at the vats.

"Then why not just add some extra leaf springs?" Morgan asks.

Bobby shakes his head. "That won't work."

"Why in the hell not?"

Bobby has a bite of ham sandwich. "Extra leafs are going to jack the ass end up high, like a dog digging a hole. Not a problem when the car is loaded with fifty or sixty gallons of busthead. The weight will drop the car down to normal height. Where you get into trouble is when the car is empty, coming home. The vehicle's going to look mighty suspicious, with the rear end sitting way on high. That's not going to fool the revenuers any. Hell, it wouldn't even fool a gasbag like Truscott Parr. They see a car sitting like that and they're bound to follow it. Which puts them right smack on your doorstep here."

"How do we get around that?" Morgan asks.

"I'm still thinking on it," Bobby says.

In the corner of the wrecking yard behind Charley Walker's Texaco sits a 1919 Model T truck. The engine has long ago been poached for another project, and the front axle, steering column and seat are also missing. But the rear cross spring and axle are intact.

"Me and my Uncle Stan are building a farm wagon for a fellow over to Alexander County," Bobby says. It's the story he decided on.

It's early afternoon; he and Charley stand looking at the skeletal truck. Bobby knows Charley to be a pious man and as such might not be open to trading the rear springs for a gallon or two of illegal hooch. Of course, Jedediah Flagg is also a pious man and he isn't overly concerned about the sins of alcohol. His situation was different though. Bobby has decided not to risk any raising of Charley Walker's suspicions.

"What would you take for the springs?" he asks.

Charley glances toward the garage. "I'll make you a deal. Buck Stafford's Oldsmobile is sitting inside, needing a valve job. Bill is swamped and I got to head to Maryville to fix a John Deere tractor. You want to do the valve job; you can have the whole rear axle out of the truck. Matter of fact, you can have the whole dang truck."

Bobby is agreeable to such a plan. By five that afternoon, he is back at the plant. He's there until midnight, fashioning brackets out of angle iron and then mounting the truck springs above the original rear suspension in the sedan. Morgan helps Bobby, or at least is of the impression that he's helping Bobby. It's late when Ava comes down from the house. Bobby removes the floor jack from under the car as she walks in.

"What in tarnation are you boys up to at this hour?"

"Have a look at this, Ava," Morgan says.

"A look at what?" she asks.

"Kneel down here," he instructs her. "See—we put the truck springs over the car springs. That way, when she's empty, she sits regular. But when she's loaded with moonshine, the truck springs take the extra weight and she still looks normal. Revenuers are looking for cars that are loaded down. But we have taken care of that."

Bobby stands off to the side, smoking and smiling at Morgan's liberal use of the word *we*.

Ava stands up, turns to Morgan. "You come up with that?"

"Well—I guess it was Bobby's idea," Morgan admits.

"You think I can't come up with an idea?" Bobby asks.

"I suspect you come up with lots of them," she says. "Some of which land you in jail." She pauses. "So now what—you put in the motor and we're ready to go?"

"It's not a motor, it's an engine," Bobby says. "I'll pick it up tomorrow. I'm going to need to borrow a Flagg truck to fetch it. You want to come along for the ride?"

"Nope," Ava says. "I got too much to do to be traipsing across the state to pick up a *motor*. When will this thing be up and running?"

"Day or two," Bobby says. "I want to remove the bench seats to give us more cargo space. I'll put in a single. My uncle has one out of a Sopwith. And I need to mount a couple of headlights above the back bumper."

"Above the *back* bumper?" Morgan asks.

Bobby nods. "Yeah, and the brighter the better. In the event we have John Law chasing us, we turn on those lights to blind them."

"You've given this some thought," Ava says.

"Come on, you Flaggs aren't the first bootleggers I ever come across," Bobby tells her. "I might say you're the first that aren't very good at it, but I won't. If we're going to do this, we're going to do it right. Keep in mind I risk going back to jail because of this. You can see how I'd like to avoid that if at all possible."

Ava turns to Morgan. "It looks as if we're about to have ourselves a vehicle. But now we need a destination. Have you thought about that?"

"Luther's man over at Johnson City is in the market for busthead," Morgan suggests. "He gets word to Luther somehow or another. As good a place as any for a trial run."

"That's right through Boone Saunders's territory," Ava says. "Didn't we learn our lesson there?"

"Boone couldn't catch this car if he was sitting astride winged Pegasus," Bobby tells her.

"You saying he don't make you nervous?" Ava asks.

"Nervous as a long-tailed cat at a rocking chair convention," Bobby laughs. "But I'm just saying he won't catch me."

"Catch *you*?" Ava repeated. "You won't be driving. We hired you to construct this here vehicle. Not drive it."

"Who will drive then?" Bobby asks.

"Morgan," Ava says. "Or Luther."

Bobby nods as he takes a cigarette from his pocket. Lighting it, he blows a couple of smoke rings into the air above his head. "In that case, I might just head on over to Nashville this weekend to play the fiddle at the Grand Ole Opry."

Ava and Morgan exchange glances.

"I didn't know you played the fiddle," Morgan says.

Bobby blows another ring. "I don't. Just like you or Luther don't know how to drive a car like this. That's just a hard fact. Truth of the matter is, there's only one man in all of Wilkes County who knows how to drive a car like this proper. You want to take a guess who that man is?"

"How do you live with that ego?" Ava asks.

"It ain't easy," Bobby says. "Especially when you keep trying to stomp on it, lady."

"My name is Ava," she informs him. "Not lady. It's Ava."

"Well, mine's Bobby Barlow. And I'm the one going to be driving this car."

The man called Spit Fletcher spends a couple of hours that afternoon trying to show Otto how to throw a curve ball. Otto is an eager student, with a lot of questions and very little talent when it comes to hurling a baseball. It is not general knowledge that Otto has purchased the team, mainly because Otto himself doesn't want it known, afraid that the fans will see him as some rich guy trying to buy his way onto the nine. That is precisely the case, but that doesn't mean that Otto wants it known. Spit knows, but only because he told Manager Hobbs earlier that he had no interest in teaching some gangster how to pitch a ball. Hobbs was then obliged to explain to Spit which way the wind was blowing.

"Where'd you get a nickname like that?" Otto asks when he meets Spit on the field. "You used to spit shine shoes for a living?"

"I never shined nobody's shoes," Spit tells him. "I'm a white man, in case you didn't notice."

"Then what?"

"I throwed a spitball."

"What is that?"

Spit hesitates, wondering just how much he's supposed to go along with this charade. "Smear a little spit—or tobaccy if you use it—on one side of the ball. Makes the pill dance all over the place."

"Did you throw your spitball to Babe Ruth?" Otto wants to know.

"I only ever played him once," Spit says. "It was spring training back in '18."

"But did you throw your spitball?"

"I throwed everything but the kitchen sink at the sonofa-bitch," Spit replies. "And he hit everything I threw. He was still with the Sox then, still pitching every four days. He could pitch better than most, but he was born to hit."

"I'd love a chance to go against him," Otto says.

Well hell, Spit thinks. Babe Ruth would hit the goddamn ball right through Otto Marx.

"Show me that grip again," Otto says. "I think I'm catching on to this. Then you can teach me the spitball. Does that suit you?"

The arrangement really doesn't suit Spit Fletcher but after talking to Manager Hobbs earlier, he knows he has no choice but to say it does.

"That goddamn lummox couldn't hit the side of a barn with a shotgun," Spit tells Hobbs later that day. "He thinks I can teach him how to pitch in two hours? I couldn't do it in ten years."

Hobbs looks across the diamond, where Otto stands talking to one of the players. "I'd be careful about calling him a lummox."

"He is a damn lummox."

"And Joe Louis is a nigger," Hobbs says. "But I wouldn't call him that."

Spit shakes his head as he considers his plight. He's fifty-three years old and forty pounds overweight. He has gout and angina and drinks too much, the booze making both conditions even more troublesome. He doesn't need problems like Otto Marx. But he does need his job. He played in the big leagues and never made more than three thousand dollars in a year. He has no savings and no prospects other than the Smokies.

"What are you going to do with the man?" he asks, still watching Otto across the field.

"Long term, I got no idea," Hobbs admits. He exhales heavily.

"Short term, he's starting tonight against the 'Birds.'"

"Good Christ." Spit turns and gives Hobbs a long look. "I suggest you keep the married men out of the infield."

Married or single, the infielders are only in harm's way for an inning. With Otto on the hill as the starting pitcher, the Redbirds score eight runs on eleven hits. The three outs recorded by Otto come on screaming line drives, all to the third baseman, who backs up a couple steps after each one. In the dugout between innings, Hobbs warily approaches Otto, who sits glaring at the Redbirds on the field.

"How's the arm?" Hobbs asks.

"What's the name of that fellow what hit the home run offa me?" Otto asks.

"Schwartz," Hobbs says. "Right fielder there. Why do you want to know that?"

Otto shrugs. "I like to keep a record of these things."

"I'm worried about your elbow," Hobbs says, even though he is not even remotely concerned about Otto's arm or any other part of his anatomy. "Looked to me like you might have been favoring it some. I suspect you may have thrown too much earlier with Spit. Could be your humerus."

"Are you making sport of me?" Otto demands.

Hobbs raises his palms. "Of course not. The humerus is a bone in your arm. Pitchers have problems with it sometimes." He pauses. "Especially the better pitchers."

Otto is quiet for a moment. "I knew that. I believe I may have put a strain on mine. My fast ball wasn't popping."

It was popping pretty good off the bats of the Redbirds, Hobbs thinks. "Might be the prudent thing for you to sit down and rest up for your next start."

"Maybe I'd better," Otto agrees.

Otto doesn't sit too long. Hobbs sends Blake out to pitch the second inning and he breezes through the Redbirds on ten pitches. Hobbs is not surprised; the 'Birds are the weakest hitting team in the league. He won't mention the fact to Otto though.

Otto leaves in a sulk after Blake blanks the opposition again in the third inning. Driving back to the hotel in his Lincoln, he decides that Spit Fletcher is a damn poor excuse for a pitching instructor. In two hours, he hadn't managed to teach Otto how to properly throw a curve. Worse than that, his instructions had left Otto with a strained humerus bone, something he didn't even know he had until today.

Boone Saunders's Cadillac is parked in the lot behind the hotel. As he pulls up, Otto sees Boone behind the wheel, smoking a cigarette, his elbow out the window. When Otto gets out, Boone does too, walking around to open the trunk to reveal the jugs of moonshine there.

"What's with the clothes?" Boone asks.

Otto has forgotten for the moment that he's still wearing his uniform. "My team played tonight. I was the winning pitcher. What do we got here, Boone?"

"Some of old Boone's best."

"Yeah?" Otto says. He's still in a foul mood from his experience at the ballpark. "Bring a jug inside then."

Boone grabs a gallon and follows Otto up the steps to the loading dock and then into the hotel backroom. Otto fetches a glass from atop the icebox and pours a couple ounces from Boone's latest delivery. He tastes it, swishing it inside his mouth before swallowing. Boone stands inside the door, watching, his hands tucked in his overall pockets. Otto has another taste then goes back to the icebox and retrieves the Mason jar containing the liquor seized from the boys from Wilkes County, the hooch intended for the dear departed Daytona Dave. He pours a measure into a glass and walks over to hand it to Boone.

"*This* is what I call a high quality busthead," Otto says. He gestures to the jug Boone has just delivered. "That is not."

Boone has a drink. He nods his head slightly before making a point of shrugging his shoulders, reluctant to heap praise on someone else's product.

"Not bad," he says. "A little on the musty side."

"Musty side my asshole," Otto says. "I never had better shine than that. And I suspect that you ain't neither."

Boone realizes now that there's something very familiar about the liquor he'd just tasted. He has another sip to be sure. "Where's it from?"

"From North Carolina, that's where," Otto says. "That would be your neck of the woods, right?"

"Where in North Carolina?"

"Couldn't say," Otto lies. "Better question is—why would I buy from you when I can purchase a superior product for the same money?"

"What are they charging?"

"None of your fucking beeswax," Otto tells him. "Does Sears Roebuck tell Monkey Ward their business?"

Boone glances around the storage room. He is surprised that Slim and Elmer—Otto's shadows—aren't there. There's no evidence of any more liquor in the place. He has driven there with a fresh batch of shine, fifty gallons, and he has no desire to drive back with it. He even left Val at home, knowing that Otto doesn't care for the boy. Val had not been happy about it. Since their last visit there, Val had been talking of doing Otto bodily harm. Boone had to constantly remind him that any attempt at that might just turn out to be a grave mistake.

"You want the shipment or not?" he asks.

"Not at your usual price," Otto says. He's rubbing his right arm now, wondering where exactly the humerus bone is. His arm never bothered him until Hobbs suggested that it might be sore. It had to be Spit's fault. Why did Otto listen to that old bugger anyway? Babe Ruth had knocked his pitching all over the place. The man even admitted as much.

If Otto's arm was sore, Boone was even sorer. "What's your offer?" he demands.

"Eight."

"Shit," Boone says. "I can't make it for eight."

"Then you should stop," Otto tells him. "But I know that's

165

bullshit. Don't take a genius to find out the price of corn. And sugar too."

"What about the expertise?" Boone asks. "And the risk?"

"You run your risks and I run mine," Otto says. "That's the way of it. As far as expertise goes, well, I think I just demonstrated that there's others out there leaving you in the dust."

Boone falls silent. Otto has been his best customer for over a year now. But he is loath to drop the price.

"How about it?" Otto says. "Or do you figure to haul that load elsewhere and sell it to somebody who doesn't possess my refined palate."

Boone has no notion what a palate is, but Otto doesn't look particularly refined at the moment, in his baggy uniform and cloth Smokies cap. He looks more like a clown. But he happens to be the clown calling the shots.

"I'll take the eight dollars," Boone says unhappily. "On one condition. You need to tell me who made that other batch."

"I don't need to tell you nothing," Otto says. "The price is eight bucks. Take it or leave it."

Boone takes it.

TWENTY-THREE

"Next thing, we need to break her in," Bobby says.

It's Friday suppertime, inside the molasses plant turned distillery. Morgan and Ava have been watching as Bobby set the timing and adjusted the carbs on the rebuilt engine, freshly installed in the Ford sedan and running now like a Swiss timepiece. Tiger Thompson provided a Buick transmission to back up the flathead. The airplane seat from the wrecked Sopwith is bolted in place and two headlights, rescued from a REO truck parked in the weeds behind Uncle Stan's barn, are now clamped to the sedan's rear bumper. A toggle switch on the dashboard controls the lights.

"How do you do that?" Morgan asks. "Break her in."

"Gotta put some miles on her," Bobby says. "But we need this here vehicle to remain incognito, as we say in the service. So I'll be driving it at night."

"Driving it where?" Ava asks.

"Thought I might take a run down to Charlotte, show old Tiger the fruits of his labor. You want to come along?"

"Nope," Ava says.

"What about you, Morgan?" Bobby asks. "Fancy a trip to the city?"

"My group is playing at the roadhouse tonight," Morgan says. "How long to—what do you call it—break her in?"

"Charlotte and back a couple times ought to do it," Bobby says. "Tiger might want to take her for a spin."

"You saying the car will be ready to run a shipment of moonshine to Johnson City tomorrow night?" Ava asks.

"The car will be ready," Bobby says. "The driver won't."

"Why not?"

"I'm racing my coupe over to the Hollow."

"You're working for us," Ava reminds him.

"After a fashion," Bobby says. "I told you before—I'm a race-car driver first and a moonshiner second. Not only that but I've been a Flagg family employee for nigh on to two weeks now and I'm every bit as broke today as when I arrived."

"You're working on contingency," Ava reminds him. "That was made clear to you from the start."

"Contingency," Bobby says. "Every time somebody throws a big word at me, I feel like my pocket's being picked."

"You figure to make your fortune driving around in Boss Harvey's hay field?" Ava asks.

"Nope, but I might pick up some cigarette money, which is more than I'm making here," Bobby replies. "Besides, I want one more race under my belt before I head to Bristol next week."

"What's in Bristol?" Morgan asks.

"They got a real track over there," Bobby says. "Half-mile oval, with banked turns."

"Whatever the hell that might mean," Ava interjects. "I don't care about Bristol, nor Boss Harvey nor none of it. Luther's got a man in Johnson City waiting on fifty gallons. You're claiming that this car will get it there. I want to know when."

"My dance card is wide open for Sunday night," Bobby says. "If that pleases you."

Ava frowns. "Run liquor on a Sunday?"

Bobby scoffs. "You figure God's okay with it one day and not the next?"

Morgan laughs. "He has a point, sister."

"I suppose so," Ava says reluctantly.

"Then Sunday it is," Bobby says. "Now if we got that straightened out, I'm going to idle this sedan down to Charlotte and back." He smiles at Ava. "Sure you don't want to tag along?"

"As sure as God made little green apples."

Saturday afternoon Bobby picks up Myrna Lee from the drugstore. She's waiting out front for him when he pulls up in the coupe, wearing sunglasses and her drugstore uniform and carrying a paper bag. When she opens the door and hops in, her hem raises, showing a little leg and the flash of a white slip.

"I got us a couple of sandwiches from yesterday," she says. "Still good."

Bobby finds first gear and pulls onto the street. "I ain't precious," he says. "Day-old is fine by me. We going to your place?"

"No," she says. "Boone's there and he's in a foul mood."

"Well shit," Bobby says. "I was looking forward to...relaxing some...over lunch."

"I know you and your relaxing," Myrna Lee says. "Why can't we just go somewhere and have a nice lunch? If all you want to do is screw me, then you can let me off right here."

"Now, now...I never knew you to be opposed to a little slap and tickle."

"I'm not," she tells him. "I thoroughly enjoy the slap and the tickle. But there are more things in life than sex, Bobby Barlow."

"Oh, I know," Bobby says. "There's cars, for instance."

She rolls her eyes and sighs. "You are impossible."

Bobby smiles. "Nothing is impossible. What do you say we take a drive out to the lake?"

The lake is really a large spring-fed pond that feeds into Cub Creek, south of town. Bobby parks the coupe on the firm sand, then retrieves a blanket from the back of the car and spreads it out for them to picnic on. Along with the chicken salad sandwiches, Myrna Lee brought sodas and a cookie for each of them. She removes her sunglasses to unpack the food and that's when Bobby sees her eye.

"What the hell happened to you?"

"Hell," Myrna Lee says, putting the glasses back on. She'd forgotten she even had the shiner. "Boone came home nasty last night and just got nastier. Wanted something to eat and when I didn't have it on the table fast enough, he delivered me a smack."

"Jesus Christ."

Myrna Lee shrugs her indifference. "Just when he started to calm down, Val came home and got him going again."

"Going about what?"

"Something to do with this big bootlegger over to Knoxville," Myrna Lee says. "Daddy says the man is lowballing him. Worse than that, he's been buying shine from somebody else around here and Daddy don't know who. He's looking to find out. Val's blood was up. He wants to kill this Knoxville character but Daddy keeps telling him no."

"Who is the Knoxville character?"

"Name of Otto Marx," Myrna Lee says. "Supposed to be the Al Capone of Tennessee."

"I've heard of Otto Marx," Bobby says. "Tell Val they got Capone for tax evasion. He ought to try that on this Otto mug."

"Very funny, Bobby. I'm not telling Val nothing." Myrna Lee has a sip of soda. "So now they're determined to find out who's been cooking shine and selling it up to Knoxville. Undermining them, is the word Daddy used. Top shelf liquor too apparently, which don't make Boone and Val any happier, let me tell you."

Bobby thinks about it. The day she bailed him out of jail, Ava Flagg told him that they'd lost a shipment of liquor to some big cheese in Knoxville. And the Flagg moonshine was indeed top shelf. She didn't mention the name Otto Marx, probably because she was afraid it might scare Bobby off. She might have been right in that. Even in backwoods North Carolina, people knew about Otto Marx. Bobby has heard enough to be more than wary.

"You got any idea who it is, might be cooking around here?" Myrna Lee asks.

"Sure," Bobby says. "Give me a pen and paper and I'll jot

down two or three hundred names. Making shine is the national pastime in these counties, babe."

"Yeah, but how many are selling it to this Otto fellow?"

"Maybe Otto Marx didn't buy it," Bobby says. "Maybe he just took it."

"Why would you say that?"

"Just a guess."

But Bobby decides to leave it alone. He couldn't say for sure that the liquor Otto Marx had confiscated from the Flaggs was the same stuff that now had Boone Saunders in a snit. And Bobby wouldn't tell Myrna Lee about it even if he could. He and Myrna Lee had a lot of fun together, in and out of bed, but at the end of the day, family was family, especially in these hills and hollows. Boone is Myrna Lee's daddy, and he would surely not be a particularly forgiving daddy if he suspected anyone in his family of being disloyal.

Bobby drains his soda and then stands and walks over to the water's edge, where he kneels and picks out a handful of flat stones. He begins to skip them across the water. Myrna Lee watches from the blanket for a while then removes her shoes and ankle socks and comes over to wade in the shallows.

"Lookit this," Bobby says. "A perfect stone. I bet I can make this one skip ten times. Wanna bet?"

"What are we betting?"

Bobby thinks. "Kisses. Ten skips, I get ten kisses. A kiss for every skip."

"How is that a bet?" she demands. "What do I get if I win?"

"Then you get ten kisses."

"Sounds to me like this game is rigged."

"For certain it is," Bobby laughs and he tosses the stone, skipping it six times. He grabs Myrna Lee around the waist. "That's six kisses."

She complies. "Just your good fortune that I happen to enjoy kissing you, Bobby Barlow."

They kiss for a while, standing along the shore. As they stand there a pair of trumpeter swans swoop in and land on the lake. Myrna Lee sees them and squeals.

"Look!" she says. "Lovebirds, just like us!"

Bobby glances over. "If you say so."

"Oh you," she says. "You ain't got a romantic bone in your body. I suppose if I was a carburetor or a radiator, you might write a poem about me."

"I just might. Not sure that I know any words that rhyme with carburetor."

She cuffs him sharply across the head and then kisses him again. "All right, I need to be getting back. I take more than an hour and old man Sutherland is like to pitch a fit. Saturday afternoons can be busy at the counter, even in these tight times."

"What does he pay you, that old fart?"

"Thirty-five cents an hour," she says.

"That's brutal, that is."

"Times we're in, it's better than no job at all," Myrna Lee reminds him. "Plus I get tips on top of that. Last week, this gentleman came in, dressed in a fine linen suit and silk tie, and had the hamburger plate, which comes with mashed potatoes and coffee. That gentleman tipped me fifty cents."

"High cotton, baby."

"What does old man Walker pay you at the garage?"

"I'm not working there anymore," Bobby says. "His mechanic came back."

"What do you do for money now?"

"This and that," Bobby says.

"This and that ain't a job," Myrna Lee tells him.

"Come on, baby. I don't need a regular job. I'm a race-car driver."

Back in town, Bobby drops Myrna Lee off in front of the drugstore and watches through the window as she hurries inside to tie her apron on and walk behind the counter. Bobby waits to see if Sutherland dresses Myrna Lee down for being five minutes late. But the owner is not in sight.

While watching for old Sutherland, Bobby suddenly gets the feeling he himself is under scrutiny. He turns to see a yellow Packard sedan parked across the street. Two men lounge outside the car, smoking cigarettes. One is tall and lean and the other has a pockmarked face. They have a long look at Bobby's stripped-down coupe before walking over.

"You look like a man who knows his way around," Slim says approaching.

Bobby smiles at the line. So that's what he looks like? "Something I can do for you boys?"

"We're just in from Nashville, on business," Elmer says. "We were admiring your car. Looks like a lot of motor under that hood."

"It's an engine," Bobby says.

"A lot of engine then," Elmer says.

"This is a sure enough one-horse town," Slim says. "What do folks do for excitement around here?"

"Same as they do in Nashville, I expect," Bobby says.

"Well, in Nashville we go to dances and restaurants and the picture show," Slim says. "And sometimes we'll take a nip, if one is offered. Would there be anybody around here makes a good corn liquor?"

Bobby gives the two a closer look. They're overdressed for Wilkesboro. A couple of mugs from some city, probably not Nashville, who think they're dealing with a dumb hick. Well, let them think it.

"I can tell you boys are strangers," Bobby says. "Else I'm sure you would know that corn liquor and other spirits are against the law in Wilkes County. Selling and imbibing both."

"Ain't you a smart sonofabitch," Elmer says.

"Why, thank you," Bobby tells him. "An expert on that, are you?"

"I ought to knock your goddamn teeth down your throat," Elmer continues.

"For being smart?" Bobby asks. "My mama used to give me hard candy."

Slim intervenes. "Making and selling moonshine is against the law in most counties," he says. "And yet damn plentiful at the same time. And we suspect it's just as plentiful in this little hillbilly town as elsewhere. So who do we see around these parts, if we want to wet our whistle?"

"Can't help you," Bobby says. "Looks like you boys are stuck with dry whistles."

"This goddamn smart mouth," Elmer says.

Bobby smiles as he hits the starter button and the coupe roars to life. Elmer is still offering threats as Bobby pops the clutch and spins the rear wheels as he drives off.

"You don't know for sure it's the same shine," Val says.

They are sitting in the farmhouse, drinking and waiting for Myrna Lee to come home from work to cook up some supper.

"I know for one hundred per cent certain," Boone replies. "I've been drinking corn liquor since I was in three cornered pants. I can tell a horse from a cow or a dog from a cat. There's boys who use buckwheat honey in their mix and that's what I'm tasting. Exact same stuff we took offa that nigger boy driving that old Ford truck that night."

"You figure he was heading to see Otto Marx?"

"He was heading to see somebody," Boone says. "But he only had ten jugs. Not sure that quantity would justify a drive all the way to Knoxville in a claptrap T. Who knows who else these boys are selling to?"

"We don't even know who these boys are," Val says. "We should have got that nigger's name. Or at least found out where he lives. You figure it's niggers cooking this stuff?"

"I suppose anything's possible," Boone says. "I knew a woman once taught her cat to play the damn piano. I suppose you could teach a nigger to make moonshine. But I kindly doubt it. That boy was just a sprite. I figure he was only transporting."

Val laughs. "Or trying to."

"We don't know who he was but we do know which direction

he was heading," Boone says. "He was heading west but what does that tell us? Could have been going to Knoxville. But he could have been heading to Johnson City too. Or even Sugar Grove or Hampton. We don't know. But we do know the road he was driving. As for a vehicle, I suspect whoever he's working for ain't about to send out that old truck again, not after last time."

"Then what?"

"I don't know what as yet," Boone says. "But I goddamn guarantee I'm going to find out."

TWENTY-FOUR

Saturday night Bobby is back at the Hollow, hoping to get in a couple of races, his last chance for a tune-up before heading up to Bristol and the real competition later in the week. He runs the first race and wins easily again. But Boss Harvey has news for Bobby as he pays him the purse.

"That's it for you, boy."

"What's it?" Bobby asks.

"You ain't racing no more," Boss says. "Not here anyway."

"Why in the hell not?"

"I'll tell you why in the hell not," Boss says. "I don't like your ugly car, I don't like your snotty attitude and for good measure I don't like your face. So get in that coupe and get offa my premises."

Bobby shrugs. "You're not the only one in the world knows how to turn a hay field into a racetrack." He waves the cash under the big man's nose. "But thanks for the dough, you load of shit."

Edgar sees Bobby leaving moments later and catches up to him at the gate.

"Where you going, Bobby?"

"Old Boss has blackballed me, Edgar. I'm all done here."

Edgar glances over at Boss Harvey, who's at the starting line, getting ready for the next heat. "Truscott Parr was here earlier, and he was talking to Boss a fair bit," he says. "This was before you

177

showed up. I just bet it's got something to do with it. Everybody knows the story about you and Ava Flagg and the bail money. Just like everybody knows that Parr isn't too happy about it."

Bobby smiles. "I'm sure he is not."

Edgar turns to Bobby. "He was definitely in Boss's ear tonight. I couldn't hear it all but I did hear your name mentioned and more than once."

Bobby nods. "So Parr figures to get back at me by ending my racing career. Well, screw him. I'm moving on anyway, Edgar. Truscott Parr can take a flying fuck in a rolling donut."

"What about those gas station charges?" Edgar says. "They're still pending, I assume?"

Bobby shrugs. "I haven't heard anything since I made bail. I don't even have a court date down there. Maybe the law over to Stony Point forgot about me. Wasn't much of a crime anyway. I doubt very much I'm on J. Edgar Hoover's Ten Most Wanted list."

"Chief Parr isn't one to forget," Edgar says.

"There's a first time for everything, Edgar."

But this isn't it, not where Truscott Parr is concerned. Late Sunday afternoon Bobby heads for Flagg's Hollow. He'd told Morgan he'd be there by five to help load the sedan with the shipment before setting out for Johnson City. Bobby had spent the afternoon at Myrna Lee's. Boone and Val were off somewhere and so Bobby brought steaks and some of Uncle Stan's homemade beer. He and Myrna Lee had eaten and drunk their fill and then lounged around in bed for a couple of hours. Bobby is feeling pretty good as he approaches Flagg's. He is looking forward to trying out the Ford sedan on a real run. But then Bobby looks forward to any endeavor that puts him behind the wheel of a fast car.

Arriving, he parks the coupe alongside the building and revs the engine before shutting it down. Ava and Morgan hear the roar from the exhaust and come out of the factory, where they had begun to pack the liquor in the sedan. Bobby gets out. He's loose and happy, after an afternoon of beer and steak and rowdy sex.

"Hello," he says. "I hope y'all been having as good a Sunday as me. We ready to load that car?"

Morgan is smiling and then he's not. It takes Bobby a moment to realize that neither he nor Ava is looking at him now, but at the crossroads behind him. Bobby turns to see a Wilkes County police car approaching.

Bobby's heart sinks. He turns back to Ava and Morgan, who are standing in near panic, unable to move.

"What the hell is this?" Bobby says.

Morgan turns to Ava. "Ezra?"

"That sonofabitch," Ava says softly.

They watch as the cruiser turns into the lane and rolls to a stop. Truscott Par climbs out first. He waits for Deputy Watson, who is having trouble finding his hat in the back seat. When he finally gets out, he rests his right hand on the revolver at his hip.

Bobby has a notion to get into his coupe and drive away. Chief Parr had obviously been tipped off about the Flagg's moonshine operation, but what did that have to do with Bobby? The law would have no way of connecting Bobby to the scheme. For all Parr knew, Bobby had just stopped by for a social visit on a Sunday afternoon. So why not just jump in his car and leave? Even if Parr was to take offense to that, there was no way he was going to catch Bobby's coupe, not in the county-issue sedan he was driving.

Bobby glances over at Ava. He mouths the words *I'm sorry* before walking to his car. He feels bad about leaving but his staying isn't going to change anything. The jig is up for the Flaggs, whether Bobby is on the premises or on the road.

"Where do you think you're going?" Parr demands, cutting Bobby off.

"Any damn where I please," Bobby tells him.

When he opens the door to his car, Parr slams it shut again with his heavy boot. "Not so fast, shitbird. I'm about to put a roof over your head again."

Now Bobby is thoroughly confused. Deputy Watson has moved over to back the chief up, his hand still caressing the butt of his .38. Neither man has so much as looked at the two Flaggs, standing thirty feet away, each as nervous as a virgin bride. Or bridegroom.

"What the hell are you talking about?" Bobby asks.

"You're going back to jail, punk," Parr tells him. "You're going back to jail today—and if you think Miss sugar-wouldn't-melt-in-her-mouth Ava Flagg is going to bail you out this time, you'd best give it another think. My deputy has learned a few things lately, one of them being that only the high sheriff can set bail."

"But I already made bail," Bobby says. "We got the paperwork. You can't go back on that, even a shifty character like you, Parr."

"You're right about that," Parr says. "I can't rescind bail on the robbery charges, not without reason. But I can sure as hell lock you up on the new charge."

Bobby finally realizes that Parr is not there for the moonshine. In fact, Parr obviously knows nothing about the moonshine. Bobby looks over at Morgan and Ava and sees they're now coming to the same conclusion. The relief washes over them like a wave. Bobby feels the same but the realization is tempered by Parr's intent to lock him away again.

"What new charge?" he asks.

"Felony assault," Parr says. "Your little accomplice has been singing again. Miss Luanne Dixon? I swear, that gal is gonna put Kate Smith out of business. She says it was you who broke a pop bottle over the head of the cashier at the gas station in Stony Point."

Shit, Bobby thinks. There was no pop bottle. The cashier was reluctant to open the till and Luanne had reached over the counter and punched him in the mouth. Apparently some significant embellishing had occurred since that day, either by the duplicitous Luanne, looking to save her own sorry skin—or by a gas station cashier too embarrassed to admit he'd taken a sock in the yap by a woman not much bigger than a schoolgirl.

"That's a load, Parr," Bobby says.

"I don't care one way or another," Parr says. "The warrant has been issued and I'm here to execute it."

Ava turns to Morgan, her eyebrows raised. The chief of police and his deputy are standing in the parking lot of the old molasses factory. Inside, over two hundred gallons of corn liquor are bottled and shelved. And it is becoming increasingly apparent that neither the chief nor his deputy have any knowledge of that. Both Morgan and Ava are hugely relieved, albeit not quite sure of just how they have dodged the bullet. But there is now a new concern; they are about to lose their driver.

"Hold on," Ava says to Parr, approaching now. "You're saying these charges are all from the same incident? Barlow has already made bail for that."

"Nice try, counselor," Parr says. "New charges, new arrest… and a brand spanking new bail hearing, I might add."

"How much?"

"How much?" Parr repeats. "Ain't that funny, coming from the woman who pulled a fast one on my deputy here the last time. Maybe you ought to bat your eyelashes and say you'll accompany me to the races some night, like you did him. But what works on my halfwit deputy ain't gonna work with me."

"I wouldn't accompany you to the outhouse, Parr," Ava said.

"Hey, wait a dang minute," Deputy Watson says, realizing he's been slandered by his own chief.

"Shut up, Turtle," Ava says before turning back to Parr. "I asked how much."

"I'd say fifty thousand dollars ought to do it," Parr tells her.

"That's ridiculous."

"Yes, it is," Parr says. "And it's also the bail. I just set it." He turns to Deputy Watson. "Handcuff the prisoner and put him in the car, Deputy."

As Watson leads Bobby away, Ava steps forward to block them.

"Hold on a minute, Parr," she says. "Can't we talk about this?"

Parr reaches out with a hand the size of a Sunday ham and pushes Ava back forcefully. "You can goddamn well stay out of it this time," he barks. "I'll lock your little behind up just as quick as Barlow's here."

"Chief Parr!"

Everybody turns at the sound of Jedediah's voice. He's walking down the hill from the big house, wearing his black Stetson and dark suit. Parr pulls his hand back from restraining Ava.

"Hello, Reverend," he says.

"What brings you to Flagg's Hollow on a Sabbath?" Jedediah asks.

Parr indicates Bobby. "Looking for this sorry excuse."

Jedediah's tone grows as hard as mica. "And just how does that involve you laying your hand on my daughter?"

"All due respect, Reverend, but she was interfering with police business," Parr says. "I'm taking Barlow here into custody."

"For what?" Jedediah asks.

"Felony assault, over to Stony Plain."

"Felony assault," Jedediah repeats. "What was he doing—manhandling a woman? You going to arrest yourself next, Parr?"

"He assaulted a gas station employee, whilst in the process of robbing said employee."

Jedediah looks at Bobby a long moment before turning back to Parr. "And when did this occur?"

Parr is obliged to remove a notebook from his breast pocket. He flips through several pages, shaking his head at the inter-ruption. "It was May fifteen, at five o'clock in the afternoon."

Jedediah gives the information some thought. "Did you say *May* fifteen?"

"That's right."

"Of this year?"

"Correct."

"May fifteen," Jedediah repeats, as if to himself. "Hold on a minute, Chief Parr. Just hold on."

He turns and goes into the plant. When he opens the door, the opaque jugs of moonshine on the shelves along the wall are clearly visible. Neither Chief Parr nor Deputy Watson react. Either they didn't see or are of the opinion they are looking at molasses. What else would they find in a molasses factory? Jedediah is gone a few moments. When he returns, he's carrying a scribbler, the type used by kids in school.

"Mr. Barlow has been working for the Flaggs off and on these past months," Jedediah says. "Fixing those old delivery trucks that require constant attention, it seems." He opens the scribbler. "Let's just go back to May. Here we are, the week of the fifteenth. It seems young Barlow was here every day. His workday would commence at seven in the morning and run until six at night. Stony Point is, I would estimate, a good four-hour trip from here. How can you put the boy there at that time and place?"

Parr's face has grown red and his breathing picks up. He wants to call Jedediah a liar but he knows better than to go that far. The preacher is highly respected, revered even.

"I expect I'll be required to make a trip to Stony Point to testify on Barlow's behalf," Jedediah says then. "I will consider that an inconvenience but I will do it in the interest of justice, if I must. At such a time, I will be remiss if I don't mention to the authorities there that I informed you that Barlow was in my employ the day he allegedly robbed the gas station. I wonder how that news will be accepted?"

Chief Parr doesn't say anything for a time. He glances over at Bobby, then at the deputy, weighing his options. None of them are particularly appealing. "All right then," he says softly. "Uncuff him."

"But Chief—" Watson protests.

"I said turn him loose."

Watson fishes the key from his pocket and frees Bobby. Parr turns to Jedediah.

"I'm not going to waste anymore of my time on this punk," he says. "I want you to know that I have my hands full, Reverend. I have a two-man force, and I'm run off my feet every day, with thieves and bootleggers and hoodlums of all stripes. Do you have any notion the extent of moonshining that goes on in this county alone?'

"I would have no idea," Jedediah replies.

"No, you would not," Parr tells him. "Although I would think that you, as a man of the cloth, would be concerned by it. But I'll leave you and your family to your little games. I have too much on my plate to be concerned about some gasbag who held up a gas station for two bits and slapped a cashier in the process. Let's go, Deputy."

"One more thing, Chief Parr," Jedediah says.

Parr turns. "What now, Reverend?"

Jedediah moves a step closer. "If you ever raise your hand to my daughter again, I will remove this coat and lay you low as David did Goliath. I have beat hell out of bigger sinners than you."

Parr stares at the older man a moment, then turns and walks to his car. Before getting in, he stops and looks back at Jedediah. He seems to want to say something. He could, in fact, charge the preacher with threatening an officer of the court. But Parr is unpopular across the county, for the most part. Locking up Jedediah Flagg would make him even more so. He eventually thinks better of it, gets in the cruiser and both he and Deputy Watson drive away.

"I don't believe I've ever held my breath for fifteen minutes before," Morgan says.

Ava walks over to her father and kisses him on the cheek.

Jedediah smiles slightly before turning to Bobby. "You had better know that I shan't make a habit of telling lies for you, Barlow. This has been a one-time occurrence. In the future, let your conscience be your guide."

"I hear you, Reverend," Bobby says. "I am obliged."

Ava still has her arm hooked in her father's. "So what's in the scribbler?"

Jedediah hands it over. Ava riffles through the pages.

"Blank," she says. "Now what if Parr had asked to look at this?"

Jedediah smiles. "I thought you had moonshine to load."

TWENTY-FIVE

"There's something we need to talk about," Ava says.

She and Morgan are standing by the loading dock outside of the molasses plant. Luther sits in a chair nearby, legs splayed out, a pint jar of liquor resting on his ample belly. Moments earlier, Bobby Barlow had driven off in the hopped-up Ford sedan, loaded down with moonshine, bound for Johnson City.

"What do we need to talk about?" Morgan asks.

"How do we know we can even trust the man?"

"Who?" Morgan asks.

"Bobby Barlow," Ava replies. "Who do you think?"

Morgan glances over at Luther before replying. "A hell of a time to ask that. We just sent the man on his way with fifty gallons of our corn liquor. And *now* you want to know if we can trust him?"

"It's been weighing on me, is all," Ava says. "You saw that he was about to take a powder when the police showed up."

"Probably a smart move on his part, with his record," Morgan says. "Besides, what would he have accomplished by sticking around?"

Ava dismisses this with a shake of her head. "Think about it. We provided the capital—well, the moonshine—for him to buy that old car and put that fancy motor in it and all the rest. Tonight we load it up with five hundred dollars' worth of mountain dew and send him on his way to Johnson City. Or is he on his way to Johnson City? Maybe he's had this planned all along. Steal the car and the liquor and do with both whatever he chooses. We couldn't exactly call the cops on him, could we?"

Luther has a drink and chuckles.

"What's so funny?" Ava demands. "We know he's a criminal. He's stole cars in the past, and he held up that gas station. Why should we ever think that he wouldn't steal from us?"

"Two things," Luther says. "First of all, he ain't had nothing planned all along. You might recall this was your idea, not his, Miss Ava. You bailed the boy out of jail and brung him here to work. And I suspect for a man like Bobby Barlow, that accounts for something, the bailing part anyhow. And two—you're forgetting about that right there." He points the neck of the bottle towards Bobby's coupe, parked in the yard. "He ain't going nowhere without that motorcar."

"I suppose you're right about that," Ava says.

"It goes back to human nature, sister," Morgan tells her. "At some point, you got to trust somebody in this old world."

"Amen," Luther says and has a nip.

"I'll trust him a whole lot more when he gets back from Johnson City with the cash," Ava says.

"Getting back from Johnson City will be easy," Morgan says. "Making it there is the tough part, as we know full well. I did hear a rumor that the revenuers don't work on Sundays."

"No truth to that," Luther tells him. "John Law don't never take a day off."

"Well, let's hope that Bobby Barlow stays one jump ahead of him then," Ava sighs. "That car doesn't look all that impressive to me. I don't care what all he did to it."

"You're turning into an awful pessimist, sister," Morgan tells her.

Ava manages a slight smile. "I fear I am."

Staying ahead of John Law isn't Bobby's problem on the road to Johnson City. Steering clear of the Saunders boys is another story. Boone and Val spend Saturday cruising the turnpike heading west, looking for what they deem to be suspicious vehicles. They pull over a few farmers in pickup trucks, and a salesman driving a sedan delivery. None of them are in the business of moving moonshine across the state. When Boone goes into a mercantile near Maple Springs for tobacco, he comes out to find Val poking through a load of wheat straw on a two-wheeled cart being pulled by a swayback mule, under the care of a colored boy of about twelve. Boone walks by without a word. If Val thinks that the local bootleggers are transporting liquor using mules and children, Boone will let him. Val is thirty-eight years old. He is as smart as he is going to get, Boone reasons.

They are back on the turnpike Sunday and as soon as Boone spots the Ford sedan rolling along the macadam, he feels a tingle at the back of his neck. It is dusk and he can't make out any details about the man behind the wheel, other than a dangling cigarette and an old fedora, an arm hanging out the driver's window. But the car is hopped up, no question; Boone can tell by the sound of it.

And by that tingle.

Driving past, Bobby spots the Cadillac, set back in a churchyard outside of Rocky Knob. He knows that it's Boone's car, and he also knows what Boone is up to, parked along the turnpike on a Sunday night. Bobby flicks his cigarette out the window as he watches in the rear-view mirror. When he sees the Caddy's headlights turn onto the road, he slips the Ford into second gear and hammers the throttle. The car jumps forward but Bobby immediately feels the difference between driving the sedan when empty and driving it when loaded down with roughly five hundred pounds of liquid cargo.

The Caddy's headlights shine brighter. Bobby lets off the gas and slams the Ford into third gear before flooring it again. He doesn't know what Boone is running under the Caddy's hood—probably a twelve cylinder—but he knows there are a number of sharp curves coming up and that the Cadillac can't stay with him there, even with the weight disadvantage. At least he thinks he knows that.

He is about to find out. Boone runs the Caddy up on his rear bumper and flicks his headlights from low to high beam, over and over, like a cop demanding that Bobby pull over. Of course, Boone is merely operating purely on a hunch for the time being. He can't know that Bobby is hauling moonshine.

Or can he?

Either way, Bobby will not oblige him. Boone knows this just as well soon enough, and begins to ram the Ford from behind, hard, knocking the sedan sideways each time. Bobby hits the gas and tries to pull away, but Boone stays with him, running the front bumper of the Cadillac on top of the Ford's rear bumper, then backing off and slamming forward again.

The road dips into a hollow, where it follows alongside a shallow creek. Bobby switches to his bright lights and a quarter mile ahead, he sees the first of the curves. Boone rams into him yet again as Bobby begins to slow down. Entering into the bend in the road, he drops the coupe into second gear and mashes the gas pedal. He slides sideways, fighting the wheel. In the Cadillac, Boone tries to stay with him, still riding the Ford's bumper. The next curve is to the left, a hairpin hugging the creek. A hundred yards out, Bobby flips the switch for the headlights mounted on the rear bumper. The lights glare against the Caddy's windshield. Bobby flies into the curve, flat out in second gear, pumps the brakes and skids through the loop, the sedan coming within ten feet of the fast-running creek, then straightening out as Bobby hits the gas again, the back wheels spinning like mad, the sedan fish-tailing crazily as it roars off.

Boone, blinded by the lights, doesn't see the curve until Bobby is through it and by then it's too late. He cranks the wheel but the Cadillac's front tires get caught up in the gravel. The car barrels forward, sliding off the road and splashing down in the creek. The front bumper slams into the bottom of the shallow stream. Boone and Val both go headlong into the windshield, shattering it. Val, about three-quarters drunk to being with, is knocked cold and falls sideways against the door. Boone remains conscious. There's a gash in his forehead, the blood flowing down into his eyes.

He cuts the engine and sits there, bleeding and hurt. And royally pissed off.

Bobby has been told to park behind the Tennessee Arms Hotel and knock at the loading door there. He's to ask for a man named Bones. Bobby pulls up a little past ten and shuts the sedan down, killing the headlights. There are dim lights on in the rear of the hotel as he climbs the steps to the dock. He knocks and a few moments later the door opens and a lanky colored man wearing a cream-colored suit comes out.

"I'm looking for Bones," Bobby says.

"I'm Bones." The man gives Bobby a quick inspection, then looks at the sedan parked below.

"Luther sends his regards," Bobby says. "And a couple jars of buckwheat honey."

It's what he's been told to say, word for word. Bobby feels somewhat foolish saying it, as if he's in a movie show where people use passwords and codes. Bones nods in slow affirmation, still looking at the car though.

"Where is all this honey you talkin' about?"

Bobby points his chin toward the sedan. "Right there."

"Luther say fifty gallons."

"That's right."

"In that car?"

"In that car," Bobby replies.

The two of them unload the jugs of moonshine and carry them inside. There's a small room there, some sort of storage area, with corrugated steel walls and a massive oak door, with hinges made of cast iron. There's a large hasp and padlock that the man Bones opens with a key from a ring hanging from his belt. It takes them a quarter hour to carry the shine up the steps and inside.

When they're finished, Bones is breathing heavily. He's an older man, at least seventy, Bobby would guess.

"How do I get paid?" Bobby asks. He wonders now if he should have asked for the money before he helped to store the shipment away under lock and key.

"Right here," Bones says, reaching into his suit coat pocket for a wad of bills. He counts out five hundred dollars in fifties and twenties and hands it over to Bobby.

"I've never seen a colored man with five hundred dollars on him before," Bobby says.

"And I ain't never seen a white man driving a car with fifty gallons of busthead in it," Bones says. "I guess we about even in the ain't-never-seen department, sir."

Ava goes to bed at ten o'clock and lays there awake until well after midnight. Finally she gives up on sleep and rises. She puts on a pair of pants and shirt and goes to sit on the front porch. It's a warm night, the air heavy and wet. There are a few mosquitoes. It's after one o'clock when she hears the sound of the vehicle approaching from the west. A minute later Bobby returns in the sedan. He pulls up to the double doors of the plant and gets out to slide them open.

Ava walks down from the house in the darkness and enters the warehouse through the front door. By the time Bobby drives the Ford inside and parks it, she's standing there watching. Bobby climbs out of the car, gives her a look as he goes to close the big doors.

"Waiting up for me, darlin'?"

"I wouldn't say that," Ava replies.

Bobby pulls the wad of money from his pocket and approaches her. "Waiting up for this then."

"I wouldn't say that either," she tells him. "Couldn't sleep." She takes a few moments to count the money. "You can understand that, right—how I might be a little nervous? Given our previous problems in this department."

"You were worried I wouldn't come back."

Ava thinks about what Luther said earlier. "Not in the least. You wouldn't leave me that fancy race car of yours."

"Not on your nelly," Bobby says. "I think you're beginning to understand me, Ava Flagg."

"I'm not so sure about that." Ava folds the money and stuffs it in her pants pocket. "No problems, I take it?"

Bobby shrugs.

"I can't interpret a shrug," Ava says.

Bobby smiles. "A nod is as good as a wink to a blind horse."

"I'm no horse. And I sure as hell ain't blind."

Bobby shrugs. "Boone Saunders took a run at me, out past Rocky Knob." Talking about it, he walks round to the rear of the car for a look at the damage. The bumper is bent and the lower fenders and tail pan dented from the Cadillac's bashing, but the taillights and extra headlights are all intact.

"What happened?" Ava asks.

"I lost him in those curves west of town."

"Lost him how?"

"He may have ended up in Turner Creek."

"Good place for the sonofabitch," Ava says. "After what he did to Jodie." She pauses. "Were you scared? I mean, when he was chasing you?"

Bobby shakes his head. "Boone Saunders is not about to catch me."

"I didn't ask you that," Ava says. "I asked if you were scared."

Bobby smiles. "I can't remember now. Why do you need to know?"

"I guess I don't," Ava says. "Go ahead and play the tough guy."

"I'm no tough guy," Bobby says. "This does create a problem though. Boone knows this car now. He's going to be looking for it. Which means we got to keep it out of sight during the day. Locked up in here, in other words. I was thinking I could throw a quick paint job on it but that's not going to fool Boone. We're just going to have to be careful."

Ava looks at the damaged sedan then nods her agreement.

"I don't know about you but I've had a long day," Bobby tells her. "I'll be going."

She watches until he is at the door. "Hold on," she says, realizing. "What do we owe you so far?" She pulls the money from her pants.

"I don't rightly know," Bobby says. And he doesn't. He'd complained about working for nothing but in truth turning the sedan into a bona fide moonshine runner had been a labor of love. Well, to a point anyway.

Ava counts out two twenties and a ten. "Take this for now. We'll have to figure out a more precise number later."

Bobby looks at the money. "You can hold off," he says. "You know—until we move more shine." He doesn't know why he's saying it; he's practically flat broke, as usual.

"No," she insists, tucking the bills in his shirt pocket. "Cigarette money."

TWENTY-SIX

The next day Bobby spends the morning helping Uncle Stan move some lumber and then he goes into town, to the Rexall for lunch. Myrna Lee is working the counter so Bobby sits there and orders the hamburger special. There's just him and two others at the counter. Mondays are the slowest day of the week, Myrna Lee tells him.

"So what are you up to nowadays?" she asks. "Whilst I'm here trying to earn a living?"

"Well, Wednesday night I'm bound for Bristol. Try my hand at that new track they got over there. I hear it's a bona fide oval, a half mile with banked turns."

"Speak English, Bobby Barlow." Myrna Lee's voice drops into a whine. "Will you take me along with you? I would like to go watch, you know."

"You told me you hate the races."

"Well, maybe I changed my mind," she says. "You ever think of that? Beats sitting around that farmhouse, looking at those four walls and trying to find a station on the wireless that plays good music instead of talking all the day long about this damn Depression."

Bobby finishes his burger and wipes his mouth with the back of his hand. "Well, maybe you can come along. What's the tally here?"

"Thirty-five cents."

Bobby makes a show of counting the change out on the countertop, a quarter and two nickels. Myrna Lee brings over the coffee pot and pours him a refill.

"What did you say that fancy dan in the suit tipped you?" Bobby asks. "Was it four bits?" He takes a one-dollar bill from his shirt pocket and smooths it out before placing it beside the change. "Piker."

"Ain't you Mr. Moneybags," Myrna Lee says.

Bobby smiles. "I'm next thing to a Rockefeller."

He sees her eyes go to the front window and then she frowns. Bobby turns to see Boone pulled up at the curb, behind the wheel of the Cadillac. The grill is smashed in, one headlight is broken, the fender dented beneath it. Boone and Val climb out, neither looking any better than the car. Val's nose is misshapen and an odd shade of purple. Boone has dried blood on a wound across his forehead. Neither man looks particularly happy as they come through the door.

"Hello, Boone," Bobby says. "What happened—you run that Cadillac into a freight train?"

"None of your goddamn business, grease monkey," Boone says. He and Val sit at the counter, away from Bobby. "Fry me a couple eggs, girl. And some sowbelly."

"Give me a hamburger and fried potatoes," Val tells his sister.

"Not real big on the please and thank-yous, are we?" Myrna Lee asks as she turns to the grill.

"Just cook the goddamn food," Boone tells her.

Bobby sips his coffee, watching the two men. "So what happened to your car, Boone?"

Val turns on him. "Daddy told you to mind your business, gasbag."

Boone has another look at Bobby though, as Myrna Lee pours coffee for him and Val.

"You know, maybe this is his business," he says, picking up his coffee cup and moving over to sit beside Bobby. "I'm looking for a fella driving a hopped-up Ford sedan. It's a shit brown color and built to run moonshine is my guess. If anybody in Wilkes County would know that car, I'd say it was you. Or maybe one of your racing pals. What do you say, Barlow?"

Bobby makes a show of thinking it over. "Ford sedan?"

"Yeah."

"Two door or four?"

"Two."

Bobby nods. "And dark brown?"

"That's it."

"And pretty fast too, right?"

"Yeah."

Bobby shakes his head. "Gee Boone—I don't recall ever seeing a car like that in these parts."

Boone stiffens. "Your type likes to stick together. You wouldn't tell me if you knew. Would you?"

"I might," Bobby says. "What do you want with this car anyway?"

"I have unfinished business with the driver."

Bobby finishes his coffee and stands up. "I'll keep my eyes peeled, Boone. I happen to run across that vehicle, by God you'll be the first to know. Well, you or Val there. What happened to your nose, Val? You been walking into screen doors again?"

"How'd you like me to flatten yours?" Val asks.

"I will decline that offer," Bobby tells him. He winks at Myrna Lee and leaves.

Boone watches him as he crosses the street outside, gets into his coupe and drives off, tires spinning.

"Why's he hanging around you?" Boone asks Myrna Lee.

At the grill, she flips his eggs onto a plate with the bacon and brings it over. "Stopped for lunch, is all."

"I got a feeling he knows about that vehicle," Boone says "Him and his ilk all run together. They're like a goddamn cult, out there at Harvey's hay field. I goddamn guarantee he knows that car."

Myrna Lee shrugs. "You heard him. He says he don't."

"His word don't cut no ice with me." Boone covers his meal in hot sauce. "Where's he working nowadays?"

"He was over at Charley Walker's Texaco," Myrna Lee says. "Not sure about now. What's so special about this car anyway?"

Boone shovels a forkful of food into his mouth. Egg yolk dribbles down his chin. "Running shine under my nose."

Myrna Lee smiles. "Looks like they ran it right *into* Val's nose."

"Go to hell, sister," Val snaps. "Where's my hamburger?"

Myrna Lee continues to laugh as she turns back to the grill.

"It ain't a joke, daughter," Boone tells her. "As that driver will eventually find out."

"His name is Schwartz," Otto tells them. "Right fielder for the Redbirds."

"But the Birds left town, didn't they?" Slim asks.

"They will be back," Otto says. "I looked at the schedule. They're back here in August. Take care of him then."

Slim looks over at Elmer, who's sitting on the steps behind the hotel. Otto and Slim stand a few yards away. Otto has been pitching to Slim in the alley and now he's tightening the laces on his baseball glove, pulling at them with his teeth.

"Are we gonna break an arm or leg on anybody what ever hits a home run offa you, boss?" Slim asks.

"Yes."

"Don't hardly seem sporting."

"They don't want to get hurt, they should strike out," Otto says. "It's up to them, not me. I expect the word will get around." He finishes with the glove, takes a ball and smacks it into the pocket a couple times. "Now give me the news from Wilkes County. Did you find those boys what made that good shine?"

"Those crackers are a tight goddamn bunch," Slim says. "And down there we was sticking out like a couple of whores in a church house. They wouldn't tell us nothing."

"Not for love nor money?" Otto asked.

"Not for money," Slim says.

Elmer laughs. "And we never offered any love. A few threats, but those hillbillies don't scare easy neither."

"Maybe you weren't persuasive enough," Otto says. "Everybody I ever met had something out there they're afraid of—or beholding to. And one is as good as the other."

He takes the ball from his glove and stretches two fingers across the seams, like Spit Fletcher showed him. He pantomimes the throwing motion.

"Sounds like you're sending us back down there," Slim says.

"I want that good goddamn busthead," Otto says. "Keep in mind those people came to this city that night looking for that piker from Florida. Looking for a buyer. I suspect that is still the case. So we'd be doing them a favor, not the other way around."

"Kinda works both ways though," Slim says. "Don't it?"

"Yup, and that's the beauty of it," Otto replies. "All we need to do is track 'em down."

"You're coming with us?" Elmer says.

"No. I got a game tonight. We're playing down to Nashville."

"You're riding the team bus?" Slim asks.

"Hell no," Otto says. "That goddamn bus smells like sweat socks and beer and farts. I got somebody driving me down." He smiles. "Ain't nothing wrong with the way she smells."

"You figuring to pitch in Nashville?"

"As the owner of the team, I'm figuring to do whatever the hell I please, in Nashville or anywhere else. Depends on how my arm feels. I got a sore humerus."

"A sore what?" Slim asks.

"Humerus," Otto repeated. "It's a bone in my arm."

"And it's called a humerus?"

"That's what it's called," Otto says. "All the better pitchers have one."

Wednesday afternoon Bobby picks up Myrna Lee at the farm, and they head for Bristol. Myrna Lee wears a yellow summer dress and patent leather shoes. She's excited to go to Bristol, a town she's never visited. Living on the farm, alone most of the time, she's excited to go anywhere.

"Where's old Boone today?" Bobby asks as they set out.

"I ain't seen him since Monday when him and Val got a free meal off me at the Rexall."

"They didn't pay?"

"They did not," Myrna Lee says. "But I got a dollar tip from a nice gentleman before that, so that covered their meals."

"That dollar was meant for your pocket."

"I know that." Myrna Lee shrugs. "I'm used to it, by now."

"Boone broke, is that it?" Bobby asks. "I always figured there was money in the moonshine business." He'd invited her along in part to quiz her on Boone's movements.

"I don't know whether he's even cooking nowadays," Myrna Lee says. "All he talks about is that Ford sedan that ran him into the creek last Sunday."

Boone driving into that stream was his own doing, Bobby knew. But of course he would never admit it.

"And you haven't seen either of them since Monday?" Bobby asks.

"Nope. He's either cooking up at Cyril's or more likely off looking for that damn car. I wouldn't want to be that fellow if Boone catches up to him. Him and Val are toting enough guns to start up the Civil War again."

"That car might not even be from Wilkes County," Bobby says. "It could have been passing through."

"It comes back this way, it better pass through quick."

Bobby has never seen the track at Bristol but he's been hearing a lot about it lately. Apparently, it started out the same as Boss Harvey's oval back in Wilkes County, just another converted corn field. But the man who owns it—a Scotsman who did contract work for the TVA—brought in one of his excavators and banked the turns while leveling out the straights. The Scot also erected permanent bleachers that would seat a few hundred people. There are hot dog stands and soda concessions. A man with a trumpet plays at the start of each race. The Scot had borrowed the idea from the thoroughbred track in Louisville.

Wednesday night is race night, with the action starting at seven o'clock. Bobby arrives at the track shortly after six. He and Myrna Lee have been in town for a couple of hours. She wanted to go to Montgomery Ward and the Woolworths to look at clothes and other sundries. Bobby follows her around for a bit and then, when she goes shopping for underthings, he goes out to wait in the coupe, at her suggestion. He isn't sure why she is bashful about him watching her buy underwear; he has seen her both in and out of her clothes for some time now. But women are strange, he knows. He doesn't anticipate ever understanding them fully, but he's okay with that. He likes them just fine nonetheless.

Admission at the track is twenty-five cents. Bobby pays for Myrna Lee and she goes off to the bleachers as he drives into the infield, looking to sign up. The other entries are parked side by side along a fence at the back of the track. The cars are a step up from those at Boss Harvey's muddy field of ruts and ragweed. Or a few steps up. Like Bobby's coupe, they're built for racing; equipped with dual exhaust and extra carbs. Some have fancy paint jobs. A few even have signs on the doors, advertising for local businesses. Bobby hasn't seen that before. He smiles to himself, thinking that he could have painted Flagg's Quality Busthead on his car and drummed up some business for the family.

He gets the sense that the other drivers are watching him, in the fenderless coupe with flat primer covering the damaged areas, like he's an oddity. He parks and climbs out of the Ford to approach a man wearing a straw hat and carrying a clipboard. Bobby assumes he is the one in charge.

"Something I can do for you?" the Straw Hat asks.

"How do I sign up?" Bobby asks.

"You give me five dollars and make your mark on this clipboard," the Straw Hat replies. "Your first time here?"

Bobby nods as he pulls a five from his pocket and hands it

over. A bright green Plymouth coupe drives up as Bobby is signing his name. The car has over-sized tires and loud exhaust. The hood sides are missing and Bobby can see the straight eight beneath the hood, topped with three Strombergs. On the door is printed DANVILLE EXPRESS. The driver gets out and takes a long look at Bobby's coupe before exchanging amused glances with the Straw Hat.

"Another one down from the hills," he says to the Straw Hat.

"What's that?" Bobby asks.

The Plymouth driver is tall and blonde and wears crisp clean white overalls. He pays the Straw Hat and writes his name on the sheet. "I said—we always welcome you boys from the mountains with open arms."

"I appreciate that," Bobby says. He doesn't care for the man's tone or the smug look he shares with the Straw Hat. "Coming from a man who don't look like he's ever crawled underneath a car."

"I pay others to do my crawling for me," the man says. He gestures to Bobby's car. "This your Ford?"

Bobby nods.

"You can't buy a gallon of paint back in those hills?" the driver smiles. "Well, you're not racing around behind Aunt Polly's barn anymore, Jethro. We'll let you play with the big boys for twenty laps and then send you on home with your tail between your legs. Do me a favor though—try and stay out of my way out there. It's hard enough driving a race car without having to worry about gomers who got no idea what they're doing."

"I appreciate the advice," Bobby says. He points to his car. "You see that there back bumper?"

The driver shrugs. "What about it?"

"I hope you like it," Bobby says. "Because in a few ten minutes, that's all of me you're gonna see, gasbag."

Moments later the cars line up. The Straw Hat drops the flag and the race starts. Bobby comes out clean and settles in, middle of the pack. The Plymouth roars out of the pack hot as a firecracker and is soon running second, tucked behind the leader, a Lincoln coupe. Bobby doesn't make a move for the first few laps, getting the feel of the track while allowing the other cars to stretch out. The dirt here is packed, firmer from that back home and Bobby finds the banked turns to his liking. He can go into them harder and come out quicker. After a half-dozen laps, he's ready to make his move. Coming out of the second turn, he hammers the coupe and the vehicle jumps like it's powered by a rocket. He passes three cars like they are going backwards and downshifts as he slides into the next turn. Barreling into the stretch, he does the same. The coupe is fast and light; it's soon obvious that there's nothing in the field that can catch him on the straights and almost nobody as skilled in the turns.

When Bobby flies by the Plymouth, he cocks his thumb and forefinger like a gun and "shoots" the unhappy driver in the head. When the race is done, Bobby has lapped half the field and beaten the second-place car by a quarter mile. He rolls through the finish line and drives into the infield where he turns a couple of donuts, spinning the coupe in circles in the dirt. He shuts the car down and gets out to wave to the crowd. Some cheer but just as many boo at his showboating. Bobby glances up to see Myrna Lee in the bleachers, on her feet and clapping. The other entries cross the finish line one by one. Bobby watches them as he makes his way over to the Straw Hat.

"Where do I get paid, pal?" he asks.

"Patience, son," the Straw Hat tells him. "Race ain't hardly finished yet."

The Plymouth idles past, and the driver shuts it down and gets out. Still speaking to the Straw Hat, Bobby raises his voice slightly.

"I'm in no hurry," he says. "It's just that I got to head back to the hills with my tail between my legs. Or so I've been told."

The Plymouth driver laughs. "You're awful touchy for a man who just cleaned our clocks real proper. What's your name anyway?"

"My name is Bobby Barlow."

"Earl Danville," the man says. He leans over for a closer look at Bobby's engine. "This thing has some giddy-up. Who built it?"

"I did," Bobby tells him.

"What do you got in there?"

"That's a stock V8 from Henry Ford."

"You are full of shit, Barlow."

Bobby smiles.

"What will you take for her?" Danville asks.

"Not for sale."

"You didn't hear my offer yet," the driver said. "Everything is for sale."

"Not everything," Bobby says. He gestures to the Plymouth parked a few yards away, to the writing on the door. "What is Danville Express?"

"That's my company."

"And what does your company do?"

"I'm in the delivery business," Earl Danville says. "I'm faster than the U.S. Mail. And I manage to make money doing it, in spite of these hard times. More than enough to buy this coupe."

"If it was for sale," Bobby tells him. "And it's not."

But Bobby is thinking now. He walks over to the coupe's passenger window and reaches into the glove box for a pint of corn liquor from the Flaggs. He has a drink, watching Earl Danville for a reaction. When Bobby offers the pint over, Danville takes it.

"Well," he says after drinking. "That's not half bad."

"It's better than that," Bobby tells him.

"Where'd you get it?"

Bobby laughs. "I can't recall."

"You're lying about that engine, and you're lying about this moonshine," Danville says smiling. "You ought to run for office."

"Maybe I will."

Danville hands the pint back. "In the event that you remember where this stuff hails from, let me know. We might be able to do business together."

Bobby tucks the bottle in his hip pocket. "I'll keep that in mind."

TWENTY-SEVEN

Luther can't say what his old friend Bones Pettifog, lately of Johnson City, is doing with the moonshine he's buying from the Flaggs, but whatever it is, he's doing it in quantity. Just two days after Bobby's first delivery, Bones sends word via the brakeman on the Great Smoky Railway that he is in need of another fifty gallons. It is agreed that Bobby would make the run again, this coming Sunday.

"What about Boone Saunders?" Ava asks.

Bobby and Morgan sit across from her in the lunchroom at the molasses plant. Luther and Cal have gone for the day. They'd been cooking since early that morning. A new batch of shine drips from the copper coils a few feet from where they sit. They had run out of sugar that afternoon; they'd have to wait for more before starting a new batch of mash.

"Boone can't catch me," Bobby says.

"They all say that," Morgan reminds him.

"Who all?"

"Billy the Kid, John Dillinger, Jesse James. They all said they couldn't be caught."

"I ain't Billy the Kid," Bobby says. "And even if I was, Boone Saunders is no Pat Garrett."

"We have to assume he'll be looking for the car," Ava says.

Bobby decides not to tell them about his encounter with Boone at the Rexall. It would serve no purpose other than to make the two of them worry, and they were already doing that.

"Maybe we could create a diversion," Morgan suggests.

"What kind of a diversion?" Ava asks.

Morgan shrugs. "Send him on a goose chase. What kind of goose would Boone Saunders chase after?"

"A goose called busthead," Bobby says. He gestures to the Ford, parked along the wall of the building. "And he's already in on that chase, looking for that sedan over there."

"We better not get too cute with him," Ava says. "The goose he cooks might be ours."

The rear door opens then and Ezra walks in, arriving so quietly that they wonder if he's been lurking outside, listening for a time. He appears hangdog and petulant, as has been his wont of late.

"Let me think about Boone," Bobby says, ending the matter for now. He doesn't want to discuss anything to do with transport in front of Ezra. The more people with knowledge of a plan, the more likely that plan will get out.

"Wondered why the lights were still on," Ezra says as he approaches. He seems surprised to see Bobby there, but he nods. "Bobby."

"Hello, Ezra."

"Wrapping up for the day," Ava tells him. She stands and collects the dirty glasses and coffee cups from the table. "I was about to come see you."

Ezra walks to the copper coils and watches the drip-drip-drip of the clear liquor into the smaller vat. His disapproval of the whole enterprise hangs from him like a shroud. "See me for what?"

"We're out of sugar," Ava says, putting the dishes in the porcelain sink. "And we need to be careful where we buy it. If we buy out the mercantile in Wilkesboro every week, the word is going to get around. You know--*what in tarnation are they making out there at Flagg's Hollow?* Everybody knows you make molasses out of cane or beets, not sugar. You see what I mean, brother?"

"I am not a dummy," Ezra tells her. "But what's it got to do with me?"

"You've been put in charge of sugar procurement for the business," Ava tells him.

"You don't put me in charge of anything, Ava," Ezra snaps. "Who made you the president of this danged company?"

"Should we vote on it?" Ava turns to Morgan and Bobby, speaking quickly. "All in favor of Ezra being our sugar procurer, raise your hands."

Morgan and Bobby have their hands up immediately. Ava joins them, smiling at Ezra. "Three to one. Congratulations, brother."

"Vote all you want," Ezra says. "And make your little jokes at my expense. You ain't going to force me into a chore I got no stomach for."

"I suppose not," Ava says.

Having made his case, Ezra nods curtly and heads for the door.

"You get that money I left with Rachel?" Ava asks.

Ezra stops, staring at the door that was almost his escape. "I got it."

"Are you under the impression that the money came from the manufacture of molasses?" she asks. "Even though we haven't produced a drop of molasses in over a month? Are you somehow under that impression, Ezra?"

Ezra still will not look at her. "No, I am not."

"Where do you think that money came from, brother?"

Ezra glances over at Morgan and Bobby, sitting at the table. Bobby is smiling.

"What are you laughing at, Barlow?" Ezra demands.

"Nothing," Bobby says, but his smile broadens. "Your sister is a hard case, isn't she?"

Ezra regards Bobby darkly for a long moment, then exhales heavily as he turns back to Ava. "Where am I going to get sugar?"

"I figure you can head east," Ava said. "Buy a bag here, a couple there. Follow the river. Hit Ronda, Jonesville, Pleasant Hill; all those little towns have general stores. They all carry sugar in bulk because everybody and his brother is cooking in those woods. You buying hither and yon won't raise an eyebrow."

Ezra glances about; his eyes come to rest on the Ford sedan. "Am I to drive that?"

"That car stays here," Bobby says.

"You ain't in charge of anything," Ezra tells him.

Bobby grins again. "We could take a vote on it."

"Take the old truck," Ava says. "And leave in the morning first thing. We need that sugar."

Ezra opens the door and looks back at her, gesturing toward the dripping coils across the building. "This will all end badly," he says. "Mark my words."

Mid-week Slim and Elmer are back in Wilkes County, trying once more to track down the moonshine that has become the object of Otto's desire. It was now bordering on obsession with Otto. His mood in general had not improved in recent days; he had pitched in Nashville Saturday and hadn't lasted an inning. He'd given up three home runs, which meant that he had three more names for Slim and Elmer, three more players to be educated as to the dangers of having success at the plate against Otto Marx. Slim and Elmer are not enthusiastic about beating up ballplayers who happened to hit home runs off Otto. Nor are they particularly enthusiastic about driving blindly around Wilkes County, where the locals all regard them as outsiders or rank opportunists. Or worse than that—Feds.

Wednesday noon they stop for lunch at a diner in Traphill. They've heard the area is rife with moonshiners, going back to the days of the Civil War. But nobody—not the farmers nor the merchants nor the tobacco-spitting old men lounging in front of the Stageline Hotel—will allow them the time of day, let alone tell them where they might purchase a jug or two of mountain dew.

"Do I look like a Fed?" Slim asks as they enter the diner.

"A Fed?" Elmer repeats.

"Yeah."

Elmer shakes his head. "Do I?"

"Not in the least."

The place is called Curly's and run by a man of that name, a fellow who may have had curly hair, back when he had hair. The only menu is scrawled in chalk on a blackboard on the wall.

"You fellows decided?" Curly finally approached after they'd been sitting at a table by the front windows for a full five minutes. The proprietor had been regaling a couple of old-timers at the counter about a bass he'd caught a few days earlier and the story—like any good fish tale—had taken a while.

"Tell me something, chief," Slim says to him as he comes over. "Do I look like a revenuer to you?"

"What's a revenuer?" Curly asks.

"What's a revenuer?" Slim scoffs. "You mugs are all the same. I bet you never heard of anybody making moonshine whiskey around here neither, have you?"

"Can't say that I have," Curly says. "Ain't that agin the law?"

Slim looks at Elmer. "I bet this piker never heard of Santy Claus nor the Easter Bunny neither."

"Just like everybody else in this damn county," Elmer says. "I got five dollars says we could find a gallon or two on the premises."

"Not these premises," Curly tells them.

"Come on now—couldn't you see clear to offer us a sample? We would surely make it worth your while."

"Ain't nothing to sample," Curly says. "Like I said, I'm for certain that making and selling spirits is agin the law. You fellows care to order some food?"

Slim throws his palms in the air. "This is useless. Gimme the liver and onions."

After eating, they walk outside and stand smoking on the sidewalk. The town isn't much more than a hamlet, with one main street and a few buildings in behind, shotgun shacks and chicken coops and woodsheds. There's a livery at the end of a side street, but not an animal in sight. Summerfield's General Store is across from the diner. There are a couple of trucks parked out front and a freight wagon hitched behind two scrawny bay geldings. Slim and Elmer had already been inside the store earlier. The proprietor, of course, had no knowledge of anybody in the Traphill area making moonshine and had, in fact, appeared to have never heard of such activities. Same old song with a different tune. The citizens of Wilkes County might just as well make up a choir and take it on the road.

They'd parked the yellow Packard at the far end of the street, in a lot between the Baptist church and a shuttered blacksmith shop. Walking to the car now, they pass the freight wagon and the trucks angle-parked in front of the mercantile. One truck is a Ford double-T with a dented grill and fenders. To Slim, it looks like every other farmer's work truck except for one thing. There's a dozen or so fifty-pound bags of sugar in the back. A tarp thrown haphazardly over the cargo doesn't manage to hide it.

"Hold on," Slim says to Elmer, who is walking ahead.

"Well, well," Elmer says when he sees the cargo. "What do we have here? Somebody's old granny making mulberry jam?"

Slim nods. "Yeah, I suspect that's just what it is."

Elmer has a look inside the cab and then walks around the truck. He notices that the passenger door has been crudely painted over with a brush.

"They covered some writing on the doors," Elmer says. "Why would a person need to do that? Unless they was hidin' something."

But Slim isn't listening. He's at the other side of the truck, looking at three round holes in the driver's door. "Lookit here."

Elmer comes around the front of the truck as Slim pulls the .45 semi-automatic from inside his jacket and releases the clip from the gun. He thumbs a shell out and fits the nose into one of the holes. He turns to Elmer.

"I thought this truck looked familiar. You'll recall I'm the one put those holes in that door, a few weeks ago in Knoxville. Those two pikers running shine to Daytona Dave. Or trying to."

"I'll be damned," Elmer says, realizing. "Those pikers what was infringing on Otto. Same damn truck—and loaded to the tits with sugar, by God."

Slim slides the clip back into the .45 and tucks the gun in his belt. "About time we caught a break."

They sit in the Packard fifty yards away to wait. It's not long before Ezra Flagg comes out of the store, a bag of sugar over his shoulder. He plunks it down in the box of the truck, then pulls the tarp over the load. He pays no attention to the Packard as he gets behind the wheel and drives off, heading west.

"He ain't one of them from that night," Elmer says. "There was a youngster and the fat colored what shat himself."

"This is one of the crew, I expect," Slim says. "Maybe even the cooker himself."

They follow Ezra at a distance for the next hour or so, watching as he stops at the general stores in Mulberry and Fairplains, picking up more sugar in each place before continuing on west, towards Wilkesboro.

Ezra chugs along at a slow pace, mindful of his heavy load. A couple miles shy of Wilkesboro, he takes the turnoff north. When he reaches Flagg's Hollow, Slim and Elmer hang back, aware that they're very conspicuous, driving the new Packard into a community where horses and mules outnumber automobiles. They park short of the crossroads and watch as Ezra backs the truck to the loading dock of the molasses plant. Luther comes out a moment later, followed by Ava.

"That's the nigger from before," Elmer says.

"Who's the dame?" Slim asks.

Elmer shrugs. "No idea. So how do we handle this?"

"I ain't too sure," Slim says. "First question is this—are they cooking here or is this just a depot for the ingredients? Most of these boys hide their stills up in the hills."

Elmer points. "Sign says it's a molasses factory."

"I don't care if the sign says they're making gingerbread," Slim says. "I shot holes in that truck and when I did, it was loaded to the gills with busthead. These people are cooking moonshine, whether it be here or somewhere else."

"One way to find out," Elmer says. "Kick that door in and have a look."

"No," Slim cautions. "We don't want to spook them. We kick the door down tonight and we might come back tomorrow and find the place cleared out."

"Not if we explain to them certain things. I mean things to do with their health."

Slim scratches his cheek as he looks out the windshield to the sky. "Nigh on to dark. I say we head back into town and get us a room. We'll come out here tomorrow first thing. People ain't scared during the day like they are at night. We come back tomorrow and see if we can't talk a little business with these people. Like Otto says, they was looking for a buyer that night in Knoxville. Why would that have changed?"

Slim drops the Packard into gear and they pull a U-turn and head towards town.

Inside the building Bobby is watching the two men in the yellow Packard. He showed up a while earlier, with ten gallons of gas for the Ford sedan, in preparation for the run to Johnson City. He couldn't drive the car into town to fill the tank, not with Boone Saunders and who knows who else on the scout for it. While dumping the jerry cans into the Ford, Bobby had heard Ezra drive up in the truck and gone to the window for a look. That's when he spotted the Packard, which had quite obviously been trailing Ezra.

It's the same car Bobby had seen a few days earlier in town, when the two city mugs had quizzed him about bootleggers in the area. They've obviously been stumbling around in the dark, without so much as a candle or a match to light it. But it's apparent now that they aren't giving up, whoever they are. So now they've been following Ezra, while he was hauling a truck full of sugar. Given the nature of his task, Ezra should have been mindful enough to notice a shiny yellow Packard on his tail. But then Ezra is a tad oblivious in general, and too busy pouting to take note of much of anything. Whatever his state of mind, he has succeeded in leading the two mugs right to the family doorstep.

They weren't stumbling around in the dark anymore.

TWENTY-EIGHT

That night Bobby finds the Packard parked beside the Wilkesboro Hotel. He takes a walk through the empty dining room, looking for the two men, then goes to the front desk, where Gus Harrigan is doing a crossword puzzle and nipping from a bottle of Coke that Bobby knows contains more whiskey than soda pop.

"Hey Bobby," Gus says. "Gimme a five-letter word for courage. Starts with V."

Bobby ignores the request. "That Packard parked outside," he says.

"What about it?"

"Where are they?"

"They got a room upstairs." Gus sips from the bottle. "They just checked in an hour ago but they been hanging around town for a week or more. Can't hardly miss that car. Couple of mugs in fancy suits and toting guns, both of them. I suspect they might be revenuers."

"They are a far cry from that," Bobby says.

Bobby leaves and walks over to Yadkin's Diner across the street, where he takes a seat by the front window and orders corned beef and hash. From there he can see the rear end of the Packard, parked in the hotel lot. Supper hour has come and gone and there is nobody else in the diner. Floyd, who works the counter after the owners go home for the day, sits at a stool, reading a paperback novel and chain-smoking Camels.

Bobby gives the situation some thought while he eats. They may not know it yet but the Flaggs are in a bind, what with Otto Marx on one side and Boone Saunders on the other. They might make an arrangement to sell to Otto but in the end, it would go sour, especially if Boone comes to the conclusion that he's being cut out of the action. Even without Boone in the mix, from what Bobby has heard of Otto Marx, he's not a man to trifle with. When it comes to criminal activity, he's way out of the Flaggs' league.

As for Boone, Bobby can't imagine any scenario between him and the Flagg family that won't result in violence. Boone is a thief, and a sadistic whiner who always finds someone to blame for his own lot in life. Not only that but revenge is an art that Boone has long cultivated, one that is fed by his insecurities and paranoia.

By the time Bobby has finished his dinner and is drinking a second cup of coffee, he has arrived at the conclusion that the smart thing for him to do now is to extricate himself from the entire situation. Get in his coupe and drive. He has been hearing that there's money to be won racing in Georgia and Florida, with the added incentive that down there he wouldn't be risking his life butting heads with the likes of Boone Saunders and Otto Marx. There's nothing keeping him in Wilkes County. In Georgia he could make a name for himself. He could even drive the coupe all the way to Florida and race at Daytona, something he'd always dreamed of doing. Hell, he could start his own business, building cars for other drivers.

If what to do is the question, then cut and run is the answer. The Flaggs went into the bootlegging game with their eyes open. Well, maybe not completely open, given that they've made every rookie mistake imaginable so far. But they knew they were getting into a business rife with violence and double-crossing. It was dangerous in the days before Prohibition, it was dangerous during Prohibition and it's still dangerous now. It isn't Bobby's job to protect the family. He'd agreed to build them a bona fide moonshine-runner and he'd come through on that.

He looks at the clock on the wall. Shortly past eight. He could leave now, drive down to Charlotte and spend the night at Tiger's place before continuing on to Georgia in the morning. Dawsonville was the place to go in Georgia, he'd heard. They might even be racing there tomorrow night.

So that's the plan. Get the hell out of Wilkes County while he's still able. He has a good car and nothing to hold him here. Georgia is full of promise, as is Florida. This here is a mess, and not one of his making. Leaving Wilkesboro seems the better part of valor.

"Valor," he says out loud. Five-letter word for courage. He wonders if Gus, in his half-drunken state, has stumbled upon it yet.

The more Bobby thinks about it, the more the notion of pulling stakes appeals to him. He hates to leave the Flagg family in the lurch but what can he do at this point? There's trouble on all sides and Bobby's first concern is keeping himself clear of it. And after all, the Flaggs came looking for him, not the other way around.

Bobby looks across the street, to the fancy yellow Packard parked there in the shadows. He thinks about the two men up in their room, with their guns and their cloudy motives. And he thinks of the Flaggs—of the naïve Morgan, the sulking Ezra, the stiff-backed preacher Jedediah who isn't above telling a white lie when he deems it right. Well, maybe not right—but necessary. And he thinks of Ava, of her sharp tongue and her beauty, her inherent integrity even when earnestly breaking the law. And then he thinks of her disdain for Bobby, how she never seems to take him seriously, even though he'd done all she had asked and more.

After a moment, he sighs heavily and turns to the counter. "Floyd, another cup of joe, bud."

"I thought you was finished here," Floyd says as he brings the pot.

"I was thinking the same thing," Bobby says. "But not quite."

The next morning Bobby gets up early and makes a couple of stops before driving into town, where he again parks across from the hotel. He sits in the car there, watching and waiting. Shortly past eight o'clock Slim and Elmer emerge from the hotel and cross the street to Yadkin's Diner. They go inside and sit at the same table Bobby had taken the night before. Bobby remains in the coupe and smokes a cigarette, watching them as they order coffee and breakfast. After their food arrives, he gets out, tosses the butt in the gutter and goes inside.

"Well, well, look at the revenuers," he says approaching the table. "How's business, boys?"

Both men give Bobby the eye. Of course they recognize him from the other day, when he'd gotten smart with them about the existence of moonshine in Wilkes County and Elmer had volunteered to rearrange his face.

"There's no revenuers here," Slim says.

"I know it," Bobby says. He pulls a chair over, turns it around backwards then sits. "There's some in Wilkes County have got you pegged for that but I kinda doubt the Feds would be driving around in a Packard the color of a canary. That would be considered conspicuous."

"What do you want, hayseed?" Elmer asks.

Bobby shrugs. "If memory serves, you mugs are looking for moonshine. That *is* why you're hanging around, right?"

The two mugs in question exchange glances. Elmer smiles. Might be they finally have a fish on the line.

"And you have decided to help us out?" Slim asks.

"You could use some help," Bobby says. "After that numbskull move last night."

Slim takes a moment. "What numbskull move was that?"

Bobby shakes his head, smiling. "Come on. Parking that big yellow boat out to Flagg's Hollow. You followed that boy home with the truckload of sugar. Then you parked in plain sight. By the

216

time you figured out just what you'd stumbled on, they'd already spotted you. And so naturally they spent all night cleaning that warehouse out."

Elmer stares at Bobby, his lips tight, before turning a bad eye on Slim. Elmer had wanted to hit the molasses factory last night but Slim had argued against it. Well, look where that had got them.

Slim puts his fork down, wipes his mouth and has a drink of coffee. "And where have they gone to?"

"Where do you think?" Bobby asks. "Into the hills. You should be able to find them, no problem. Might take you twenty or thirty years."

"Funny man," Elmer says.

"Why have you decided to share this with us?" Slim asks.

"Because I got a proposition for you," Bobby says. "I haul moonshine for the Flaggs. Not only that but I built them a runner that nothing in the goddamn state can keep up to. I'm supposed to deliver a hundred gallons to Johnson City come Sunday night. Given the proper incentive, I could be persuaded to alter that plan."

Slim smiles. "Looks like this country boy is right ambitious."

"What kind of incentive?" Elmer asks.

"The busthead alone runs ten dollars a jug," Bobby says. "That's a thousand there. And I expect the car is worth nigh onto that much again. She's a sure enough moonshine-running machine. I'll hand over lock, stock and barrel for a thousand. That's half price. Question is—can you two mugs handle that?"

"We can handle whatever you got," Elmer snaps. "But that's a lot of cash."

"It's a lot of moonshine," Bobby tells him.

"What's a dummy like you going to do with a thousand dollars?"

"How about none of your fucking business?" Bobby replies.

"You'd better try that again," Slim tells him. He opens his coat slightly, enough to show Bobby the .45.

Bobby shows his palms. "Hold on now. Fact of the matter is, I'm looking to get out of the bootlegging game. I got me a first-class race car and it's my intention to take it down to Georgia to run it. I could use a stake."

Slim shovels the last forkful of scrambled eggs into his mouth and then leans back in his chair with his coffee. "We might be able to work something out. This is the same shine like we got last time?"

"Precise same recipe," Bobby says. "Best in the county."

Elmer leans towards Bobby. "You'd better not be jerking our chains here, hayseed."

"You guys are the ones packing iron," Bobby says. "I ain't about to get sideways of you."

Slim lights a cigarette and tosses the spent match onto his dirty plate. "Then you got a deal, son. Providing you can hold up your end. Where are these hundred gallons at the moment?"

"Nice try," Bobby says smiling. "I can tell you it's where you won't find it. Which means you need me and I need you."

Slim nods. "How do you want to do this?"

"I'll have the Ford loaded and ready to roll, come Sunday dusk," Bobby says. "I'll meet you behind the hotel across the street there."

Slim looks at Elmer for a moment, then back to Bobby. "We'll be there."

TWENTY-NINE

Saturday morning Bobby gets up with the sun and makes the long drive up to Bristol, looking for Earl Danville. It turns out that Danville is well-known in the city, with his thumb in any number of pies. Bobby finds him in a small music studio on Cumberland Street. It turns out that Earl Danville is a banjo player of some renown. He and two other men are recording a song when Bobby shows up. He doesn't take a whole lot of their time.

It's late afternoon when Bobby arrives back in Wilkesboro. Myrna Lee's shift at the Rexall is nearly over so Bobby sits at the counter and waits while she finishes up. There are no other customers. Bobby drinks a soda and watches Myrna Lee wash dishes and clean the milkshake machine. The mouse beneath her eye is almost gone.

"Where's old Boone these days?" Bobby asks.

"Who knows?" Myrna Lee replies. "He was out to the house when I left earlier, sleeping off a drunk on that ratty old couch on the porch. Val's off in the Caddy somewheres. Up to no good, if I know Val."

"I might have some information for Boone."

"What kind of information?" Myrna Lee asks.

"You know," Bobby says. "Business."

Boone is still at the farm when Bobby drives Myrna Lee

home, sitting on the creaky top step to the porch, with a sawed-off shotgun between his knees, cleaning the weapon. Boone's eyes darken when he sees the coupe pull into the yard.

"If looks could kill," Bobby says.

"You know he's very protective of me," Myrna Lee says.

"When he ain't slapping you around," Bobby reminds her.

She gives him a look. "You better let that go. You know Boone. You don't want to mess with him."

"I do not."

"All right. I'm gonna go change out of this uniform." She gets out of the car and goes into the house.

Bobby reaches into the glove box for a pint of liquor and then gets out to approach Boone. The old man eyes the bottle as he snaps the forestock on the twelve gauge back into place and then slides five shells into the gun. He chambers one round while eyeballing Bobby.

"Tell me if this tastes just a little bit familiar," Bobby says, offering over the shine.

Boone hesitates a long moment before reaching for the pint. He removes the cork and has a short drink, then a longer one, all the while watching Bobby warily over the neck of the bottle.

"Where'd you get this?" he demands.

"At the getting place, Boone. Don't you know nothing?"

"I know lots," Boone says, lifting the barrel of the gun higher. "And what I don't—you're about to tell me, you fucking pipsqueak."

"You got people in Wilkes County laughing at you, Boone," Bobby says. "Never thought I'd see the day."

"What are you talking about?"

"I come across these two mugs in town, been running shine right under your nose. They sold me that pint outside Yadkin's Diner just last night."

"What mugs?"

Bobby shrugs. "Couple of city boys in suits. Been hanging around a while now, buying busthead from them that's selling. Shipping it back to the city, I suspect."

"What city?"

"Knoxville, so I hear. Some character named Otto something-or-other been buying up busthead hither and yon. Or at least these boys have been buying it for him."

Boone has another sip from the pint before tucking it in his overall pocket. He has no intention of giving it back to Bobby. "I suppose next you're gonna tell me they're driving that Ford sedan I been looking for."

"I don't know what they're driving," Bobby says. "I told you—I ran into them in town."

A pair of pigeons fly out of the mow window of the barn. Boone raises the shotgun and follows them but doesn't shoot. Shooting pigeons is a job for a twenty gauge or a .410. Lowering the barrel, he glances toward the house, where Myrna Lee has gone.

"For what reason you telling me this?" he asks. "Looking to get in my good books so you can keep sniffing around my Myrna?"

"Just passing on some information," Bobby says. "You recall you asked me to keep a lookout for people running shine in your bailiwick. As for your good books, Boone—I never figured you to have any."

Boone points the pump shotgun at Bobby's coupe. "I got five loads of double-ought buck in this here gun, boy. Wouldn't take me but thirty seconds to turn that precious Ford of yours into a pile of scrap metal if I take a mind to."

"You don't want to shoot my car, Boone."

"I'll shoot whatever I please," Boone says. Now he swings the barrel toward Bobby. "You need to keep that in mind. And next time you run across those so-called bootleggers, you better let me know about it. Or you can stay the hell away from my Myrna."

Bobby reaches over and calmly pushes the barrel aside. "You got it, Boone. Truth is, I don't like these city mugs coming around anyway." He smiles. "Making us country boys look bad."

"You just point 'em out and we'll see who looks bad," Boone says.

"Tell Myrna Lee I'll see her later," Bobby tells him.

"I ain't telling her nothing," Boone snorts.

Bobby laughs as he walks off the porch and gets into the coupe and drives off.

On Sunday afternoon Bobby finds Edgar at home with his parents on Locust Street. The house is one of the oldest in town, a fieldstone two-story with a porch across the front and down one side. The place is surrounded by leafy burl oaks and the black locust trees that gave the street its name. Out back is an old carriage house, left over from the past century. With the horses long gone, Edgar's father a few years ago turned the building into an artist's studio for his wife. She spends most of her days there, working on oil paintings—landscapes and kittens and such—which she tries and fails to sell. Most end up on the walls of the funeral parlor downtown.

Edgar and his folks are in the backyard, playing a game of croquet, when Bobby comes around the side of the house. Edgar's father is tall and taciturn, not a man given to frivolous behavior or pursuits. In temperament, Edgar favors his mother more.

"Good Sunday," Bobby says. It seems to him that the family—even though Edgar and his father are in their shirtsleeves—are still dressed from church. Both men wear bow ties and Edgar's mother is in a long brown dress with tortoise shell buttons down the front.

Edgar's father says good Sunday back but it's plain he's not terribly happy to see Bobby there. He's heard the stories—about stolen cars and gas station robberies and the rest. Not only that but it has been years since he's seen Bobby in church on Sunday.

"What's going on?" Edgar asks.

"I need a favor, pal," Bobby says.

"It's Sunday," Edgar says.

"I know what day it is," Bobby tells him. "I might need you to drive my car somewhere tonight."

Edgar's eyes pop. "Your coupe?"

"That's right."

Edgar can barely hide his excitement. "I just need to change my clothes."

"Finish your game," Bobby tells him. "I got some things to tend to and then I'll be back."

"Will you stay for lemonade?" Edgar's mother asks.

"I can't just now," Bobby tells her. "Thank you just the same."

It's nearly dark when Bobby pulls up behind the Wilkesboro Hotel in the Ford sedan. He has managed to cram eighty gallons in the vehicle, packed in straw. Eighty gallons is all the car will hold and maybe all that the beefed suspension will handle. The cargo weighs roughly eight hundred pounds; the weight has the sedan squatting on the Model T springs Bobby had added to the rear end.

Across the street, Edgar is behind the wheel of Bobby's coupe, parked in the alley beside Yadkin's Diner. He's been told to wait for Bobby's signal. His right leg, foot on the gas pedal, bounces nervously in anticipation.

The yellow Packard is behind the hotel, where Bobby had seen it last. Slim and Elmer must have been keeping watch from their room upstairs because within two minutes of Bobby's arrival, they come down, walking out the back door of the hotel, dressed in their wide-lapelled suits and raked fedoras.

"Well, well," Elmer says. "And here we thought you was all talk."

Slim says nothing but walks around the sedan, looking it over. He drops to the pavement for a glance at the rear suspension then straightens and opens the trunk. He pries a jug of moonshine out of the straw packing and uncorks it to have a taste. Putting it back, he lifts out another jug and tries it as well.

"That the stuff?" Elmer asks.

"Would appear so."

Elmer turns to Bobby. "And you squeezed a hundred gallons in this heap?"

"Eighty," Bobby says. "And this heap, as you call it, will outrun anything you've ever seen, city boy. Now what do you say we conclude our business? I make it eight hundred for the busthead and a thousand for the car. Half that is nine hundred American greenbacks. And that is cash on the barrelhead, gentlemen."

Elmer smiles at Slim before turning on Bobby. "Yeah, there's been a little hitch in things."

"What kind of hitch?" Bobby asks.

Elmer produces the snub-nosed Smith & Wesson from his coat. The hitch is obvious and really of no surprise to Bobby. The two men have no intention of paying him anything. But before Elmer can explain that which Bobby already knows, a pair of headlights sweep across the alley as a black Model T truck comes bouncing off the street and into the lot. The men squint into the lights, trying to make out the driver. Slim produces the .45 and both men level their guns at the headlights until they shut down.

Ava Flagg gets out.

"What the hell are you trying to pull?" she shouts, charging across the lot at Bobby.

"Hold on—" he begins, his palms forward.

"You wait 'til my family is at church and then rob us?" Ava accuses. "We took you in, you thieving sonofabitch. We bailed you out of jail and took you in. We treated you like family."

"Whoa now," Slim says laughing. "Who's the harpy?"

"You go to hell," Ava fires back. She turns on Bobby again. "Your game is up, Barabbas. You're going to drive this car back to the Hollow and I'm going to follow you every inch of the way. I was told not to trust you; I should have listened from the start."

Bobby hesitates. "Well, we got us a bit of a situation here."

"No, we don't," Slim says, carelessly pointing the .45 at the two of them. "Elmer, get behind the wheel of that Ford."

"We had a deal, goddamnit," Bobby says.

"We don't got nothing of the kind," Slim says. "According to Miss Firecracker here, you're trying to sell us stolen moonshine. That ain't going to fly. Why would we pay for stolen goods? We'll just confiscate this shipment."

"That liquor belongs to me," Ava tells him.

Elmer turns to her. "Not anymore, it don't. So shut up, lady, and take your medicine. I will kill the pair of you dead, right here."

When Ava starts to protest, Elmer points the barrel of the

revolver at her head. She holds her tongue. Elmer climbs into the Ford and hits the starter. The engine roars to life. Elmer looks at Slim and smiles.

"This here is gonna be fun," he says. "Let's get a move on."

Slim wags the barrel of the semi-automatic at Bobby and Ava, like a schoolmarm warning her students to behave, then gets behind the wheel of the Packard. Elmer revs the Ford and pops the clutch, the rear wheels throwing gravel across the lot. The Packard follows as the two vehicles pull out onto Main Street and head north out of town.

The instant they're gone, Bobby turns and runs to the street out front. He waves both arms to catch Edgar's attention and points to the north.

"Go!" he shouts.

Edgar fires the coupe up, peels out of the alley and hits the pavement. Bobby sees the euphoric look on Edgar's face as he puts the flathead through the gears. Bobby watches anxiously until he's out of sight.

"Keep her between the ditches, Edgar," he says aloud and then heads back to the alley behind the hotel, where Ava is waiting, her eyes dark.

"Mary Pickford has got nothing on you," Bobby tells her.

Ava smiles. "Why, thank you, sir."

Bobby walks past her to look in the back of the truck. There's a tarp there; he pulls back a corner and sees the glass jugs packed tightly in the box.

"What do we have?"

"Fifty," Ava says. "Like you said."

"Then let's go to Bristol."

THIRTY

The story comes out in dribs and drabs over the course of the next few days. When Edgar arrived at the Saunders farm, Boone and Val were on the porch, where they had a game of cribbage going beneath a forty-watt bulb. They'd opened a jug from Cyril's and were working their way through it. In Edgar's telling, Boone was about three quarters drunk and Val was all the way there. Myrna Lee, tired of their cruel and slothful ways, had gone into town with a friend, to the picture show. The movie had been Bobby's idea. He'd even given Myrna Lee money for admission and popcorn.

Edgar said that he was there at the bequest of Bobby Barlow, doing the Saunders boys a favor. When he told them that the Ford sedan they'd been seeking for the past week was at that moment loaded down with moonshine and headed for Knoxville with a bright yellow Packard in tow, Boone and Val practically fell over each other loading weapons into the Cadillac.

They caught up to Elmer and Slim a few miles out of Blowing Rock. Val was behind the wheel of the Cadillac. First he side-swiped the Packard, pushing it into a ravine beside the road, and then roared up to crash into the rear of the Ford, propelling it into a stand of saplings. Both Elmer and Slim came out of the cars with guns in hand. When the shooting was finished, Elmer and Boone were dead and Slim close to it, having taken a load of buckshot in the chest. Val was shot in the shoulder and jawbone. He and Slim lay out in the woods until morning, when a farmer happened along and discovered the carnage. The Caldwell County Police came and called an ambulance for Slim and Val and a hearse for the others.

The Feds showed up shortly afterward, tipped off by somebody with knowledge of the gun battle, possibly a deputy looking for brownie points or maybe someone from the hospital. Seeing that the sedan was packed with jugs of moonshine, the Feds took over. They were eventually to find out that the car wasn't quite as filled with liquor as they thought. Only the half-dozen jugs in the rear that were easily accessible were moonshine. The rest were filled with mountain spring water from Flagg's Hollow.

On the other hand, the fifty gallons in the rear of the double-T Ford driven that night by Ava Flagg were in fact filled with genuine Flagg's Hollow moonshine. Bobby took the wheel when they left the lot behind the Wilkesboro Hotel. He knew the back roads to Bristol. And he could drive better than Ava, even she had to admit.

"How did you know they were going to steal the shipment?" she asks as they head north along the red dirt road.

"They stole from Morgan and Luther, didn't they?" Bobby says. "Why would tonight be any different?"

"I suppose." Ava thinks about it. "But how do you know that Boone will chase after them?"

"That's one thing that I got no pause about," Bobby says. "Boone is as predictable as the sun coming up. He figures he's been wronged, even though he hasn't. That don't matter to Boone. Vengeance is like mother's milk to him. And Val—well, that's an acorn that never fell far."

In the slow-moving truck, it takes them the better part of four hours to reach Bristol. Earl Danville is waiting at his place, sitting in a wicker rocking chair on the front porch, a flyswatter in one hand and a glass of bathtub gin in the other. After the introductions are made, and the liquor sampled, he counts six hundred dollars cash into Ava's hand.

"We said ten dollars a gallon," she reminds him.

"I'll pay twelve," Danville says. "Providing I get first crack at the supply."

"There could be a problem there," Bobby says. "There's competition from Knoxville. You should know that the game could get rough."

"What competition is that?" Danville asks.

"You know the name Otto Marx?"

Danville smiles. "Everybody knows who Otto Marx is."

Ava frowns, puzzled by the smile. "We hear he's not a man to trifle with."

"The news out of Knoxville is that Otto himself got trifled with," Danville says.

"How so?"

"Bunch of baseball players beat the living hell out of him and ran him out of town," Danville says. "From what I hear, it couldn't have happened to a nicer guy."

It is nearly dawn when they get back to Flagg's Hollow. Ava is sleeping against the door when Bobby eases the truck into the parking lot behind the old molasses factory. He sits quietly for a while, wondering what transpired after they had left last night. Did Edgar find Boone and deliver the message—more importantly—did Boone find the two mugs bound for Knoxville? Bobby decides he can wait to find out. Right now he needs a place to lay his head.

He reaches over and shakes Ava. She comes awake slowly, blinking into the sunshine just now showing on the horizon to the east.

"Where are we?"

"Home," is all Bobby says.

*****